THE BENCH

To Tami,

John Carns

Christmas 2004

THE BENCH

above Boothbay

A novel

John H. Corns

iUniverse, Inc.
New York Lincoln Shanghai

The Bench
above Boothbay

All Rights Reserved © 2003 by John H. Corns

No part of this book may be reproduced or transmitted in any form or by any means, graphic, electronic, or mechanical, including photocopying, recording, taping, or by any information storage retrieval system, without the written permission of the publisher.

iUniverse, Inc.

For information address:
iUniverse, Inc.
2021 Pine Lake Road, Suite 100
Lincoln, NE 68512
www.iuniverse.com

Cover photo by the author

ISBN: 0-595-27348-3 (pbk)
ISBN: 0-595-65669-2 (cloth)

Printed in the United States of America

For Susan
and
her Loving Care of Parents

Prologue

Himalayan Mountains—Nepal—1981. Dorothy adjusted her goggles and looked up at the snow-covered peaks. The mid morning sun was just rising over the white skyline, fusing the snow and ice and the blue sky beyond in a silvery glare. The tinted lenses did not soften the rays enough to entertain the image long. She looked back at John, standing just below her on the narrow, ice-crusted path. The warmth of the sun lessened the chill of the air except when the winds swept along the steep incline of the mountain. The summer was gone but the season for trekking parties was not quite over, and she had enjoyed the freedom of the last ten days. As soon as they had left Katmandu, she felt like a bird fleeing a cage, the door thrown wide after years of confinement.

Last night she had lain in the compact tent as the wind maintained a steady and disquieting rush against the taunt skin of the igloo. The liberty of their vacation in the awesome beauty of the mountains was threatened by the wailing tent wall, the confining sleeping bag, and the unsettling darkness. Only her face felt the cold, but it helped to steal her sleep. She knew that her husband was warm with the flap of his sleeping bag pulled snugly over his head. John could do that; she could not. The single candle burning in the small vertical cylinder of glass was more to provide her light than warmth. She could not stand darkness. It had frightened her since childhood, but it was the added noise of the high wind that denied her sleep for the first night on the trek. She had pulled the wool cap down to cover her ears and tried to block out the sound, but she failed, and it had been a long night. Now she was tired and wished they were going to rest for the day. There was only this one more day. Tomorrow they would be back at the pick up point. She and John had walked the trail selected by their two guides who allowed them little movement off the course. The pace had permitted her to take many pictures and to rest frequently. Now she would like to stop for the day, but she did not say so.

"You okay, Dot?" John asked.

"Sure."

And she was. Just tired, but she would push on. He would be proud of her later when she told him of her fatigue and lack of sleep.

Dot wished they had taken a less rigorous vacation that could have included their son, Stephen, six years old and back in Seattle with Grandmother Grace, but John and Grandmother Grace had decided on Nepal, and Dorothy had hoped to include a visit to India, but the flight had been to Tokyo, Hong Kong, and then into Katmandu. It was the only time she had feared flying because the aircraft they had boarded in Hong Kong seemed ancient, but John had tried to reassure her: It was a charter, sound, and had cost a lot of money. Not that the Grace family had to worry about money. Grandmother and Grandfather Grace had plenty, and the old lady knew how to use it to control the people around her, especially John.

It was Grandmother Grace from whom Dorothy felt free—at least for a while.

"We can stop at the next sheltered spot if you'd like," John said.

She watched the two guides: both once Ghurka soldiers in one of the British infantry companies. They seemed to understand English well, even that of the Pacific Northwest of America.

"We should not stop," the older guide said. "Best to get by next two miles now. Rest tonight."

"See, John, it's best to keep on. Let's go," she said.

"My Mountain Gal," he said, smiling as he zipped up the front of his interior jacket. It was cooler than it had been just an hour earlier, and the wind was whipping down the slopes harder than at any time during their hike.

She heard it. Then she felt it—a rumble—as if standing on an elevated platform when a train roars into the station. But there were no trains, not on this mountain above Katmandu.

She looked up the steep slope. There was no glare now. No sun. No blue sky, just white. She turned and reached for John. She saw his lips moving, but she heard only the roar above. She wished she could see his eyes but they were hidden under the brown glasses. Her mind worked and her lips moved as their hands met, arms outstretched. Then an invisible force ripped them apart and propelled them out over open space. John's face disappeared behind a curtain of gray. Her mind and lips expressed but one word—one name—*Stephen*.

A gray, granite wall slammed against her. Then there was darkness…blackness.

CHAPTER 1

Boothbay Harbor, Maine—2000. The white vase lay on the floor, the spilled water painting the carpet a darker blue beneath the tumbled splay of carnations. Rachel had heard the vase thump against the floor as soon as she closed the door of her mother's bedroom, and she had pushed the door open again. The plush carpet pulled the water down and shaped it in an oval pool. Her mother lay with her head and shoulders extended over the side of the bed, her hand inches from the vase, palm toward the ceiling. She turned her head as Rachel reentered the room. Rachel looked at her and longed for a sound—a word or a cry. But her mother's eyes held no surprise, or puzzlement or interest, even in the spilled flowers.

"Mom. You're going to hurt yourself." She said it as if to a small child or to someone she knew to have no hearing. But her mother could hear. They told her that. With such great authority and confidence, the white coated men and women told her, she could hear. But could she understand? Rachel placed her arm around her mother's shoulders and swung her back onto the bed, and then supported her as she groped for the pillow lodged between the headboard and the mattress. A year ago Rachel could not have done this, but she guessed her mother was now a spare one hundred pounds, thirty less than her weight then.

"You really must be more careful, and Mrs. Clausen should not put the flowers so close to the bed," she said and pulled the covers up to her mother's shoulders and folded the sheet down and tucked it under her arms. There was a stain, orange juice she guessed, on the sheet. She thought of changing the bedclothes, but she would wait and do that in the morning. She was glad her father had encouraged Mrs. Clausen to take the two days off to be with her family, but she did not share his confidence that the two of them could care for her mother as well as Mrs. Clausen. Still, it was Thanksgiving, and families, like the Clausens, should share the holiday. Rachel took a towel from the adjoining bathroom and laid it on the damp carpet and placed the flowers back in the vase. She patted the towel to draw up the water, ran new water into the vase, and put it well out of the reach of her mother—on the table beside the doorway. She went out of the bedroom leaving the door slightly ajar and walked to her room to change into jeans and running shoes. She heard her father's soft footsteps in the hallway and the click as the door to her mother's room closed.

The holidays this year probably would have no meaning for her mother, but they had at one time and, for Rachel, Thanksgiving had been a fun time until her early teens. When she was a child, the Thanksgiving symbols had been the boys' tall, black paper hats and the girls' bonnets and white aprons over long black skirts. They had reenacted the rescue of the hungry Pilgrims by the Indians who knew how to grow corn. She had enjoyed the early holidays when Uncle Ted and Aunt Ellen visited with their three girls. She had learned to eat turkey by pretending it was made from the large paper silhouettes of the proud bird in the food market window. She admired the meal laid out on her mother's dining room table: the browned turkey with white, paper balls for feet at the center of the table, settings of white china and crystal glasses, and gleaming silver flatware that seemed too pretty to touch. Even when her older cousins laughed at her version of where her father had gotten the turkey, she liked having them there—the company.

That was before her mother's illness and before Aunt Ellen and Uncle Ted stopped coming, after the big argument that started between the sisters—her mother and Aunt Ellen—then included the fathers and forced the girls out of the dining room and into the cool, damp air outside their house. That Thanksgiving night her father told her that her mother was ill; that they were not sure what her sickness was, but that she would recover. Somehow, the doctors' inability to say what was wrong caused Rachel to believe that it could not be too serious, although she knew her mother forgot things, a matter of light joking within the family of three.

Rachel was fifteen that year and she recalled it as an end of something, like leaving home to attend college, but far more unsettling despite her father's effort to reassure her. So much had changed from that day. She heard from her aunt now only by rare phone calls and Christmas cards, and she had come to think little of her mother's sister, and the thoughts she had were not without some resentment. In her senior year of high school, her father explained that even with today's medical knowledge some families chose to whisper about illnesses such as her mother's. By then they had put a name to the ailment. It seemed to be so unscientific—not the name—the process of elimination that told the doctors it was not any of several other diseases, and so, probably, it was Alzheimer's disease. They were not even definite then. President Reagan had the same thing. She guessed the doctors could only tell even him that it probably was Alzheimer's disease. A past president of the world's richest nation with its most advanced medical research had to be told that he probably had this Alzheimer's disease. Her father told her she should not be bitter. Hurt and anger were normal, but the bitterness would be like a disease; so she had tried.

She read a book on the disease. People seemed to read a book on everything, and she thought sometimes that they looked for easy answers rather than trying to think through problems on their own, but she had not yet found answers, so she read the book. The names of people who historians said probably had the disease were surprising and remarkable, victims of a disease not named until the early twentieth century. A German Doctor Alzheimer observed a woman patient, before and after her death, and introduced some new thinking about the ages of people affected by this and similar diseases and challenged ideas about senility and something they called senility dementia. She did not find solace in the knowledge that people had suffered with it two thousand years before, or that the number of people afflicted around the world was growing rapidly.

As she read the experiences of daughters, sons, fathers and mothers of probable Alzheimer sufferers, she had little doubt. They were describing her mother. Rachel cried often and laid the book aside, but she would retrieve it and read anew. Her eyes grew moist when the writer so unequivocally wrote: *and there is no known cure; the process is not reversible; the patient in time returns in a process not unlike the reverse of the development of a baby, a toddler, a pre-schooler, an alert and learning student of life.* She would set aside the book for days, but always she was drawn back, feeling that she was being punished as she read, but unable to believe that there was not, somewhere, a bright spot to be found.

Rachel guessed her aunt had never read such a book and had never mustered the strength to visit her sister more than the one time. That was over four years ago, when her mother still looked healthy. But even then she might make coffee and put the nearly full coffee can in the trash, or tell her sister the same story for the third time in her visit, unaware she had told the story at all that day. Those were little things—Rachel thought. Then one day her mother told Rachel of her great embarrassment during her sister's visit; of the terror she felt knowing that there would come a time when she would remember no one—not Rachel, not her husband.

"I know it sounds weak, Rachel, but I would rather die than have you go through that with me. Promise me you won't stay around me to see that."

Rachel had not promised. She had held her mother's hand and they cried almost without sound. She had never let her mother see her cry after that day. Her mother had wiped Rachel's tears and told her that the white china in the Rosewood breakfront was hers. Rachel protested, but her mother said it was something she wanted to tell her now—she did not want to forget. The china had belonged to Rachel's grandmother, a fact often stated by Aunt Ellen at the holiday dinners. Aunt Ellen could have the china, Rachel thought, if it would delay just one day her mother losing her thoughts and self.

For a while she was at her mother's side regularly when not at school. Both her father and her mother would tell her to go visit friends, go to a movie, or just take a walk. Gradually she began to take longer walks; then jogs, but her thoughts drove her pace faster and faster. She had become a runner—a compulsive runner. It helped her as nothing else did; yet, it gave no lasting help.

Her mother's health worsened in rapid stages once Rachel was in college, almost measurable by each of her academic semesters. Part of it was the prolonged interruptions in seeing her mother, although she tried to get home frequently. The longer she stayed away the more marked the changes appeared to be: more forgetful, more difficult, quicker to anger, more prone to accidents, and more in need of someone whenever she left the house. Finally, her dad told her, it was unsafe for her mother to drive the car or to be let outside the home alone.

Rachel had considered the field of medicine during her second year of college, but she rejected it. During one trip home she had met two women who regularly visited and talked with her mother. They had no medical degree; they specialized in talking with people with diseases or difficult social relationships. Her mother seemed happier and more observant after talking to either of the two women than after any of her regular days with the doctors or after taking her daily pills. Rachel walked out of the house with them following one of their visits and asked how she could talk to her mother as they did. One of the women said that she should not expect to draw her mother out with conversation as they did. The woman seemed to take some pride from that, but at least the women did more for her mother than the doctors did—and more than Rachel.

No one had said as much, but in those early days she had felt that she must be part of her mother's problem. Once, a so-called family psychiatrist in somber tones told her that she was not at fault. Rachel replied that she knew that. But she didn't. She must have done something. She did not know what, and she felt that she should know what it was. She had never been able to accept that she was of no help to her mother. It had bothered her all her senior year in high school and especially during the summer before college. She had cried in the night—many nights. She would awaken in the morning irritated and angry and run through the town, around the streets overlooking the bay, and tell herself that she must accept what was happening and recognize the limits of what she could do for her mother. However, once in college, she caught herself even in the midst of laughter picturing her mother's more frequent vacant look, and she would grow quiet, moving to the side of the room to find a private spot. She had done that often when she was out with Craig—too often.

She still hoped to regain some of the special memories of Thanksgiving. At least it brought her home to The Harbor. Moreover, it gave her a break from her junior year at Northbern College. She was a good student, not great, but a good student. She had gone off to become a lawyer but changed her mind the previous school year. It seemed that every third girl she met was going to be a lawyer, and all had identified their post-law school goals. Many predicted what their first year salary would be, and estimated higher income than that of her father, an engineer for twenty years. She doubted their numbers, but not their determination. Whether their path was strewn with as large obstacles as some suggested, she did not know, but seven years of study she viewed as challenge enough, and she knew that there were firms where the top jobs tended to go to the roommates and early confidants of the people at the top. Few of those at the top were women. Still it was not the challenge of the years of study or whether opportunities in the practice of law were limited that caused her to drift away from the goal. She told herself that she wanted a challenge. She wanted to do battle for a worthy cause. She was not convinced that the best challenges and most deserving causes were in the fixation on the big salary, entitlements, and stock options.

She recalled the movie. She and her father and mother had watched it on a rented videotape—before the time of the Thanksgiving argument. The young woman, Maggie, is a corporate lawyer in the story, pitted against her father representing several complainants who charge that her client's company has manufactured faulty automobiles. Rachel's mother had excused herself, picked up a soda in the kitchen, and gone up to her room. At the end of the movie, as Maggie and her father express their love for one another and begin to dance, Rachel had hugged her dad and told him that she loved him.

"Me too, Pumpkin," he said.

She knew that he had enjoyed the movie, and she guessed that he admired Maggie as much as she did. At that point, she had decided she would be a lawyer.

The cool air brushed her face as she opened the kitchen door at the side of their home. She walked the short distance along Sea Street to the corner and turned up the steep roadway. One of her favorite memories was running along the street and over this hill. She had walked or run here for as long as she could remember, up the street and then along the dirt and patchy grass path that cut across the lawn behind Holmes Cottage. From there you could look out on the harbor inlet and the larger bay beyond. Her strolls had mostly been with her mother when she was small, and later with her father, but in the last three or four years she had run alone. It was a private time to make sense of things, or like today, to let her feelings flow; mull over thoughts and settle on the most positive, if not the most pleasant, of them by the time she returned home. It had worked better for her when she was younger. She smiled to herself: younger, a high school freshman, or sophomore. Lately, positive thinking did not come easily when she was back in Boothbay Harbor. Still, many of her most pleasant times had been along this short path behind Holmes Cottage—and sitting on the bench.

The steep incline of the street had grown no easier over the years, but the reward of the bench and the view had always put the extra spring in her step. Her father seldom walked over the top now, but took the near level Todd or Howard Street to get to McKown and Townsend and then to the footbridge to the east side of the harbor. The path went over the top and left the street at the short driveway beside the cottage, dropped down slightly along a bank of shrubbery, and opened on the view of the old wrought-iron bench sitting just below the top of the long knoll and well above the water and sailboats and the finger of wooded land that pointed south into the bay. The bench had been black at one time, but for many years the enamel had continued to peel to reveal a dull metal gray that took on the familiar rust of iron near salt water. The rust was primarily near the bottoms of the legs, and the middle of the back and seat kept a glossy gray, for the bench was not a secret, and many people came, polishing the sitting surfaces.

One of Rachel's early walks alone to the bench had been on a Sunday. She had forgotten the fullness of her white summer dress and had swept the skirt along the lower surface of the bench's leg. Her mother's irritated prediction that the rust would never come off proved correct. The dress was discarded, and it was weeks before she returned to the bench. Her Grandfather Malcomb, her mother's father, had been visiting then and had comforted her, telling her and her mother that he would pay for a new dress; that she was not to worry. Her mother had smiled then. She always smiled around Grandfather Malcomb, but then he made everyone smile. He had made boats all his life but in those days he was retired and he just sailed around in the Odyssey. He called it Tilley's boat. Tilley was the grandmother Rachel could not remember, and Rachel was saddened when her mother remarked to her father one day that Mother Tilley had never liked the boat—or any boat. Rachel had been on the boat one time and she remembered the shiny red wood of the cabin that reflected her hair blowing in the wind that cascaded off the sail of the flying boat. That had been when she was twelve and her parents had taken her to visit him at his home near Belfast. He had died two years later. He had told her about the purpose of quiet walks—to pick out and cast away the negative and timid weeds of fear and disappointment and to open to the light the confident and positive plants of brightness and beauty. Sometimes the positive plants are tiny, nearly covered, and you have to look closely to find them. It was an uncomplicated story. All of his stories were, and he had a story for everything. All had good endings. She often wished now that she had talked to him more, asked more about his stories, his love for the smooth woods in his boats and his Tilley. He had sat with Rachel one day on the bench. She tried to recall which of his stories he told her that day, but she could not. It had been warm then, unlike the cold weather today. Now above the scuffed summer sneakers and comfortable jeans, she wore a sloppy, cream sweater with rolled turtleneck and a hem that tucked below her hips. It had felt cozy when she stepped out of the house, but now she felt the chill that was so familiar in the fall under low clouds that capped the harbor and, out in the bay, made the line between water and sky hard to make out. She knew she had under-dressed, but she was not going to shorten her run. She needed the time alone.

She saw it as soon as she neared the drive beside the cottage. It was a fence, and it was ugly—orange vinyl, horizontal bands and vertical, unpainted wood slats. It sagged for lack of adequate support from green metal stakes set too far apart. It had not been there before. It cut across the lawn leaving no way except down the steep hillside into a group of houses with no view of the bay or back out on the street in front of the cottage.

It might be a safety fence, but she saw no erosion of the bank or unsafe situation, nor signs of construction. She walked along the line of the fence although its sagging height would have allowed her to step over it. The fence ran back some forty feet from the edge of the embankment and anchored to the corner of Holmes Cottage. She did not walk up to the cottage window, but she could see light beyond the curtains. She saw no sign of anyone inside. The cottage normally was not let at this time of year. No one from the Holmes family had lived there for years, but one of the town's rental agencies let it out in the summer at monthly and weekly rates. No one had used it the past summer—unusual.

She felt the urge to walk down the slope and pull up the end of the fence, lying on the steep hillside beyond the last stake, but the wood and metal stakes were lashed together with coils of heavy wire. The wire had probably been twisted with pliers, and a similar tool would be needed to cut or work them loose.

She returned to the sidewalk and walked along the front of the cottage. The same type of fence attached to the other rear corner of the building. The unsightly fence ran diagonally to the edge of the knoll and disappeared down the slope. On the grass just inside the fence but close enough to touch was a pole with a hand painted sign, black lettering on white wood, telling her to keep out. She did not think the path could be blocked this way. At least it never had been and it should not be now. However, if the bench was on the Holmes Cottage property she was afraid that the owner might have the right to fence it off. She started to turn back toward her home but decided to continue her run. She walked down the steep street on the other side of the knoll, then along Townsend, and then to the right and across the footbridge. The far end of the bridge was roughly the halfway point on her run to the entrance to the Spruce Point compound, where she usually turned back. It was well over a four-mile run out and back. Often she ran slowly, looking out for people along McKown and Townsend Streets and the footbridge, and then took up a faster pace as she ran along Atlantic Avenue that paralleled the other side of the harbor.

She began to run as soon as she crossed the bridge although there had been few people to keep her from running sooner. Thoughts about her mother and then of the fence and the loss of her bench soon slowed her pace again. She hoped that the bench was not the property of Holmes Cottage.

By the time she made the turn at the stone pillars that marked the entrance to Spruce Point, she knew the sweater gave more than adequate warmth despite a strong breeze that whipped along the rocky beach and toward the point. Her thought turned again to her mother's health. Mrs. Clausen was now staying at their house full time. Rachel's father had decided that reluctantly, and she was glad that he had not put her mother in the home. She hoped that would never be necessary. But her recollections of the book's specific words on the care needed by a baby-like, fully-grown adult, told her that they might not always be able to find or keep someone like Mrs. Clausen or that the task would grow too great for one person without special facilities. Rachel had talked little with her father after she arrived earlier in the day. He had just returned from one of his frequent inspection trips. She would talk to him before she went to see the town authorities about the fence. It occurred to her that she should go see the person living in or caring for the cottage and ask why the fence was there. Yes, she would do that. But not today. She needed to get home and help her father.

Later she watched him at dinner. Her mother had ceased to take meals with them over a year before, and now the dining room table seemed cold and immense. She had placed her setting to her father's right before he came to sit at the end of the table. He looked tired, and she did not know if it was the cold weather, his trip, or the weight of her mother's illness. Rachel had made spaghetti and needed only to boil the noodles when she returned from her run. Her mother was resting quietly when Rachel came back into the house, and she could hear her father in the basement before he went upstairs to freshen up for dinner. She ought to tell him that she and Craig had broken up. He had taken a liking to the young man visiting the Harbor with her the past summer. She would wait, hoping for some pleasant conversation to raise his name. She and her father had not talked a lot since about the time she told him she was no longer preparing to be a lawyer. Her father had not liked it when she gave up her pre-law curriculum, but she knew that he had been worried about how he would meet the cost of her education and the rising expense of her mother's care. Her parents had been paying for long-term health insurance but the policy did not cover all the costs.

Her decision to drop the law idea had bothered him more than she had expected, but there was little reason to discuss law school. Even now she was considering a part-time job second semester. It might mean staying in Boston through the summer with a full time job. He would not like that.

"You going up to see Becky today?" He asked.

"She's not here this weekend, Dad."

"What keeps her at school over Thanksgiving?"

"She's not at school. Her family is down in Portsmouth visiting with her grandmother over the holidays."

He nodded and twirled up more spaghetti. Becky was her childhood friend who had never quite forgiven Rachel for not enrolling at the University of Maine at Orono as she had done. Rachel had been drawn to her dad's old school in Massachusetts. She talked to Becky on the phone from time to time, but not often. They had not spent a lot of time together the past summer either. Rachel did not like that. She needed to spend more time with Becky. In high school they had been inseparable, and Becky's mother, Vicky, had been the most frequent visitor to Rachel's mother from the early days of her mother's concern as the symptoms of her mysterious illness first appeared. Even now, Vicky was her mother's most frequent visitor.

"How's school?" He asked.

"Okay."

"Your mother seemed to rest pretty well today."

"Yes, at least from what I have seen since I got here and since Mrs. Clausen left. I think Mom may have noticed that Mrs. Clausen was not here, at least by early afternoon. She knocked the flower vase off the table. Right before you came in. Dad, do you think she really knows me?"

"Sure."

Rachel did not think so. Oh, she had gotten her mother to smile when she showed her the flowers that she had brought to her last month, but she guessed that her mother did not know that Rachel was her daughter, or even that she had a daughter. Her mind had seemed to lose recognition quickly. Between Easter two years ago and Easter break of the prior school year she felt like she had lost her mother, and she still felt the shock of that first meeting at Easter time.

They ate in silence for a couple of minutes.

"How's that Craig friend of yours? He's in engineering?"

"Yes. I guess his studies are going fine. Peggy just told me last week that he gave her a system to figure out what Dr. Sterling will cover on his exams."

"You mean the cough routine? Where he coughs to let you know that the next lecture point will be a question on a quiz or exam?"

"Yeah, how did you know?"

"I guess you don't know how many years old Jeffrey has been lecturing there. He did that when I was a student."

"Does it work?"

"Did then."

"I think that's terrible."

"Then you're not going to use the system?"

"I didn't say that, but maybe I won't."

"There's nothing wrong with it. It encourages students to learn what he thinks is most important, and I don't think you can sit there waiting for the coughs and ignore all the other points he makes."

"Maybe."

"But that's not what I was asking with regard to Craig. You two seemed to be getting pretty serious up here this summer. I mean how are the two of you getting along?"

He paused and waited.

"We aren't dating anymore, Dad. No big squabble or anything. I think we both just realized we were not having that much fun together."

"I'm sorry to hear that, Rachel. You seeing anyone else special?"

"No."

She knew that he liked Craig; so did her roommate, Peggy. With Peggy, she wound up feeling guilty somehow; like there was something she should have done or said to avoid a breakup. She was not good company to Peggy or anyone else. She knew that, and she, not Craig, had suggested they ought not to be tied to one another. He had laughed at her choice of words, but she knew that they had angered him a little.

She had felt freer—a little more alone, but freer—since they ceased seeing so much of each other. Actually, they had not dated since, but had shared a few activities where other people were present. He was dating; she knew that. She was not. She did not like talking about it with her roommate. Peggy's comments had suggested that Rachel did not appreciate Craig; that she had not been aware of the interests of other girls in him. Peggy had offered her a shoulder, but she clearly was sympathetic toward Craig.

"I'm fine. I have fun," Rachel said to her father.

"I hope so." He swirled up another bite of spaghetti.

The next morning she lingered over a slice of dry toast and orange juice, waiting for her father to come down. Finally he bounced into the kitchen, dressed in running shoes, Dockers slacks and a Patriots sweatshirt. He looked younger and much fresher than the previous night. His dark hair was graying, but evenly and with the affect that can make a man appear more mature, and handsome. And she had always thought of him as handsome. He was a little heavier; not enough to affect his good looks, but enough to make him a less frequent runner—or maybe it was the other way around.

"Your mom slept well."

"I heard you go into her room a couple of times," Rachel said.

"Yeah, with Mrs. Clausen not in there I think I slept a little lighter than usual. But she was sleeping each time I looked in."

She knew that it bothered him. Just last summer he had said that he would not move out of the room when Mrs. Clausen and the doctor had suggested such a change. Then it was to give Mrs. Clausen more flexibility when she stayed late in the evening, before she started staying full time.

"I'm going for a walk along the path," he said. "Sorry you can't join me." There was a slight flush to his face as soon as he said it. He had embarrassed himself. He seemed to start to say something else, but did not.

"Another time. When Mrs. Clausen is here. Maybe I'll run as soon as you get back and it warms up a little," Rachel said. "But I'd like to ask you something before you go. Have you seen the fence at the Holmes Cottage?"

"I don't recall any fence there. Is it new?"

"Yes. It's a big, orange fence, like a snow fence or the kind they put around construction sites."

"No, I haven't seen it. Why?"

"There's a *Keep Out* sign too and the fence blocks the path behind the cottage. You can't get to the bench without stepping over the fence and just ignoring the sign. Can someone do that? The fence, I mean?"

"Well, I guess so." He chuckled before sipping his coffee. "Sounds like someone has."

"Oh, you know what I mean, Dad. Is it allowed in the rules of the town, in the ordinances?"

"Now that's a good question. But I think that's private property. Actually, the landowner has probably just tolerated public use of the path. But the bench has been there as long as I can remember, and everybody uses it."

"Would this be like the paper streets thing in the *Register* articles a year or so ago?"

"I don't think so. Those were based on agreements between the town and the land developers that some of the planned streets might be extended for public access to the waters of the bay. The path is not covered by those agreements; besides, it's well up from the water. I don't know, Pumpkin, but it seems to me the local codes favor the property owner, except for the flats, of course; that's open to the public."

He had not called her Pumpkin in a long time.

"Well, if I'm going to do it, I had better do it right now." He rose from the chair. "Wait any longer and I'll find a way to keep myself from getting all sweaty and mad at cigarette companies."

"Cigarette companies don't smoke your cigarettes," she said.

"Spoken like the Maggie of old" he said, turned, and went out the door.

He still had not accepted her abandoning the law. He was gone before she could think of a quip in return. Was it the feeling of hurt; the feeling once again that she had disappointed him?

He opened the door and stuck his head back inside.

"You trying to make me feel bad—your running thing? Guess you'll run over the topside too," he said with a smile.

"You bet."

He waved and closed the door again. He was gone. He had tried to soften the Maggie comment, but he had not taken it back. Maybe she should talk to him about the job and their financial situation. Maybe he just did not recognize how much cheaper it would be now that she was not going on to law school.

She went up the stairs and stepped into her mother's room. She was awake, and turned her head as Rachel opened the door. Then she turned her head back, looking at the ceiling. Rachel looked up too, but there was nothing there, just the soft white texture of the ceiling and the slowly turning fan.

She went back to the kitchen and found little that needed to be done so she wiped down the counter top, sink and stove and went to her room and slipped on her mint green running suit.

She was still in her room scanning the *Boothbay Register* newspaper when she heard her father downstairs in the kitchen. She was nearly running as she passed him standing at the sink and draining a large glass of water.

"That water won't stop the heavy breathing," she called out as she passed.

"It's that damned hilltop of yours," he responded as she let the screen door slam closed behind her. He said something else but she could not make it out. Something about the worth of a great view—or lack thereof.

He had gone over the top. She smiled.

CHAPTER 2

William pulled on the black mountain boots with the lug soles and tied the strings, the arthritis in his fingers making the task more difficult in the morning cold. He would have to figure out a better way to heat the cottage, and soon. The realtor had said the cottage was seldom used in the winter, but he had never guessed the one baseboard heater in the front room would provide so little heat for the bedroom. It was an old building, and not well insulated. That had been clear in the spring when he looked it over. It would never have passed the test for an Alaskan cabin. He had lived in Alaska the last seventeen years, and even his cabin on the Kenai River would have been warmer with just one candle than this cottage had been last night.

Not that cold weather normally bothered him that much; he had always prided himself on taking the cold well. He preferred the cold anytime to the heat of Fort Benning, Georgia. But in the last seven or eight years, the arthritis, the osteoarthritis in his knees and fingers, made things harder. That was why he had left his job with the North Slope security people and retired down on the Kenai five years ago. That and the salmon runs. He already missed them, and he had been in the lower forty-eight States only two weeks. The runs would be over by now, the last Reds struggling up the Russian River and the acrobatic Silvers springing out of the surface of Seward Bay.

He had not shaved yet, but he would. He could count on one hand the number of days he had not shaved in the last fifty-six years—except for his days in combat in Korea and Vietnam. He tucked the Wooly-Pulley sweater down into his olive drab, wool trousers. The long johns underneath felt good, and the olive sweater was already holding in his body heat as he shoved his arms into the forest camouflage jacket of his old Army fatigue uniform. The large jacket draped loosely over his six feet, five-inch frame, but he had seldom worn it since he left the Army in '82. But he had worn it on occasion, and mixed with some experimental cold weather clothing that a couple of manufacturers provided at the cost only of a report on their use, he stayed warm up on the slope, even in temperatures seventy degrees below zero. It was quite warm so far here in Maine. A lot like the weather down on the Kenai. It certainly would not be as cold here as at Prudhoe Bay, but the poor heat in the cottage had caused him the day before to dig into his boxes and find the cold weather clothing.

He wished he had not slept so late. It was his second night in the cottage, and he had thought he would need no alarm, but he had been wrong. It was after eight o'clock. He would hate his old Alaska buddies to know what a pansy he had been. He needed a clock. While the coffee water was heating, he rummaged through one of three foot lockers looking for the clock that an old, retired sergeant had given him at the time of his departure from the northern oil field. It was a white plastic, standing kitty cat with one black eye, a bugle in one hand, and a round, battery operated clock embedded in the belly. He guessed that the batteries were dead. Then the cat went into its act:

"Rise and Shine. Rise and Shine. Rise and Shine," was the loud report. He struggled to find the switch he had inadvertently flipped. Then came the cat's real wake-up call: Reveille—the same bugle call he had heard so many mornings during his thirty-three years of service, but he had never heard a bugler as loud as this little cat was right now.

There was a knock at the door. Who the hell could that be? He disliked interruptions and uninvited company, and he had not yet shut the cat up. He dropped it, but caught the loud kitty before it hit the floor. Then he looked through the glass panes of the doorway and saw a woman—a girl. He wished he had let the cat hit the floor. That might have shut it up, but now it looked like the girl could hear the loud animal. She was smiling.

Rachel watched in amusement as the tall man struggled with the white object that seemed to be the source of the loud sounds. Finally the sound stopped and the man stepped forward and pulled the door ajar. The tip of her tongue touched the warm, salty moisture above her lip and her hand stroked back the dampness of her hair along the side of her face. The awful music and the loud shouts had reminded her of Gomer Pyle television reruns. The bald man stood with a white toy animal—a cat—in his left hand. His right hand went to the top of his head as if to brush back hair that was not there. He was tall, and tanned. He wore the clothing she had seen on street people in Boston in the wintertime; however, his boots were shiny black, like those of Boston's finest police officers. He was a lot older than her father, and deep markings like a spider's web cut the skin at the corners of his eyes. They were the eyes of an older person, one who has fought off some kind of illness, or health trauma that left the eyes more deeply set and a little less lively. The gray stubble of his beard added to the appearance of general fatigue and age. His brow and cheeks were furrowed, but the flesh below his chin sagged little, owing in part to the manner in which he thrust out his chin and tipped his head back. He reminded her of the pose struck by the old actor, Gregory Peck, in his portrayal of General MacArthur. The clothing she recognized was military, maybe Army. She waited for the man to say something. Anything. But he just stood there holding the door, and she realized that she was not welcome.

"Sir," she said, and chided herself for addressing him so formally. "Mister…ah, Mister…." She received no help from him.

"Well," she said, "my name is Rachel, and I'm wondering why the fence is blocking the path."

He did not respond. Except maybe to grow an inch taller.

"Did you put up the fence?" She asked.

"Do you represent some government agency or something?"

"Well, no, but I wanted to ask about this before I went to the authorities."

"Why would you go to the authorities?"

"To find out if the fence is legal."

"It's on my land. I bought the property seven months ago."

"But you can't block the path. I mean, you shouldn't fence off the bench."

"Why not? It's my bench. Came with the property. The real estate woman was clear about that. Not that I care one way or another. Planned to take the bench to the dump. Already would have, but I don't have a way to haul it and the damn thing is bolted down to concrete. Don't need it and it's rusted. Prefer things made of brass."

"I wish you wouldn't do anything to that bench, Mister. It means a lot to the people around here. Lots of people use it. I really wish you would consider…"

William slammed the door before she was finished. Damned aggressive sort. Let her go see the authorities. He could not believe that he had bought land that he couldn't keep free of trespassers. Sure would be different from Alaska if that were the case. However, even as he jerked the smoking, empty teakettle off the stove, he remembered Hawaii. You could not block the path there, but that was along the beach, public beach. The girl had spunk. But she had caused him to burn up his old teakettle. Or maybe he had already let it boil down. No, she caused it. Getting into his business. He did not like that. Not one damn bit.

Rachel thought that she probably should not spend time on the old man, but the bench was as much a part of the Harbor to her as her home. Her father was in the kitchen when she returned, reading the paper and drinking a cup of his extra-strength coffee. He listened to her account of the exchange with the old man.

"What do you think?" She asked.

"He's probably right."

"I know."

Her father went to shower, and she found the cereal, her father's favorite—raisin bran. She did not like it. She closed the cupboard door and popped two slices of whole wheat into the toaster. Then she stood as she had as a child and watched her reflection on the side of the toaster.

"They don't make them like that any more," her father would say as he rubbed the surface that shone like a pair of reflective, silver sunglasses. She heard her father's generation make such claims so often that she tired of it, but in the case of her parents' wedding gift toaster, he was right.

She ate the toast with a little jelly and thought of the few days until she had to go back to school. Her grades were slipping and she had little enthusiasm for her classes. And there would not be Craig to help her over the times when she felt like she really did not even want to go to class. Her father had no idea that she was not enjoying college. He never spoke of his days as a student there with anything but appreciation and happy memories. She should do better. She knew that.

She went to her mother's room, and cracked the door. Her mother was awake. And alone. She told her mom hello, hugged her, and picked up the book. She was continuing to read *The Notebook* to her. She had read the book right after it had come out; thought it was a marvelous story and in a way instructive. She guessed it was what they called a sensitive story, but she doubted that her mother understood.

Before her departure Mrs. Clausen had left fresh sheets and pillowcases on the bench at the foot of the bed. After reading half a chapter Rachel decided to go ahead and change the linens. Her mother accepted being rolled from one side of the bed to the other. She was more docile than any child would be. She tucked her mother in again and sat in the cane-backed chair and continued to read the book aloud.

Weeks earlier she was home for a weekend and had been reading the book as Mrs. Clausen came into the bedroom. Rachel had paused.

"Don't stop. I've heard some of your reading. It's an unusual story. I'd like to borrow it when you're finished. If you don't mind."

"I'm afraid she doesn't hear, or doesn't understand."

"Oh she hears you; of that I'm certain. I'm afraid I don't know how much she understands."

Rachel watched the woman who cared for her mother all hours of the day. She was not a registered nurse, but she had worked for years in the Portland area and more recently out of the home care service here at Boothbay Harbor, and she had come to specialize in caring for those suffering from Alzheimer's. Even when she had attended to her mother only during the daytime, Rachel had found her a caring and industrious person. She liked both traits.

"But I don't know if it helps her," Rachel said.

"You can't know that, but it helps you, and that counts." She left the room and Rachel guessed that she left for her. To make it easier. And maybe…for her mother.

Later Rachel showered and decided to drive rather than walk to the town office. She was anxious to get the whole matter of the fence and the bench at Holmes Cottage settled. She put on a dark blue wool skirt and a white sweater, and the gray walking shoes that she wore regularly at college. She pulled on her green wool vest and opened the door of the 1990 Accord. Her father called it the most reliable car in America. That had been when the car was already six years old.

An hour later she was back beside the house, sitting at the wheel of the car in disappointment with what she had been told. She could understand that the bench belonged to the cottage, but the path had been in use for more years than she knew; yet they had said it: if the tall man wanted to deny access across his property, that was his right.

They did offer to look into the fence. It did not sound like a proper fence for a tourist-minded village.

"I had hoped for a different answer, but thanks," she had said as she left the town office.

Her remaining option was to appeal again to the tall man's better nature.

She saw him through the window of the cottage door and knocked. He walked away from her into the front room. She could hear music. She knew that it was classical, performed by a large orchestra. It was mournful, and she did not care for it. It stopped. He reappeared in the doorway between the front room and kitchen, looked in her direction, and then set a paper bag under the kitchen sink and pulled the cloth curtain to cover the opening. He walked over and opened the door.

"Yes?" He said and held the door slightly ajar as if to keep out the cold air. This was better; at least he seemed civil.

"Sir," she said, "my name is Rachel Connor, and I've lived in the Harbor all my life. I've walked on the path that goes across your property, and I've sat on that bench out there since before I began grade school. I know that it's your bench and your land, but I wonder, would you just consider letting people continue to use the path and the bench?"

He did not reply, simply looked at her.

"People will respect your property. Can I help you take down the sign and fence?"

She saw that she had gone too far.

"No," he said, and closed the door. She wanted to break the dirt-streaked glass panes of the door, scaling paint flakes the size of her thumbnail. She watched his big, camouflaged back move away into the other room, heard the music again. She looked around. Surely someone would object to the jarring, sad bass of the music. She did not know much classical music, but she thought of Wagner. Whatever the piece and its composer, she had never heard it—not in church—not even at a funeral.

She knocked on the door again, but he stayed in the far room, and the music was even louder. She turned from the door and started the short walk to her home. She slowed as she walked down the steep roadway. Tomorrow was Thanksgiving Day and she knew that she simply wanted to get it over. She felt the guilt that she was wishing away time with her family. The feeling of helplessness returned. It was a feeling present so often at school and when she sat in her mother's room. Get on with your life she said to herself; and knew how easily that was said but how callous it seemed if it meant going back to Boston to keep her mother out of her mind. There was so little she could do.

At least she might have made a difference about the path and the bench. But she had not.

CHAPTER 3

Mrs. Clausen returned Friday morning and Rachel and her father were pleased to see her. The holiday meal had been okay, but it had been mostly warmed up dishes that Mrs. Clausen had prepared before she left. Rachel's father had sliced the cold turkey breast and they ate in silence. Neither of them complained, but she knew it had not been special for her or for him. She had been a little disappointed when he asked her to see if her mother would eat some of the turkey and cranberry sauce. She did not mind doing it, but she would have preferred to know that he wanted to spend the time with her mother. Instead, he moved to the den and turned on a professional football game. For the first time in at least five Thanksgivings she did not join him. She sat in her mother's room, read aloud from the novel, and tried to get her mother to eat more turkey. She thought that her mother ate about as much as she needed for someone seldom out of bed. When she went into the den in the early evening her father was asleep in his big chair. She turned down the television volume and went to her room.

She did not see him again until morning. When she heard his voice she pulled on her robe and went downstairs. He was talking to her mother, and he stopped when Rachel entered her mother's room. He said he was going to shower and shave. He looked a little embarrassed and was wearing the clothes he had on when she left him in the den the evening before.

Mrs. Clausen had come in shortly after that, bouncy and asking right away how Mrs. Connor had done. Rachel told her of the spilled vase and her mother's position when she had entered the bedroom. The nurse did not seem much concerned.

"She got out of bed on her own just the other day and was trying to use the bathroom. I got there in time to help her and then she went back to bed on her own," Mrs. Clausen said. "Would help her to get up and walk more—the doctor has told us that more than once." Was there counseling in Mrs. Clausen's voice? Did she mean that Rachel or her dad should take her mother out for a walk? Mrs. Clausen stopped as she moved back toward her mother's room. "I sometimes walk her along the hallway and to the front door and back. Three or four times."

"But I thought that she—well; doesn't she give you some problems?"

"Oh, you mean wanting to walk into the other rooms, or to the bathroom? I think the bathroom is her favorite room. If you mean does she dictate where to walk, the answer is yes. But I let her do that. It's a small thing. It's not a very big house, and I go along with most anything she wants to do if it isn't harmful to her—even pounding the piano keys with her kitchen spatula."

"But you don't let her go up or down the stairs, do you?"

"That's never a problem. She shows no desire to go up or down the stairs—or to go outside. And there's the restraining gate your dad put at the top of the basement stairs. But your dad and I always keep that door closed anyway. Since your father agreed to move her bedroom downstairs, she has shown no desire to go back up. We're alert to the stairs—they could be dangerous for her."

Rachel had read about the need to go along with the Alzheimer patient, to avoid trying to invoke our rules or social expectations when those of the patient are different and not dangerous. She had found that hard at first, but Mrs. Clausen never seemed to mind at all. It had introduced some unusual activities around the house, especially at the time of her second year in college. She had watched one weekend as Mrs. Clausen sat patiently while her mother helped in the kitchen, placing some pots and pans in the refrigerator in place of the carton of milk that she set in the drawer below the oven. Later Rachel went to put the items back in their proper place only to find that Mrs. Clausen had already done so—at least she was quite sure her mother had not redone it all. Rachel had been there when her mother felt she had finished the chore and wiped her hands on a dish towel, folded it on the oven door handle as she had done for years, and with apparent pride in her efficient housekeeping, walked back to do some other chore in the bathroom. Rachel had walked outside the kitchen door to hide her tears, but Mrs. Clausen had remained, ever present, ever smiling, and ever patient. She knew now that she should make an effort to get her mother up and walking; so should her father. Or maybe he did when she was not there. She had stopped that months ago. Out of fear for her mother, she thought, but now she knew it was probably for herself. She recalled the time that she and her mother had walked down to the wharf, and coming home her mother had insisted that their house was to the north along Townsend, not to the south. And the time her mother had refused to leave the kitchen, grabbing the kitchen table leg and screaming until her father came to rescue her mother from whomever she had decided Rachel had become. It had been the first time that Rachel thought that her Mom did not know who she was, and it terrified Rachel until her father had settled her mother down. Yet less than an hour later she went into her mother's room and found her pleasant—unaware it seemed of the incident in the kitchen.

No, Rachel did not get her mother up for walks now, and she would. She would also suggest the need again to her father, but she did not mention it to him before his departure later that evening for Portland and a business meeting on Saturday morning. The next two days seemed like a week to her. She got her mother up twice and walked with her about the house. One time her mother moved a small, crystal swan figurine on one of the living room tables, as if the one-inch change accomplished something. Rachel was thrilled by the small move and hoped for more attention to the house by her mother. She stopped her before the breakfront with the white china, but her mother made no sign of recognition or interest. She let her mother move at her will, but then saw signs of fatigue and guessed that her mom did not recall where the bedroom was. She nudged her by the elbow and guided her with ease back to her bed. Rachel felt a little better after those walks and told herself that they had to be good for her mother. For her body, physically. Rachel decided against a run or walk, but helped Mrs. Clausen with the cleaning and spent some time with her mother, reading the book. On Sunday afternoon she handed the book over to Mrs. Clausen and drove back to school.

Peggy tried to include her in every activity she could, but Rachel did not want to socialize or party as much as her roommate did; never had, and particularly had no desire to do so now. She did go to a few parties; she learned that while she missed the time with Craig, it was really over, and no one else interested her. She turned more intently to her studies and when the Christmas break came, she felt that she was regaining some of her enthusiasm for her subjects.

She drove up to Boothbay on the twenty-third, two days later than she had planned, but she had been interviewing for a part-time job running a folding press in a printing shop. The elderly owner of the shop sounded encouraging, but said he would let her know if she would check back right after Christmas. "Never had a girl run one of our machines before," he said as he let her out the front door of his shop. His was a non-union shop. He had told her that with some apparent pride.

Her father was home when she arrived, just finishing the installation of a six-foot pine tree in its customary seasonal place in the living room near the bay window. Tonight they would decorate, but now he asked her to put down her bag and join him in going to the grocery. She went back to say hello to her mother and he did not rush her. Neither spoke of her mother's lack of attention or awareness as they chatted briefly with Mrs. Clausen before leaving the house. Rachel learned during the short drive that she and her father were to cook Christmas dinner. The prior year Mrs. Clausen had insisted on cooking the meal and Rachel had helped little, but as much as Mrs. Clausen seemed to want. This year her father had insisted that Mrs. Clausen spend the Christmas Eve and day with her daughter and her family. He told Rachel that all the medication information and phone numbers were pinned to the kitchen corkboard just like during the Thanksgiving holiday.

Rachel suggested TV turkey dinners in jest, and her father seemed offended. Said it was to be ham, and not pre-cooked ham, but an in-house baked ham complete with pineapple rings, clove buds, and knife scoring on the surface.

"If you really think you can handle that," she said. "I'll spring for making the salad."

"Waldorf," he said.

"Ouch, I had in mind tossing something. What part of the meal do I get to select?"

"Dessert. We're not going to make the dessert. You can pick one out."

"What if I decide that I want to make one myself?"

"What? Peanut-flavored chocolate sauce on store-bought vanilla ice cream?"

"I just may bake a pumpkin pie. That's my favorite…and Mom's, you know."

"Yes, I know," he said. They drove on in silence.

After the shopping and as he drove back home, he suggested that she take a little run. Back home they put the groceries away and her father said, "Now go for your run."

"I don't quite feel like a run. I'll wait until later."

"No, I'm throwing you out of the house, daughter. Walk if you want, but get out and breathe some of the good, Harbor air."

"Walk? If I'm going to the trouble right now, I'm at least going to get in a good run."

"Macho," he said as she left to change clothes.

The weather was overcast and windy, and she wore her old ski jacket over the green running suit. She had not been skiing so far this season. She and Craig had enjoyed racing down the slopes, a tall pilsner of beer, hot popcorn, and the warmth of the chalet....

The fence was gone. The bench appeared to top off a coronation with its pattern of interlocking leaves and stems of the grape that contrasted with the green grass of the slope behind it. The bench was white. White like snow, much brighter than the low clouds that hung above the bay. She dropped to one knee and, ignoring the damp earth, examined the legs, down low, where the rust had been the greatest. Even the metal nuts holding the bench seemed new. The metal of the entire bench, scraped and sanded no doubt before painting, was smooth under the white enamel.

Maybe it was a new bench.

Then she saw the missing tip of one leaf, near the top left of the back of the seat. Bobby Thigpen had broken that with a baseball bat. Not in swinging, but in using the bat as a crowbar to try to remove the bench from the concrete base to which it was bolted. She had taken the bat from him, chased him down the hill, all the way to his house, and thrown the bat up on his front porch as he slammed his front door. He had been nine, and she was eight. But she was bigger.

She looked at the other side of the cottage and saw that the other section of fence and the sign were gone.

Rachel cut short her run and ran back down the street to her house.

"Who?" She asked her father who was bending over some papers at his desk in the den.

"The Brigadier. General William Jennings," her father had said. "A Brigadier Jennings."

"How do you know?"

"Buck, down at Grover's Hardware, sold him the wire brush, paint, scraper...some naval jelly to remove rust. Buck said he had thought he was working on an old boat but the Brigadier said he would never get caught dead on a boat, or an airplane. Said he had had his fill of all of them."

"Seems he was pretty talkative with Buck. And Buck learned all that in selling him paint?"

"Yeah, and that he was redoing the bench, actually had dragged it right in the cottage. Paid for the paint and all with a check from a bank in Anchorage, Alaska. Buck said he couldn't recall that he, personally, had ever taken in a check written on an Alaska bank; said the old guy bought a lot of paint, and the check cleared just fine."

"How many coats of paint did he put on it?"

"Well, the paint was not just for the bench, it was for the outside and inside of the cottage. I don't know how much, but Buck said a lot. Buck told him it might be quite a while before it got warm enough to paint the outside of the cottage. The Brigadier said that was not a problem, that he had plenty of room to store the paint, and he liked to be prepared. He lives there alone."

It had not occurred to her that he did not live alone. He just seemed alone—struck her as someone who would be alone.

"How old is he?" She asked.

"That I don't know, and I doubt that Buck needed to know that to sell him paint. You saw him up close. How old do you think he is?"

She did not have a good guess.

"I don't know. I mean his voice is strong, but his eyes look…they look older. I don't know. I would guess he's somewhere between sixty and seventy."

Her father laughed. "You would not make a great witness at a crime scene."

"Well, I told you that I didn't know. You asked me." She didn't like him faulting her ability as a witness. It was too close to her potential as a lawyer. She did not want any criticism from him in that area.

"Why don't you go back and knock on the door and tell him that we appreciate the bench and use of the path," he said.

"Maybe later today," she said. But she did not think that she wanted to do that. He had only done what he should have done from the start.

Still, she was curious about the man. The white bench. She was not ready to thank him. He might not even listen to her long enough for that.

Late Christmas day she carried a small basket to the door of Holmes Cottage. Her father had not been aware that she was leaving. He was watching football on television. She would be back before he missed her. She listened. There was a continuous scratching sound, and light shone from the front area of the cottage. She ought to leave. He may not even be at home. She hoped that he was not. Even as she helped prepare the meal, she had thought of him and worried where he would eat his Christmas meal. At the dinner table where she talked of Peggy's efforts to get her to date more often, her father helped little with the conversation, but he did take a tray up to her mother. He returned shortly.

"She just doesn't want to eat right now. Ate a little of your ice cream without the sauce. She eats a good breakfast you know. Seems like that's all the food she needs for the entire day." They both knew that she needed to eat more. The doctor and Mrs. Clausen had told them that.

"I'll try again later," he had said.

Rachel knocked at the cottage door. She waited.

She knocked again. Twice. And harder.

Still nothing. She had better leave.

But the scratching had stopped. She leaned her head against the door and heard what she guessed were shoeless feet shuffling over the floor. She looked again. Nothing.

Maybe he knew she was here. Probably he still didn't want to see her—or anyone.

She heard the sound of a heavy object hit the floor. Then the cursing, and judging by the selected words, he did not know that she was out here. Yet he had to know that someone was knocking on his door. And it was Christmas.

His silhouette almost blocked the doorway between the front room and the kitchen. She guessed he was wearing a great robe, but when he turned on the light and entered the kitchen, she saw that it was a large Army wool blanket.

"Who is it?" He called out.

"Rachel, Rachel Connor."

"Who? What do you want for Pete's sake? It's Christmas."

"I came by to see if—to wish you a Merry Christmas."

"Merry Christmas," he said as he turned his back to her and walked back into the front room.

"General, General Jennings, are you all right?"

He stopped. He paused. But he did not turn.

"Wait a minute," he said. "I have to put something on over my long johns."

He was a long time, and he cursed twice again, both times after what she thought was a heavy shoe dropped or thrown to the floor.

William slipped on the wool trousers. Why was she here? It was a bad time. His fingers felt the pain as he fumbled to tie his mountain boots, and he had dropped one twice already in trying to put them on. His chest hurt from the lingering cold. It reminded him of the affects of the cold air when he used to run with the airborne troops at thirty below zero in Alaska. His chest and even his throat burned. And his jaw ached. Especially now as he made the effort to get dressed. Putting on his boots was the hardest thing he had tried to do in the past few days. He grimaced and rose to see why this snippy girl was interrupting his Christmas.

He opened the door. He knew it was cold and that he should invite her in, but the place was a mess. He hadn't felt like keeping things tidy. Eight gallons of paint still sat atop the kitchen table and in one of the two chairs. There was hardly room to stand in the kitchen, and the front room floor was covered with the contents of three foot lockers. He could not ask her in. And he didn't want to.

"Yes, young lady," he said as he opened the door. He saw in her eyes that she didn't approve of how he looked. But that was none of her damn business.

"What do you want?" He asked.

"I brought you some Christmas dinner."

"I already ate."

"Oh? Could I ask what you had for dinner?"

My, the girl is pushy. "A bowl of chicken noodle soup if you must know," he said. "And in style. I ate my dinner in bed."

He seemed to have shut her up. She just stood there. He smelled the ham, and cranberries, or cranberry sauce, and, he guessed, Waldorf salad.

"Do you have Waldorf salad there?" He asked and opened the door wider.

"Yes."

"Well, I haven't had Waldorf since…well I can't remember."

"May I come in?"

"Yeah, uh…yes, if we can find a place for you to stand—or sit."

They cleared the table and chairs and carried the cans of paint to the front of the cottage, and then she laid the food out as he started water for tea. He heated the water in the number ten vegetable can that had carried socks all the way from Alaska. He was glad she agreed to share his tea.

He knew that she was watching him closely as he ate.

"This is very good tea," she said.

"It's Earl Grey," he said. "My favorite."

"Were you really a general?" She asked.

It was as if she had thrown ice water in his face. It was a normal kind of question. He had been asked that before. But not in recent years. And not by a young girl who smelled of expensive perfume, and spoke with the diction and control of fine schooling. He tried to remember when he had sat alone with a woman who was anything other than a brief interruption in his security work on the slope. The food seemed to lose its taste. He remembered the last time he had sat with a beautiful young girl like this. It was a memory too many years old, a memory layered by hundreds of different efforts to forget in more countries than he cared to recall. He knew it was not the "general" thing. It was what she would expect him to have done and to have experienced—things that he had found it comforting in the last twenty years to forget or avoid. He glanced around the room. He felt the stubble of his beard. He had not shaved. Even his speech had come to reflect the language of the rough and hard living men that the oil industry in Alaska had tended to attract. They were good men. But they were not graduates of American colleges and universities, save the engineers and a few managers. But he had preferred time with the workers and security guards who demanded little of him except to carry out his share of the weight from a moose kill and to share some of his less guarded secrets on where to catch the graylings and dolly varden. But all that and this room were far away from the world of this girl and the faintly remembered world that she caused him to recall. He should have never opened the door.

"I don't think I can eat more. You ought to go now," he said.

"Are you ill?" She asked.

"No," he said and looked at her closely. "I'm just old. And I should never have come here. I should have stayed where I was."

"Alaska?"

"I really think you should leave." He rose with difficulty, the knees stiff from too little exercise since his cold set in.

"You should see a doctor," she said.

"You should go," he replied as he walked slowly to the front room, and then through the door to his bedroom. "You can let yourself out." He lay down on the bed, the pain in his chest again. "Thanks," he said, but he did not know if it was loud enough for her to hear. He was not going to say it again. The throat hurt too much. He heard her say something as she closed the door.

Rachel told her father of her visit after the game ended. She watched most of the last quarter. It was not a good game. She had come to prefer college football to the professional game. But she still sometimes shared the NFL games with her father. He was hooked on the New England Patriots who seemed to vacillate between a team with a defense and no quarterback to one with a quarterback but no defense to one with no defense and a quarterback who seemed no longer to produce. She had liked the coach who had moved to New York, but she guessed that she would not want to work for him.

"Dad, I think that he thanked me at the end. I told him Merry Christmas, but he didn't say a thing. I worry about him."

"Well, I'll look in on him, Rachel, tomorrow, but why do you have to go back to Boston tomorrow? You don't have classes until January. I'm disappointed. We've always had a good time over the holidays."

"I'm having trouble in a couple of my subjects, Dad. I've made a resolution to do a lot better next year. I promised Becky I would have lunch with her tomorrow. I haven't seen her since summer. I'm going back tomorrow after our lunch."

"That's good. Vicky was by just the other day and said it worried her that you and Becky seem to have drifted apart. I told her that you were pretty tied up in your studies."

"Well, you didn't need to say that, Dad. We just have different friends now, that's all. But I'll see her tomorrow."

"Good. Well, let me check the weather channel and see what kind of driving weather you'll have."

She watched as he surfed through the channels rather than go directly to the weather channel, a number that both of them knew well.

"Looks like you won't run into any ice or snow." He rose and walked to her chair, reaching out his hands. She took them as she stood and then he released her hands and hugged her. She hung on, felt her eyes water, and fought off tears.

"I'm sorry, Rachel. I know that things aren't going too well for you right now. I miss your laughter, but then I know I'm not all that cheerful a fellow either. We don't laugh much around here anymore."

He was right. She found it impossible to be happy in this house. Even a smile made her feel guilty. It was not fair to her mother. But it was not fair to her father not to smile.

"Any chance you two will patch it up? Craig, I mean?"

"No. He already has someone else. I don't really need that right now."

"Not bitter, are you?"

"No. I don't really make good company for anyone."

"You're really wrong on that one. Why don't you stay another day or two?"

"I do have to get back." She stepped away and turned to avoid his eyes. She was not ready to tell him of the job that she might have. It would hurt or anger him—or both.

He turned back to the television, searching again for sports—any sports. He put down the remote and looked again at her.

"What about Tom? He's back, you know. Why not look him up? Should be easy. I hear he's taking over his dad's fishing boat."

She was sorry to hear that Tom was back. His dream had been to become a professional baseball pitcher, and he had played well in college and left early to sign with one of the major league teams, Atlanta she thought.

"So he's back for good? I thought it took a little longer to find out if a pitcher was good enough for the majors. He's only two years older than I am."

"His dad says that he damaged his arm, and they can't fix it. But I think he was just not quite good enough. Probably the best pitcher that the Boothbay Seahawks ever produced, but it's another story up there, Rachel. Best hitters in the country. Besides, Tom always had a little trouble with his control."

Rachel recalled one game. A big one for the local high school. Tom had started and walked the first five batters. He was a senior, she was a sophomore, and they had only had a couple of dates. Both walks down along the wharf and a hotdog snack. The walks were all her father would allow, but the times had been special and she hurt for him even as she wanted to scream out to him to throw the ball over the plate. She knew that he could. Why didn't he just throw the ball over the plate. She knew he was angry, and stubborn. But she knew also that people talked about his refusal to quit or to "give in" her dad would say. "He won't give in to a batter on a single pitch," her dad would say of the young pitcher. She had found herself saying under her breath, "Give in, give in, Tom." But he had not. She had never known anyone who could be quite so intense. Even during their stroll on the wharf, he had never gotten far from baseball. He believed in himself. He was going to pitch in the major leagues, he told her.

"Wow, check the speed on that last pitch," a man near her in the stands had said. And she thought that she could hear the difference—the loud smack of the catcher's glove. He struck the man out, and the next, and the next to end the first inning for the visitors. The Seahawks won the game, and the visiting team never moved beyond the two runs scored on Tom's walks. Part of the Seahawks' six runs was the three that Tom drove in with a double off the left field fence. After the game Tom and his father dropped Rachel off at her home. She was embarrassed with his steady faulting of his pitching and the failure of the ball to clear the fence for a home run when he hit the double. His father complimented him on the game and said he was impressed at how Tom bounced back from the early walks. When she said simply that she thought he had played very well, he did not bother to look at her.

"What do you know about baseball," he said. It was not a question. It was a declaration. She could not recall ever feeling so hurt. By the time the car reached her house, she was angry and disappointed with him. She guessed it showed, because Tom made no move to get out of the car when his dad stopped in front of Rachel's house.

"Tom, I thought you were staying to visit for a while," Tom's father said.

"I really am bushed. I think I'll just go on home with you, Dad. See you at school tomorrow, Rachel," Tom said.

And he did. And they talked. Briefly. He apologized for not staying to visit, but there was no discussion of the ballgame or his reaction to it. It remained that way through the spring and to the end of school, his senior year. It seemed they never got past that day even though they never again talked about it. It was as if he did not want to hear her thoughts of baseball even though it was the only thing he ever managed to talk about—his pitching and hitting and her watching. She finally concluded that he had meant what he had implied, that she knew nothing about baseball. He asked her to attend the school prom, and she went. They had not dated again, and she seldom had seen him in the four or so years since.

"I'm sorry for him. Dad. I don't think that he ever saw himself as a lobster fisherman. I don't think he would want to see me." Her Dad did not respond, discovering the replay of highlights of the game he had watched earlier in the day.

The lunch the next day was not what she had expected. Becky picked her up as planned, and she admired the late model BMW that her friend was driving.

"This yours?" Rachel asked.

"Yes, as long as my GPA stays up at least near a three point. I am so tired of school, Rachel. How about you?"

"It's hard. I don't seem to be able to study like I used to. But I have done a little better in the last few weeks."

"How'd you do that? Lose your boyfriend?"

Rachel remarked on Becky's mind reading abilities and then made light of her friendship with Craig that she, not he, had terminated.

"That surprises me. You know I couldn't get five minutes with you the three weeks he was here last summer," Becky said.

"Don't pick on me," Rachel said with a chuckle. "Dad has already beaten me up on Craig. He really liked him I guess."

"Beware of men that your father likes. They are likely to be conservative, overly serious, and boring."

"Craig was not boring. If anyone was boring, you're looking at her."

"Have you seen Tom?"

"No. Have you?" Rachel asked, too quickly she thought.

"Yes. I though he might have called you. You were all that he talked about."

"Really?"

"Yes. Really. You still interested?"

"In him as a person, yes. But not romantically."

"He says he blew it with you; that he hurt your feelings at a ball game one time. I asked him what he meant, but he wouldn't talk about it any more. What did he mean?"

Rachel told Becky the story and was glad when they pulled up at the house overlooking Linekin Bay.

"What are we doing here, Becky?" Rachel had thought they were going to eat at a restaurant near the wharf, but had been too absorbed in the conversation to ask their destination as they had swung around Union to Atlantic and then up Lobster Cove Drive beside the church. She recognized the house. It was owned by Becky's older sister and brother in law, Doctor Kline. Much of the year and all of the summer, it was leased by the week to large families or groups from the south.

"The Klines and the Marslands are eating leftovers for lunch today, and you are invited."

Becky was a Marsland and not close to becoming anything else from what she had told Rachel over the past three years. She had boyfriends, and more available, and she had no serious intention to settle down with any of them in the next ten years. Hers was a life that Rachel did not think she could enjoy—or afford.

Most of the people there Rachel had come to know during high school. They were nice people. Easy to talk to, and without exception considerate of other people in their conversations. They all asked about her mother, but they did not linger, and she liked that. Two of the men and one of the women were doctors. She though that maybe that was one reason that they did not seem obliged to spend all their time with her talking about her mother's illness. They all knew about Alzheimer's and knew you could not, with today's knowledge, greatly alter the course that it took with her mother. They all knew there were major research efforts going on and some promising areas being explored, but they probably knew, or guessed, that Rachel was aware of these.

The food was not leftovers, but an attractive assortment of raw and cooked creatures of the sea or dips and finger food in which sea life was the primary ingredient. She tried only one of the several wines, leaving the glass not quite empty when she and Becky left. It had been the only laughter-filled activity of the holidays.

"Thank you," she said as she and Becky hugged by the open car door in front of Rachel's home.

"Rachel, get out and have some fun. I hate to say so, but you look tired out of your eyes. And don't give me that story that you ran ten miles this morning."

"But I did run ten miles this morning, or almost ten—out to the point and back twice."

"Well, hooray for you, but that won't get you out with friends where you can have some fun. Find a man, Rachel. Any man."

Rachel watched as Becky sent the dark convertible surging up the street at a speed that might have been double the town speed limit. Rachel was relieved that her father's car was not in the driveway. She had already packed her car and she got in and hastily drove away, but she saw the drapery moved back just inside the big window in the front room. The face was Mrs. Clausen's. She reduced the pressure on the accelerator, a response to guilt. But she sped up again. She was running away. The laugher of the lunch at the Kline house was gone, replaced by the heaviness of thoughts about her mother, and of William, and of the empty spot on the wharf where Tom Boyd's lobster boat would have been this morning if he were not already out checking his lobster traps.

On the drive back she rambled through a field of thoughts, finally settling on a resented discomfort about the job in the printing plant. She knew that her father could not help with what really bothered her. If she could just one time do something to help her mother, just one time see her smile in recognition—of anyone—or show some joy or happiness…She recalled a minister, in a movie, who spoke of how we often find ourselves unable to help those closest to us; those we love most. But the actor had portrayed some peace or acceptance of that in his sermon. She could not find that peace, or accept her mother's condition. She knew she should. She knew it was considered a strength to handle such sickness as a reality that one neither ignored nor let dominate with sadness, but she didn't know how to do that. She knew that she was avoiding her mother, even when she sat in the room with her, and she was not helped with the thought that right now only her mother's death could make her sadder.

CHAPTER 4

In February Rachel called her boss at the printing shop to tell him that she could not work as planned on Friday afternoon and Saturday. His hesitation caused her concern until he inquired about her mother's condition and listened as she told him the new development. He told her to take the time she needed and then said that hiring her was the best decision he had made the last year. She knew he was trying to make her feel good, and normally it would have worked.

She flew to Portland where her father picked her up and drove to the Harbor. It had come without warning. Mrs. Clausen had simply said it was too much for one person to care for Mrs. Connor in the home; that they needed to make other arrangements. Her father said that he had not been that surprised. He had seen a change in Mrs. Clausen over the past few months. It was one of the reasons he had pushed her to take the holidays with her daughter. It was probably depression, he told Rachel. A doctor had told him about it many months before—the phenomenon of the caregiver of an Alzheimer patient who becomes ill, depressed, or at least "burned out" by the difficulty of the task. Something like guilt lay in the car as thick as coastal fog as they sped north and east toward home. It was the step they had hoped to avoid. Her father interrupted Rachel before she could complete her proposal to quit school and come home to help Mrs. Clausen.

"Don't complicate this by suggesting that you're going to care for your mother, Rachel. I know you want to help, but our only option is a place where her illness is understood and people are trained and equipped to help her."

"But what kind of a place must it be, Dad? How can they give her the love that..."

"The right kind of place. We'll meet a woman tomorrow who'll tell us about a nice and safe home. It's right in the Harbor, Rachel."

"But, Dad, there must be some way to keep her in her own house." She stopped and concentrated on holding back the tears.

"We've done that, Rachel. We've stretched our time together as a family just as long as we could. Now we need to look at another way; one that will be better for your mother although you may find it hard to see that."

She did.

They met the woman the next day for lunch, Mrs. Clausen agreeing to stay on until they made a decision on her mother's new home. Rachel had thought they would go to the facility, but her father told her that he had suggested they meet at the restaurant. Rachel preferred that, and she guessed her father had done that for her. She had eaten on occasion at the seafood restaurant, one of the few that remained open after November in the Harbor. Her father and Ms. Polan seemed to enjoy the food. Rachel picked at hers. The woman's quick answers and emphasis on compassionate care and her constant reference to "the home" were somewhat reassuring. Then it came time to take the next step—the arrangement to visit the home—the new home. Rachel nodded in agreement. Later, she was thankful when her father did not give her a pep talk or even chide her when she elected not to go with him to "inspect" her mother's potential new home. Instead, the next day she would read to her mother and then visit the brigadier. William, her dad had called him. She would just ask him a few questions. About his family, or where he had lived other than Alaska while in the Army, anything to try to see how he could be encouraged to be at least friendly. Maybe she could thank him for the bench. Maybe she could start anew and welcome him to town. He should have taken down the fence, and painted the bench, but she wanted to know why he had. It had seemed so unlikely...what made him change?

Her father had not been punctual in his visit to the old man. He said that he had just put it off and did not get there until the twenty-ninth of December. He had found the kitchen empty of furniture and the old man painting the ceiling. Now she looked in through the clean and polished glass of the door window. It looked like a new room. The walls were painted, but it appeared that he had just completed the work, and had not removed the newspapers from the floor or put the room back in order. Only the stove and sink showed signs of use, and she could not see the table or chairs.

She knocked several times and, although she could hear him moving about, he did not answer or come to the door. Finally she called out.

"William…William, are you there?"

"Hold your horses, girl. I'll be right there."

When he did come into the kitchen, she saw that he was pale. She guessed it was the lack of sun. He had a rich tan when she had first seen him; it was gone now. He wore a khaki shirt and trousers. The shirt had epaulets, and she guessed it might be one of his old uniform items. He was wearing a pair of moccasins, and they looked new.

"I knew it was you," he said. "Heard about your mother. I'm sorry."

"Who from?" She asked.

"The clerk at the grocery store. She said she has known both you and your mother all your lives."

Information shoots through this village, she thought.

"You had lunch?" He asked.

"I'm not hungry."

"But it's lunch time. I never miss a meal; even out hunting or fishing I have my jerky or fruit bars. Never miss a meal. Not good for you. Now, would you like some lunch?"

"I don't want to be a problem."

"You already are. You come here at my lunchtime, tell me you're not hungry, and force me either to miss my lunch or to show a total lack of hospitality and sit here and eat with you watching. I'd rather not do that again."

"Okay, okay. Thank you. I would be happy to have lunch with you."

He nodded as if to say—finally—and opened the door of a cupboard above the sink. Then he went into the front room and she heard the scratching sound again and then soft music—classical—waltz music. He returned with a pair of black-rimmed reading glasses dangling near the end of his long nose. He turned his attention again to the cupboard.

"Let's see. We have chicken noodle, and chicken noodle, and—oh yes—we also have chicken noodle." He turned to display the triple stacks of soup. And he was not kidding; there was just one soup—chicken noodle. Surely he needed no eyeglasses to determine that. There must have been two dozen cans stacked on the two shelves. He smiled at her. She had never seen him smile. She did not like chicken soup.

"I'll have chicken soup with my chicken soup," she said as if ordering at a restaurant.

"That's the first time I've seen you smile since you made fun of my Reveille Cat. Could you give me a hand?"

She waited while he removed paint cans and papers from the kitchen table that he had moved to the front room and stacked them again on a loveseat and over-stuffed chair. Then she helped him carry the maple table and two straight back chairs into the kitchen.

He began heating the soup in a small saucepan, and reached for the number ten can to heat water for tea.

Rachel rose to open the door and retrieved a paper bag from the front stoop.

"A man should have a decent teakettle for Earl Grey tea," she said and handed the teakettle to William. She had found one on the way to the airport in Boston. It shone like her parents' toaster.

"Yes, a man should," William said. "Thank you." He decided not to tell her that it was her fault that his perfectly good teakettle had wound up in the trashcan.

❦   ❦   ❦

William emptied his bowl of soup and watched Rachel sip at hers. He stood to refill his bowl, and the cold or virus hit him again. This time the pain was greater in his throat and left shoulder. He sat back down and attempted to place the empty bowl on the table. He missed. It bounced around the floor on the layer of papers. He looked at her. He could see that she was alarmed. He wished she were not here. He preferred to deal with discomfort alone. But this was more than discomfort.

"William, we're going to the hospital." She rose and began to put on her coat.

"Not me. I don't need to go to any hospital."

"Well you need medicine for that cold—if that's all you have."

"I'm not going to a hospital."

"Then the clinic. It's close, and I know the people there. They won't hurt you, William."

"Maybe the clinic."

"Where's your coat?" She asked.

He pointed to the front room. "The bedroom." He did not want to say more. He wished the front of the cottage were not so untidy.

She drove him to the clinic.

"Looks like a hospital to me," William said.

"The emergency clinic is part of the hospital, William."

She had tricked him, but he didn't feel like objecting.

Inside, the burly doctor on duty made light of William's explanation of cold or virus.

"Sounds like angina. I think you should see our cardiologist, and right away."

"Don't want in any hospital. Not been in one in fifty years, except to visit some poor soul."

"Well, now you're the poor soul, William," Rachel said

"You don't have much choice, Mr. Jennings," the doctor said. I'm not going to let you drive anywhere."

"He'll stay,' she said.

"Are you related?" The doctor asked.

"Yes." She said. The doctor was fairly new to the community, and she guessed he would ask for more information, but he did not.

"I don't think I want to do this," William said.

"William, I think you should stay, but if you really are afraid, I'll drive you home," she said.

"I'm not afraid of a hospital. I just don't like them."

"Sure," said Rachel. "Well, what's it going to be Doctor?"

The doctor fumbled around with a pad of paper, wrote a note, and said, "Ill get an attendant in here to help you get him checked in, and I'll talk to cardiology. Give me just a minute." He opened a metal framed cabinet window and handed Rachel a small, white paper box. "If the pains come back, put one of these under his tongue."

"I can handle my own tongue," William said.

"Quiet, William," she said.

Spunky girl, William thought and accepted her assistance as she guided him into the wheel chair that the attendant brought in. Then he was being wheeled along by the attendant and hooked up to something electrical in the admissions room.

"A man could sleep in this chair if there was a little more leg-room. You can tell these chairs were made for short people."

"No, they were made for normal people, and you are not normal, William."

"I thought you were coming to like me."

"You confuse liking with what I would call parental concern," she said.

He was feeling normal right now, but he elected not to laugh. He was glad the clinic was part of the hospital and that they had not needed to put him in an ambulance. Just the sterile ceiling, lights, and sirens would have been unsettling, not to speak of all the tubes and electronic boxes lying around just in case. He tried to shove the picture of the ambulance interior from his mind. It was making his jaw hurt. He wondered if the fancy electrical monitor he was hooked to was picking up the cause of his aching jaw.

The cardiologist and his staff reminded William of a well trained Army squad or detachment. After he was settled into a room, the team members visited him in tandem, each a specialist who was to play a role in the exploration of his heart the next morning. He had made it easy for the cardiologist. The discomfort that began in his left arm as Rachel assisted him through the admissions process told him that he needed to know, and not the hard way. He had agreed quickly to what the doctors considered the appropriate procedure.

During the break in the parade of examiners, Rachel had seemed to lose patience and he did not think it was from nervousness on her part.

"Discomfort, hell, William. Why don't you tell them you have pain in your chest and in that left arm that you were rubbing down in the admissions room. You were about as subtle as the Red Sox third base coach in a close game with the Yankees."

He couldn't help smiling. When they wheeled him down the hallway the next morning and he felt the mild euphoria of the light sedation he had been given, he had to smile again. She reminded him so much of Carol.

He was awake nearly the whole time. He spoke to every member of the operating room staff and the doctors. He told one of the technicians that they reminded him of a well-trained Army squad. He guessed that she did not regard it as a compliment. But it was. Later she asked him how he was doing.

"I'll be okay if you stop tripping over my IV line," he told her. Of course it was not an IV line. He didn't know what it was as it wound its way across the operating room floor. But he was confident that they knew. Later still the same nurse said, "Keep that right arm down to your side."

Well into the procedure, he watched the monitor as the tube that had been inserted in his thigh entered his heart, and another specialist said, "Hold your right arm up over and across your forehead like this." She wrenched the arm into the desired position, and he could not see how nurses had ever gotten reputations as gentle and caring.

A little later the original specialist came along and thrust his arm down along his side. "I told you to keep your arm down here along your side."

"I told you that I have a military background. I do what the last captain or sergeant tells me to do," William responded. The efficient specialist said nothing. But he kept his arm where she directed.

William continued to talk with anyone who got near his head, particularly after they pointed out the spot in the left anterior descending artery where there was a "plus ninety per cent blockage." The big man, the chief cardiologist, came back to confirm that he wanted to continue and have the artery expanded and a stint put in. William had already decided this the night before. He wanted to tell them—Press On—as he guessed the old Brigadier test pilot, Chuck Yeager, would have done. But he had gone far enough to convince the cardiology staff that he had the right stuff. He knew that he should not overdo his garrulous and bombastic act. These guys were professionals—they knew how scared he was.

He was pleased when they let Rachel in to see him. She had stayed all night at the hospital. She had been a lot of help. What an inadequate description—she may have saved his life.

"You have the 'right stuff,'" he said. Her puzzled look made him wonder if she understood. After all, when they released the movie that made Yeager the hero he had deserved to be all along, Rachel was only four or five years old. But she did have the right stuff.

"What did you think of my doctor?"

"Which one?"

He guessed that she had been impressed with the specialist with the psychedelic cap who had been in the evening before. The handsome young man spent more time examining Rachel from eight feet away than he did looking at the notepad on which he was recording Williams' answers to the questions. William did not mind, but it seemed this guy was to be sitting near his head during the procedure and would be counted upon to give him the right amount of everything—including oxygen. He was glad that Doctor Kildare had apparently put all the answers in the right blanks.

"The one who just left, the 'Lady' doctor," he said.

Rachel gave him a look that a mother bestows on a nine year old licking her fingers at the mother-in-law's Sunday dinner table.

William wouldn't tell her what he thought. That the doc was prettier than the beautiful actress who portrayed the would-be doctor in "Patch Adams." If Rachel asked, he would refer to the "Lady" doctor's clear professionalism and competence. He didn't want to push his luck with her by admitting his chauvinistic leanings. Her presence the last two days had meant too much.

He was relieved to learn that the doctors had the same medical opinion that he had as to his recovery. He had not been a bleeder; he felt and looked fine; so he was going home. While he awaited the official release, Rachel received a call on the phone just outside his room. He did not intend to listen, but her words, despite a hand clasped around the mouthpiece, were clear. It was her father, and she was needed at home with some urgency.

On the drive to his cottage she had little to say, but responded to each of his attempts at small talk. He was not good at it; never had been, but especially in the past five years. He decided to ask about her mother.

"Dad had decided to take her over to her new home today, but he didn't. He wants me to be with them when they go."

She had been with him. Rachel had spent her time with William when she should have been with her mother.

"Well, you ought to have been there. That's your mother. You should…"

"Oh William, please shut up."

He had to get out of all of this. She was right. He knew it. He should not be trying to deal with normal people. He should not be trying to deal with anybody. He sat in silence and knew that the tears on her cheeks were caused as much by his clumsy and belated effort to assert his independence as by concern for her mother.

He vowed that when he got home he was going to put up the fence again. He would leave a walkway and the damned bench, but he was going to encircle his entire cottage. He would put up signs on all sides of the fence:

STAY OUT

CHAPTER 5

He did not see her again until June. Not even at Easter time, yet he guessed that she would have been home then to see her parents. He had decided it was best that she not come back. The nagging memories did him no good. He knew that. He finished painting the interior of the house, sorted through the belongings from his footlockers, and stacked the old Army wooden boxes in the storeroom on the side of the house. One of the boxes still bore the markings of his rifle company in Korea. He wanted to keep it although he had no use for the green box. He knew he could not paint the outside of the cottage for another few weeks; so he had set up the art easel he had made on the Kenai River and began mixing oils.

 He did not think a lot about fate, but he was amused at times by the coincidence of things. The day after he had set up and mixed a few oils, aware he was working backwards and not sure what he wanted to portray, he had seen the crane. It was a Red-Cap, one that he had not expected to see in Maine. He had first seen them while in college during a hike with two college buddies in southeast Washington near the Snake River. George, the real bird watcher of the three, said they were in migration north; that most would be flying up over the mid-western states. Thousands, he said, could be seen at one time in Nebraska. They migrated in large flocks. Some would go as far as Alaska. And many years later William had seen them in Alaska, not at Prudhoe Bay, but while fishing the streams around the lowlands of the Brooks Range and the Yukon River in the interior of the state.

 But in March he had seen one Red-Capped Crane, alone, flying up Mill Cove west of the cottage. The bird seemed to look up at the cottage before gliding low across the water toward the marshes just beyond the end of the cove.

He had not seen the bird again. But he remembered, and with his recollections from Alaska, he set out to paint the gray bird with the rust-brown tint on the feathers of the breast and wings. He would have to think of some common item to include in the picture to communicate the four-foot height of the bird.

He dabbed at the oil painting of the crane for the amount of time each day that the pain in his fingers permitted; then he would sit on the bench and smoke his pipe and form the lines of his poem. He had started to write again. Right after the heart procedure and Rachel's return to college he had begun to write his first poem in forty-five years.

"Hi."

He turned to see her walking toward him from the corner of the cottage. She was wearing white shorts and canvas sailing shoes with a light blue, short-sleeved shirt with button down collar. He pulled his ivory colored cardigan more snugly around his shoulders. She was rushing the season a little. She stopped ten feet away from where he sat on the bench.

"Hello," he said.

"Why aren't you down enjoying the Windjammer festivities?" She asked.

"Thought I'd go down later. Why aren't you?"

"Same for me," she said and stopped at the bench. "May I join you?"

"Sure." He took the pipe in his left hand and tapped it against the leg of the bench to remove the near cool ashes.

"Should you be smoking that pipe?" Her manner told him that he should not.

"Yes. I quit cigarettes." He waited for a pert response. There was none. She looked out over the bay as if she had made no comment about his pipe smoking.

"Never seen this many tall ships in the bay before," she said.

"Thought this was normal for Windjammer Days."

"It is, and there are always lots of boats, but I can't recall this many tall ships at one time. Aren't they beautiful?"

"Yes they are."

"Do you sail, William?"

"Not if I can help it. I might have, years ago. But just couldn't afford the sailing crowd."

"Oh? And how was that?"

"Well, how have you been?" He asked. He wanted to move the conversation in another direction—any other direction.

"Oh, fine. How are you; I mean is everything okay following the heart repair?"

He had not thought of it in those terms. He liked to call it the "procedure" when he thought of it at all. Mostly he made no attempt to think about it. He had decided not to return for the sixty-day follow-up. He had felt fine, and did now.

"I know I just dropped out of sight, but I asked my friend Becky to spy on you for me. She drove me to the airport right after your release and my mom's moving to the home. Becky's family is loaded with doctors, but she said they had trouble finding out much about you."

"This Becky, she's an old friend, a good friend?"

"Yes, as a matter of fact, I'm using her reservations at the Tugboat. They reserve a couple of rooms every year at Windjammer time. She called and offered one to me; so here I am."

"Well, good for Becky."

"She also told me that you still don't like to go to doctors. She did find out though, that you seemed to be doing okay. Are you?"

"I'm fine. Just like my old self."

"I hope not."

Then she turned to look at him directly. "Sorry, I didn't mean that," she said through a nice smile.

"Yes you did." He looked at her, expecting another quick response, but there was none. He looked beyond her at the high cumulus clouds against the Atlantic blue sky. The town fathers would be happy with today's weather.

He waited for her to say something. She was bothered. Her lips were now a straight line and tight. Why had she not been back to see him?

"William, I don't live here anymore. I mean, in the Harbor. I don't live here now."

"Oh?" He waited for her to say more. She seemed to be searching.

"Something happened that has bothered me a lot. I can't seem to just forget it and get on with my life. I may not return to college next fall."

"I knew that you had some problem. I figured that you had solved it; why I guessed you hadn't been around."

"But, how did you learn? I had thought…I had hoped that no one in Boothbay knew…that…"

"I just guessed that there was a problem, or maybe had been, and something was missing in your life."

"Oh?" She said.

William was a little uncomfortable. He wasn't sure he wanted to say or hear any more. It was none of his business.

"Would you like to walk down to see the tall ships?" He asked.

She stared at him. Not with a smile. Not with approval or disapproval.

"William, do you have a friend? Just one person that you call a friend?"

He stood too quickly. The pain in his left knee pushed him back down without cushion or ceremony.

Damn. His knees were as strong as they had been twenty years ago. They were not weak, but he had given in to the pain and sat down. He took no pills. Except one aspirin, and that had been to satisfy the pretty heart doctor. He started to rise again, more slowly.

"William, haven't you ever needed to talk to anybody?"

The question hung out there. He had known the answer since he was a young man.

"No." He sat back down. Who needs to talk he asked himself. I don't need anything, but this girl does. He wished she would seek it somewhere else.

She touched his arm. The immediate impulse was to pull away, but he did not. Her hand fell away and he watched it return to her lap.

"Have you never, ever had someone to talk to?"

He wanted to get up and run away. To run up Oak Street to route 27 and right out of Maine.

"Have you never had someone who just wanted to talk to you?" She spoke so softly that he barely heard the words, but they burrowed into him and reverberated in his head and burned in a place that he knew could only be his heart.

He knew that he could not get up now. He turned toward her. Her hands rested on her lap. Then as he watched, one hand grasped at the other; then the hands reversed. It was as loud a cry for help as he would ever see or hear. He would have to listen.

"What's wrong?" He asked.

Rachel was hesitant even though she knew she had come here to talk. And she had come to ask him to tell her about his life; about why he seldom smiled; why he was at first so awful with her when it was clear that something made him take down the fence, paint the bench. He was not just a grumpy old man. She wanted to know the person who painted the bench. She liked to see him smile. But first, she needed to tell him.

What a mixed-up person I am, she thought. But she was not sure she wanted to tell him why. It was embarrassing for one thing, and for another, it was not loyal.

"My mother is not going to get well, William. I think she will always be right there in that home." This was not what she had needed to talk about—not what she had come to tell him. She was not sure what to say next.

"No one can know that for sure can they, Rachel? I mean has something new happened? Is she worse?"

"Well, no, but she's no better."

"What have you been told? Are the doctors saying something different now?"

"Oh, the doctors. No, they haven't changed, but they never told us very much anyway. Just talked about the complex human brain and how I couldn't do anything to help her." She stopped talking abruptly. It had been a long time since any doctor or counselor had talked to her about her relationship with her mother. She knew it was not quite accurate, or fair, to them. Still, she felt the choking emotion so common late at night when she remembered the words: You should not expect to be able to get her to open up like we do. The woman had not even been a doctor. And that was over three years ago. And that was what she now told William even though it was not what she had planned to talk about. But the words flowed, as did the tears.

William listened, and watched her tortured face and saw the tears well up and heard the deep hurt. And he heard the guilt. He was sure. This girl was more than sad about her mother's sickness and fearful for her mother's life.

She had stopped talking and had checked the brimming tears. He groped for something to say, something to soothe her, but he felt quite empty. He could tell her that it was not her fault; that she was no doctor; that she should not expect to be able to heal her mother, but he knew that she knew that. And he knew that she could still feel guilty. Even be overcome by guilt. He felt again a strong discomfort with sitting and listening to her. It was a discomfort with the subject and with this young person, a stranger just seven months earlier and not seen often since then. But it was also a discomfort that had its roots many years in his past. William was no stranger to guilt.

He suggested they go in and have some soup even though he guessed that Rachel had not gotten what she might have hoped for in sharing her thoughts. Still, she seemed to jump at the suggestion, apparently happy to have at least spoken of her problem with someone. But there must be more. Why did she think that he could help her?

They had chicken noodle soup, and Rachel made the tea. He put on his Herb Alpert record, set on a low volume.

"What's the music?" She asked.

"Tijuana Brass, the Taste of Honey. Don't you like it?"
"It's fine. I just don't recall hearing it."
"It was a hit about the time of my second tour in Vietnam. Let's see, that would be '66. How many years was that before you were born?"
"Thirteen," Rachel said.
"How old were you then?" She asked.
"Aha," he said.
"It's fair enough. You know my age. Are you that vain?"
William realized that he was. Not normally, but right now, with her, he was. But he would never hint it.
"I was thirty-eight."
"A mere babe," she smiled.
William looked at her bowl. She had eaten little of her soup.
"You don't like it, do you?"
"No. I'm sorry. I don't."
"Well, I'm afraid there's not much else: some of those artificial eggs, some cereal, and…"
She laughed.
He laughed.
"But I do have some coconut chocolate chip cookies." William offered his last try.
"Oh, chocolate chips are great, especially with tea."
William took several of the cookies from a bag in the cupboard and put them on the table in a saucer in place of the soup bowl that he retrieved. He watched her eat two in short order.
"I don't think I have eaten them with the coconut," she said between munching and sipping.
"Can't always find them now. I ran into them in the fifties right after I got back to the states from Korea, the second time. Fifty-two, I guess." He remembered the year too well. He remembered well the first two years of that decade, the happiest and saddest years of his life.
"You would have been what, twenty-four or five, then?"
"In fifty-two? Twenty-four."
"William, may I ask, were you married then?"
"No."
"No you weren't married, or no I can't ask you?"
"No, I wasn't married."
"You did have a girlfriend, didn't you?"

"Rachel, that was half a century ago. This is now. What about you? You do have a boyfriend, don't you?"

"I'll tell you if you tell me," she said and crunched another cookie.

William knew the discussion had gone too far. Now it was probing, like he was on the stand, exposed to questions that he did not want to hear, the judge telling him that he had to answer the questions of the lawyer. Maybe he could end the questions, once and for all.

"No, I did not have a girlfriend."

Rachel returned to the Tugboat Inn. She could have stayed with friends, or at her father's house, but she preferred the Inn. She especially did not want to go back to the house. The Tugboat sat as if a tide had ebbed and left her by the bow high on the harbor shore. But Rachel knew the story—how men with great care and final ceremony settled the boat, once proudly named the "Maine," into her place of honor. Retired, in a way, much as an old sea captain, free to ponder the many dark nights when the crushing seas threatened lesser vessels until the Maine arrived and saved the threatened boat and its crew. As a small girl she had a book, thin but full of richly painted pictures of a little tugboat—Tess, she recalled its name—that chronicled a brave and heroic rescue. This one had been of a fish-catching trawler, a sturdy and seaworthy boat herself with able crew, but heavy with her catch in a howling storm out of the northeast. Rachel had told her mother then that she was going to captain her own boat someday—a tugboat. Her mother had not laughed. "Well, you can do just whatever you set your mind to, Rachel. But you will have to work hard." But her mother later had encouraged her toward music and, over time, she forgot the seagoing ambition.

But she had never forgotten the Tugboat Inn and Restaurant. It was her favorite place to eat in the entire Harbor although her family had not eaten there in the last few years. One of the signals of the coming of each spring was their annual first outing of the New Year at the Tugboat. Always in May, shortly after the winter cold was pushed north and the restaurant reopened its doors to the steady local customers and the visitors of summer. It was an exciting time. A triumph of Nature over herself, her grandfather would say. Or a "bursting out" as proclaimed on the old 33 rpm record that her mother had played from time to time. He would listen too—her father—and glance at her mother with just the slightest twist of a smile. It was their record, their story, but when she had shared the movie with her mother on a rented VCR tape, she wondered why they liked so much a story that ended in such a sad manner. Maybe it was the other song, "walking through a storm," that made them smile despite the sad ending. Rachel liked that song. She had not seen the record or heard its music in a long time.

She and Craig had enjoyed the Tugboat Restaurant. She remembered the meals with him, their own special table in the corner toward the bay. Now she sat at the table and sipped at a glass of house Chardonnay. She looked out the window at the harbor where everyday except in the foulest of weather Tom Boyd ran his boat out to pull up one trap after another, take out the lobster, rebait, and lower the trap again into a proven spot or another nearby. She had seen him at Easter time, and he had invited her to go with him to check and refresh the bait in his traps. It had not been a good harvest. He had few keepers, and they seemed unable to find a subject to talk about that could last longer than the run of the boat from one specially colored buoy to the other. Fortunately, it was not cold and the bay was not choppy. He handled everything well with no real need of her help. Just as well, she thought, for she had learned less in growing up about the lobster business than she had learned about baseball. The thought embarrassed her, and she felt her face grow warm but she knew that he did not notice. He was too busy guiding the boat skillfully between the many buoys and pulling on the ropes that brought the trap up along the gunnels of the boat and on board. He had a routine in opening the door of the trap, removing the lobster if there was one, placing it in his crate or tossing it back overboard if it did not meet the criteria, replacing the bait and lowering the crate. She thought of his baseball, now in a pleasant way. The routine that he went through on the mound before every pitch. She understood that routine, explained to her by her father as they watched baseball on television many months before she first saw Tom pitch. But Tom did not know that, and she guessed that he never would. When they got back to the wharf, the goodbye was easy and brief, as if each understood that there was no need for further words. She had seen him twice since in town. They had said hello, smiled, and went their own ways.

She still had not ordered, although the cordial waitress had been back twice to see if she was ready. The restaurant was packed already with tourists and several locals who nodded and smiled at her. She had waited over thirty minutes for the table, stretching the glass of wine and thinking of the midday visit with William. The waitress was new to her, but she was nice, agreeing to let her wait when she could easily have pushed her toward one of the tables for two tucked nicely into intimate spots in the restaurant. Maybe the young woman sensed the table was special for her, because it surely was the choice of many regular customers. From the corner window, one could look out toward the picturesque boathouse that sat with the larger bay and ocean beyond. She had not in years climbed the short ladder to the pilothouse of the old boat. Even with Craig, she had not shared the small cubicle of imagination of her childhood. But tonight she climbed up to the pilot's wheel. She felt warmth here, and it was not just, or primarily, the wine. It was memories and imaginings of a small girl, safe and secure in the strongest of ships, unafraid of anything or anybody and looking forward to a future of even greater happiness. The mood carried her to the review of the menu when the table became available and she ordered as if she had spent the day at hard sailing, working to bring a boat to its peak performance, hearing and feeling the strain of canvas, rope and wood as the boat keeled and raced along the bay.

She chose the scallops Monhegan and ate slowly, savoring the delicately sweet meat and the special flavor of the herbs and seasoned breadcrumbs. She had another glass of wine but turned down the invitation for a dessert, something her mother could seldom get her to do voluntarily as a young girl. The loneliness hit her as she closed the handbag, a gift from her mother three Christmases earlier. The edges of the flap were worn, and there was a split in the liner of the small change pocket. She carried it often now, especially during the summer, but the ivory-shaded leather had lost most of its luster. She had others. Newer and brighter. She thanked the waitress and nodded again at an older couple, long time friends of her father and mother, and stepped out of the restaurant.

The air had cooled a bit, but she did not go directly to her room, walking out on the Tugboat's deck. She thought again of William. He had bothered her. He had been uneasy and that had made her uneasy too—should have gone ahead with the other story, her real problem. Maybe she had found it easier to talk about her mother's illness. But she had not planned to do that and the words about her mother had just spilled out. And William was not much help. His expressions, his responses—he seemed to be the loneliest person she had ever met—he did not want to talk about his past; about why he was so alone. When might he have been married; had he ever been married; if he had, where was his wife, or what had happened to her? Maybe he had known some tragedy, a soldier's loss, maybe he had lost many men in battle, but still, somewhere, sometime he must have had a girlfriend.

She looked across the bay at the tall white steeple of Our Lady of Peace Church. She loved to look down at it in the daytime from the bench, but down here, at night, the boldly illuminated white clapboard church with its tall, slim steeple appeared so much larger and even more striking. The moon was full and silvery bright. It hung above and to the left of the church's cross-topped peak. The church was reflected in the harbor and the mirrored steeple pointed directly at her, the tip of the reflected cross reaching halfway across the harbor. And still nearer, and to the left was the shimmering reflection of the moon. The mirrored view wiggled as the slow tidal wakes from the many boats moored in the harbor danced across the water. In winter she had viewed the same reflection in a harbor all but free of boats and it was like a flawless painting. It was her mother's favorite view in all New England—the church. Would she recognize it now? Had William come down and seen this?

Rachel was sure that he welcomed her company, maybe looked forward to it. But he reeled against any probing of his life. He was about the age her Grandfather Malcomb had been during the last few summers she had shared with him. But her grandfather was not guarded, or sad. It clearly was not a matter of age. But of course she knew about Grandmother Tilley, and that her grandfather was alone, like this man. But her grandfather had laughed a lot. She looked out at the night scene of her childhood town and thought again of her mother, her father, William…One she could not help; one she did not want to help, and one she thought she could help—if she could bring him to let her. And she was going to try again to do that. Tomorrow.

CHAPTER 6

Rachel took a long walk the next morning, unable to recall the last time she had been content to walk—not run—on her first outing back from school. She did not walk over the top. She intended to visit William early in the afternoon, and she did not want to bother him this morning. She reserved her gray sweat trousers and long-sleeved sweatshirt for occasions like this morning when she wanted to fade into the scenery. They were comfortable, but baggy and seldom drew anyone's attention. She wore one of her dad's old golfing caps, her ponytail standing out boldly above the adjustable band. She crossed the footbridge and walked along Atlantic Avenue. It went by the church she had admired the previous night. She paused and looked across the bay at the restaurant and inn, the boat docks with the sailboats and their tall-masts, and the bustle of people in the mid-morning sunlight.

She walked by the pillars at the entrance to Spruce Point and continued out past the Inn, the scene of many weddings, especially right after the summer ending Labor Day. On the walk back, she picked up her pace. As she reentered the crowded harbor area and neared the tall, white church, she heard and gave way to a vehicle coming from behind her. The vehicle rattled as if it had loose parts. It slowed; then stopped alongside her.

"Like a ride in my new truck?"

Oh my, it was William. She had never thought of him driving. Suddenly she did not consider Boothbay Harbor a safe place.

"William, where did you get that—that thing?"

"What? My truck? Just bought it this morning."

"Where are you going?"

"Nowhere. Everywhere. Just a joyride. Been out on Roads End tinkering with the carburetor. You ever been on a joyride?"

"William. I've seen this truck before. Is it actually yours?"

"Sure is. You saw it on River Road beside the big Victorian two-story. They told me it had been up on those blocks for three years. Replaced some rubber hoses and put in new plugs and points, and she fired right up. Runs as smooth as Eskimo ice cream."

The smoothness had been lost somewhere. She reached for the handle and it turned loosely, but the door did not open.

"Safety feature," he said. "Only opens from inside."

She heard him grunt in his effort to reach across the seat and still keep his foot on the clutch, but he got the door open. She decided it was a bad idea. The seat looked like a mechanic's bench where someone had set a cracked oil pump and had not bothered to wipe up the leaking, black liquid. There were also leaves, cat or dog fur, and the sharp end of one coiled spring pointing up toward a once-lined roof. The dull vinyl cover of the seat might have one time been tan.

"Wait," he said. He pulled a piece of card board from behind the passenger seat and placed it on the seat, then from the same spot took a clean white towel that he handed to her.

"All set for company you can see," he said.

She folded the towel, placed it on the cardboard that restrained the menacing spring and gingerly took her seat.

"You all right there?" He asked.

"Yes," she replied with little confidence.

"Then we're off!" The car bucked as he popped the clutch. The tired truck jumped forward—and stopped. The engine was quiet. The whole, ancient truck was quiet. And so was William.

He tried to start the engine, but soon the air smelled like a gas station. She knew he had flooded it.

"You might try without pushing down on the accelerator," she said.

"Humph," his large upper body exhaled as he turned the key again with his foot cemented to the floor with the accelerator pad pinned in between.

Finally he gave up and, despite his protest that he could do it all alone, accepted her help in pushing the truck onto a graveled spot beside the road. The dented and dull-colored truck bed stuck out far enough to ensure one of the Harbor's police officers would want to find the owner within a couple of hours.

"Why don't I take you to lunch?" He asked.

She questioned if a man who could afford no better transportation than this truck could afford to pay for lunch. "We can go Dutch," she said.

"Go where?" He asked.

"Come on, William, you're not that old."

"You can't be too sure."

"Yes I can. You're seventy-one." That curbed him. They walked the short distance to the footbridge and crossed to the west side of the harbor, but when they climbed the steep Bridge Street to Townsend she heard some discomfort in his voice.

"Where we going? We're passing up some pretty good restaurants here."

"Just a little farther," she said, and they turned across from an old bank building, so labeled by a lettered sign on the front, and walked toward the intersection.

"This is the heart of our town, William: where McKown becomes Townsend and intersects with Oak to the northwest and Commercial to the southeast." William looked for a bench but what he saw was one of those mobile hotdog carts, this one powered, and a man about William's age, maybe older, sat at the wheel. He was looking in their direction. He smiled and waived. William felt a little silly, but Rachel waved back.

"Hi, Brud," she said. "I've brought a friend to lunch."

By this time they were walking across Commercial Street to the corner where Broad was set up for business.

"Rachel, how are you? How's your father?" He looked at William like the stranger that he was, but his eyes under the gold-rimmed spectacles glinted as he looked back at Rachel. He did not let her respond.

"You gonna have a hot dog? Whatcha want on it? You want mayonnaise? You want mayonnaise," he repeated. William guessed that was for affect. He had never eaten mayonnaise on a hot dog. Hamburger, yes, with lettuce and tomato, but not on a hotdog.

"You want everything?" Brud asked. Again he left no time for an answer. "You want everything. Tain't a hotdog unless it has every thing. You want two? You say he's eating with you?" Brud looked up at William, and William thought that for the first time Brud noticed his height. Brud got out of the seat, stepped over to William, close, almost touching, and extended his hand and looked up.

"I'm the King, the hot dog king of this whole Boothbay Region," he said, and turned brusquely, but not before applying a firm pressure in the handshake that caught William slightly off guard. He was accustomed, after years in the Army, to men testing his grip with a handshake, and at one time he could grip with the best, owing to the leverage brought by longer than average fingers. But this time he gripped only enough to respond with similar pressure to the test of the hot dog king, and the other man pulled his hand back in a natural and friendly manner.

"Two with everything," Brud said as he turned to his small truck and lifted the stainless steel cover, unleashing a steamy cloud and an appetizing aroma of wieners, buns, and a variety of colorful condiments. The man worked with precision, reminding William of the medical technicians just around the cove in their green and psychedelic operating room attire. He looked at Rachel, expecting an amused expression, but what he saw directed to Brud was a look of pride and affection. Any impulse he had felt to speak up, William set aside and patiently waited as Brud did his thing and handed first a hotdog to Rachel, and then one to him. Still no conversation. He guessed this was where they were to eat—on the street corner—and he took a large bite. Smooth, soft, tangy, and delicious.

"You make hotdogs?" Brud asked. William looked up from his second big bite and realized the question was to him. He waited until he chewed and swallowed the bite.

"Yes, sometimes."

"You use mustard?"

"Yes." William was about to tell him that he did not use mayonnaise on hot dogs, but then he caught the taste, faint, not that obvious. It fit. It worked—the mayonnaise.

"Well, when you open the mustard jar the first time, scoop out just a little and put it on a platter or something. You can stir it back into the jar later. Then just add about a half a teaspoon full of vinegar into the jar and stir it up real good. That's what gives you that little special tang. You can't get that just with regular mustard or even relish. You need that little bit of vinegar. But now don't go telling everybody I gave you my secret." Brud winked at Rachel and this time she showed the amusement William had looked for earlier. He thought that Brud probably shared widely his vinegar additive suggestion. William chewed slowly, aware that Rachel was enjoying the first bite she had taken of her lunch. He could easily eat a second.

"You want two more? With everything?" Brud asked. William looked at Rachel.

"No thank you, Brud. I think one is our limit today." She looked at William as the pretty cardiologist had when she talked diet with him the morning after the procedure. Then as if she had almost forgotten something, she handed her hotdog to William.

"Wait here. Don't eat my dog," she said and did a short run down Commercial and ducked in a doorway.

"Gone to Sherman's," Brud said. "Tain't Sherman that operates the bookstore now. It's a man from Florida. I'm told he just traded a bookstore down there for one up here. Right smart judgment for a young man, you know."

William stepped off the curb to see the sign better. Sherman's Book and Stationery Store. William finished off his hotdog and looked longingly at Rachel's.

"You have that summertime?" Brud asked. William was trying to make out what Brud might mean. The man pointed to a stack of papers beside the doorway to the shop just four steps away. William walked over, and looked down. *Summertime, and the living is easy in the Boothbay Harbor Region.* It was a newspaper-style guide to region activities.

"It's free," Brud said, closing the lid on his cart.

...and this is your 2001 PRICELESS GUIDE the cover further announced. William picked one up, careful not to drop the hotdog and the wrapper from his own. Rachel hurried back up.

"Got you something," she said. It was a book, a shiny sepia soft cover book on the Boothbay Harbor Region. "Look here," she said, pointing to the page opened near the back of the book. It was a picture of a young man sitting behind the wheel of his hot dog cart. The name on the cart was spelled B-r-u-d, Brud. William thought of the after-shave lotion named similarly, that he had used for a quarter century.

Rachel handed the book to Brud. She had been very busy in that bookstore. She also handed Brud a pen. "Would you please write something for my friend, Brud? He's new to the Harbor; came here from Alaska."

"That shows real good judgment," Brud said. William noted that he did not include, "for a young man."

Brud wrote slowly and carefully, his baseball style hat shading his eyes. He finished and handed the book back to Rachel.

Written just beside a picture of Brud playing spoons over thirty years before were the words:

    The King "Brud"
    1943–2001
      58 years
Newbert William Alfred
    Pierce

William knew that the 58 represented Brud's year's becoming and reigning as the king of hot dogs, not his years on earth. The picture of him on the cart suggested a man in his very early twenties with late 1940's model cars in the background. William guessed that Brud had started his great experiment on earth about the same time William had been born—maybe a few years before.

A middle-aged couple walked by, hesitated, the woman seeming ready to stop, but the man continued on.

"Great hot dogs," William said to the couple. Rachel was just trying to finish hers and could manage only, "Hmmm," and a nod of her head. The woman tugged at the man's sleeve. He stopped. Then they walked back, and Brud went into action.

"Would you like a hot dog? Two of them? What do you want on them? Mayonnaise? You want everything?" He had opened the lid on the cart again and the aroma floated toward the couple like a perfume of desire. The man stepped closer.

"Everything? Why not," the man said and smiled down at his lady. She ran her hand over his broad back, tenderly, expressing more, William thought, than if he were to pick the finest restaurant later in the evening and offered his lady the meal of her dreams.

He and Rachel walked on toward the hill that featured Holmes Cottage. He had the *Summertime* issue and the book in his hand, and opened it to Brud's autograph. What a fine life, he thought. What a gift to a town and its people. He understood Rachel's pride and affection. What a great life.

"Thanks for the lunch, Rachel. But you know I didn't pay. It was great. Too great to walk off and not pay the man."

"Brud knows I'm good for it; so do the nice folks at Sherman's. It's all on me, William."

"Thank you," he said, and doubted if she knew how much he really meant it.

When they got to the cottage, she suggested they sit on the bench. It was cooler than the day before; so he slipped back on the cardigan that he had taken off in their walk. Rachel crossed her arms and pulled the gray sweatshirt about her shoulders. She liked his cardigan. It was a heavy acrylic, probably one that could be thrown in the washer and then laid out to dry. Its bulkiness suggested warmth, but the weave was loose, so air could flow through it. It looked clean, but sagged at the elbows and in the back hem like it had not been washed in a long time.

She did not know where to start as they sat down. She guessed that he assumed her worry about her mother was all that she wanted to talk about, and she wished that were true. But unlike yesterday's subject, she hoped that he could help her with this in a way that no one else could. Not Peggy. And definitely not her father. Her problem was her father.

"William, the reason I haven't been back to see you; that I moved, is my father."

"Maybe you shouldn't tell me this, Rachel. I mean I don't want to interfere in your family's affairs."

Rachel was aware that he was trying to push her away, but she wanted to make this happen. She needed to tell someone, and she needed help. She had been unable to resolve it in her mind and heart. Maybe someone could help her. Maybe he could.

She began her story. He listened, and at some point, she thought that she got inside the barrier. If she was right, his eyes told her. The eyes, which were always rimmed with the redness of irritant or age, softened and misted. While she told her story, somewhere, the eyes changed, seemed to open up, to anticipate, and to try to understand.

It was the past March. She and Peggy had gone shopping, simply because Peggy had made the suggestion. She was still trying to get Rachel out and interested in more than the casual dates she infrequently had with boys that Peggy knew she regarded as cousin-like friends. It was a breezy and cold day, but pleasant enough if they were on the streets for short periods. So they had lingered inside three or four shops before an early lunch at the Papillion. Rachel had never been to the restaurant before, or even in this part of the city except to drive through on the way to Fenway Park to see the Red Sox games.

Peggy impressed her with her French as she read aloud from the menu, but Rachel had already decided on the chowder and a house salad with oil and vinegar. Peggy frowned as she heard Rachel's order and then presented her own preferences in French to a waitress who seemed impressed.

"Rachel, isn't that your father?"

Peggy was off her chair tilting her head to see over Rachel's left shoulder. Rachel turned. At first she saw no one that resembled her father. Then she spotted the man to whom Peggy was no doubt referring.

"No. A strong resemblance, but no, it's not him." She turned back and looked down at her half-eaten salad. She had been unable to say—My Father—in answering Peggy. Of course it was him. And he had his hand extended across the table to hold that of an attractive brunette. Just in one quick glance it had the allure of an intimate meeting, a meal shared with someone special. She checked herself as she remembered the foolishness and unfairness of jumping to conclusions in the manner of a reader of gossip columns. She would not believe it. She looked up at Peggy, busy with her food and eating at a pace that would have offended any French chef with her indifferent haste. Rachel picked at the salad, her head down, and hoped he did not see her when he and the woman departed.

Peggy handed her the near empty pitcher of iced tea and she emptied it into her glass. As she turned her head to place the pitcher on the table, the two faces appeared just outside the restaurant front window, fogged by the warm building and the contrasting cold on the sidewalk. They kissed. It was a long kiss. Her father's right eye would be looking right at her if it were not closed. Then it opened. And opened wider. He pushed the brunette away. The woman turned in Rachel's direction. She was pretty, in the look of an older woman, but much younger than her mother. The two separated farther. They were saying goodbye. Anger flushed Rachel's cheeks as she saw her father pull the woman to him again and kiss her on the cheek. Then she was gone, and Rachel and her father were no more than six feet apart, separated by the steamy pane of glass. She felt like she was looking at a stranger that she had been forewarned was her enemy, and a person that she had easily been able to hate.

"He's coming in," Peggy said.

She was right. His long strides already had him at the door. Rachel rose.

"Peggy, I'm going to the restroom...."

"Oh, no. Don't leave me here alone."

"Tell him that I don't want to see him—ever. Never again in my whole life."

When Rachel returned to the table, she found Peggy waiting and her father gone.

"Did you tell him?"

"Yes."

"What did he say?"
"That he insisted on paying for our lunch."
"That's all?"
"To tell you he's sorry, and that he'll call."
"That will be the longest ring he'll ever hear."
"Rachel, you ought to give him a chance. He is your father."
"Give him a…" Rachel could not finish. She could only think of the lady alone in the home at the Harbor, who had so little, asked for nothing, and maybe didn't even know them anymore, but who deserved something. Deserved something if only in memory of the loved and loving woman she once had been.

William reminded himself how out of hand the whole matter was. Rachel was crying now. She was sobbing—convulsive sobs that shook her entire body. He reached for her, let her head rest on his chest, the long billed cap slipping back off her head to hang on the soft ponytail. He cupped her shoulder in his left hand. Then she quieted. Spent, he guessed, her eyes closed in half sleep. He was glad. Glad that she could not see that the mist in his eyes that had clouded his view of her face and the bay was now releasing. The tears sought out the valleys of his wrinkled cheeks and jaw and made their way down toward the girl who unknowingly had brought back the pain of Carol and that day on the rainy street of Tokyo, fifty years ago.

She awakened to the smell of paint—oil paints—like those in Alice's dormitory room, and in the art class that she had struggled through as a sophomore. Then she started as she remembered where she was and pushed herself back to the end of the bench. The cap fell to the grass and lay there.

"Oh, William, I am sorry. Have I been sleeping long?" She looked at the light and knew the sun was low. She had been asleep, and too long.

"No. I rested a little myself," he said.

He looked like he too had been crying, but she knew the pollens were bad in June. She had cried, and now she could not remember when she felt so relaxed.

"William, do you paint?"

Her question was so abrupt and unanticipated that he laughed.

"A little, why?"

She was slow to answer, but smiled when she touched his off-white sweater.

"I could smell the paints. In the fiber of your sweater."

"This is my painting sweater. Bought it up in Anchorage in '94.

"Did you study painting?"

"Oh no, I'm an amateur, which my few paintings show. Self taught you might say. Only lesson I ever had was from a couple of books and the paintings by other people." He knew it was not the truth—but almost.

"Have you painted for a long time?"

"No. Started in Alaska."

"What prompted you?"

"The country. The beauty of the mountains and the rivers, the vast forests, the wildlife, the people, all of it."

"What was the first thing you painted?"

"You'll laugh."

"No, I won't. What?"

"A drop zone."

"A what?"

"A drop zone. It's the open area on the ground where parachute troops land when they do parachute jumps."

"Did you do that? Jump out of airplanes, I mean?"

"Yes."

"Why?"

"To get to the ground. Simple as that. You can't always find places to land airplanes in war, so you drop in a small or large unit of paratroopers. Sometimes a few men jump and maybe make it safe for airplanes then to land. That's just a couple of uses of airborne troops."

"And women."

"What?" He asked.

"And women. Don't they have women parachutists too?"

"Yeah, I guess so."

"You don't approve?"

"I don't have to."

"That's an easy way out."

"But I am out…have been for eighteen years.

"Why did you paint the drop zone?"

"It was after my last jump. It was a training jump, a Hollywood jump we called them. We went up to a little higher altitude than normal and pushed ourselves out of a helicopter from a sitting position. No extra equipment. Landed in a foot of snow."

"Was there a lot of risk, in that jump, I mean?"

"No, not really."

"Then why the painting?"

"Because of what it meant. We jumped from a high enough altitude that, once I checked the chute, saw it was deployed and saw that our drift toward the drop zone was what we had calculated, I just looked out and enjoyed the view."

"Which was?"

"It was early afternoon, mid-winter, so we were about out of sunlight. The entire southern sky was a golden yellow and it reflected off the mountains to the east. The snow covered the ground and the frozen edges of the bay and river to our west. A pine forest ran along the base of the mountains, and the drop zone had been cut out of a wooded area, mostly leafless birch and alder. The sky directly above us was a clear, light blue. In the painting, I tried to show the vastness of the sky and the huge expanse of the land we were floating down to. In your mind that drop zone on a night jump, from low altitude, can be pretty small. I painted this drop zone extra large and welcoming."

"Do you miss that? The Army and the parachute jumping?"

"Oh that was a lot of years ago. I can't say that I miss it any longer. I'm proud of my service, of the Army and the memories, and, yes, I miss the men I trained and fought with."

"And the women?"

"Why don't you let that rest?"

"Weren't there women in the Army when you were?"

"Of course. I didn't exactly fight with Custer, or even Sergeant York."

"Who is Sergeant York?"

"Man, is there no history taught anymore?"

"Can I see your paintings?" She asked, bending down to pick up her cap.

"No."

"Oh, come on William. That's not going to work any more. Let me see them, please."

"I'll show you two or three. That's all."

They rose and walked to the cottage. She felt better. He had offered nothing, but she felt better. She wondered where the paintings could be.

He had a pull-down stairway to the attic. He rejected Rachel's offer to do the climbing, and she watched his obvious discomfort as he slowly climbed the stairs and disappeared in the dark rectangle above the cottage room kitchen.

"Here," she heard, and then saw a cloth-draped rectangle being extended down. He passed down two more, and then he came down even more slowly than he had gone up, carrying an unwrapped painting. She looked around at the kitchen floor and the front room. He apparently had scrubbed the vinyl floor in the kitchen until the old, patterned vinyl surface was rubbed away in two large spots, one in front of the stove, and the other in front of the sink. But the room was tidy and clean. The maple chairs were strong and the surfaces highly polished. The table had been refinished, but not recently. The front room had two wicker chairs in addition to the wicker love seat she had noticed before. They were all in a tarnished beige or white made dull by time. The seat cushions were covered with a faded pattern of violets and green leaves. The white, wooden bookcases contained few books, most paperbacks. She could make out author names of Alistair MacLean and Jack Higgins.

She waited until he was down and let him select the first painting to uncover. It was the head of a moose, the large rack dominating the picture. The animal stood by the branches of a pine tree, as if to gain some shelter from the falling snow. It depicted the majesty of the animal, with eyes that were not doe-like, but more combative. The second was a view of mountains with a quiet stream flowing out of the mists near the foothills. The single, small birch tree in the foreground gave a sense of depth to the scene. The third was of a sunset, the colors ranging from a dark red at the surface of the mouth of a bay through a range of colors that ended high in the evening sky.

"Turnagain Bay," he said. "That's just south of Anchorage."

"I've heard of it," she said. "And this one?" She asked.

"The mountain ranges of the Cascades in Washington, looking from the east. I grew up there."

Progress.

"This," he said, "is a much maligned animal." He was pointing at the painting of the moose.

"They deserve to live separate from people. People seem to push closer to them and then not give them the room to move about and forage."

"Looks sad," she said.

"Maybe. This one other painting I started after I came here. Careful, the paints aren't dry."

It was clear that the incomplete painting was of a bird and the background, which appeared in nearly complete form, reminded her of the head of the cove just west of her family home.

"Do you have a picture of the bird?"

"No."

"How do you paint it? I've never seen one like it before."

"Well, from memory. I saw them as a young man in southeast Washington and Oregon and then many times in Alaska."

"How long before you finish it?"

"Not long…when I get free of interruptions."

"William, I'm going back to the Tug. I feel more welcomed there." He had not smiled as he spoke of interruptions.

"How long are you staying at the Inn?" This time he did smile, but she thought that he was ready for her to leave, to be left alone.

"This is my last night. I have to get back to school. Have you eaten at their restaurant—the Tugboat?"

"No. Why did you come back?"

"To talk with you."

"You've done that. Now you can get on with your life. Go find you a young man and have him take you to Bali, or Rio or, or, anywhere."

"You haven't answered my questions. Why don't you join me for dinner at the Tugboat?"

"What questions?"

"What should I do about my father?"

"You didn't ask me, and I wouldn't try to tell you if you did."

"What have you done in your life, William? I mean, other than the Army, what did you do?" She paused. "What happened to you?" She smiled to soften the question.

"I told you that."

"Oh, you told me so little."

"That's all you need to know, and all that I'm going to tell you. I appreciate your invitation to dinner, but not tonight. Some other time." He moved all the paintings close to the table edge nearest the pull down stairway.

"Can't I at least come back and see how you're doing on the painting?"

"Okay, but not tomorrow. I'm going to go get my truck tomorrow."

"Take you all day to do that? You must be expecting real trouble with that old truck."

"No. But after I pick it up I have some shopping to do down in Freeport."

"Really William, you're not going to drive that truck all the way to Freeport are you?"

"Sure am. You didn't think I paid good cash for a truck just for local joyriding, did you?"

CHAPTER 7

Rachel missed her run again the next morning, had a late breakfast in the restaurant, and took a quick spin in her car around the Harbor. One of William's joyrides. She went by the spot where they had left the truck, but it was gone. She drove by the Gulf station on Townsend, and it was not there either. Then she drove to the cottage.

The truck was not there, and she was glad. Her hunch was right: he did not lock the door, or at least he had not today, and she let herself in after knocking to see if he was there. She walked under the pull down for the stairway but she could not reach it. She took one of the kitchen chairs as a stool and pulled down on the wooden handle at the end of the rope. The stair swung down, creaking to suggest its age. She unfolded the bottom section of the stairs, set it against the floor, and scampered up the steps. She wore jeans and a black Tee shirt in anticipation of the task, and soon found her choice of clothing appropriate. She tugged the pull string, and one naked bulb cast light over a low attic with a few sections of plywood thrown over the rafters. She could see the light from the kitchen through seams between some of the ceiling sections nailed to the bottom edge of the rafters. A folded easel lay near the top of the stair. Beside it a chair like the two in the kitchen lay on its side partially draped by a piece of bed sheet. Under the sheet and the frame of the chair was the painting of the crane. He had worked on the painting either after she left the day before or this morning. The bird now sported a bright red spot that covered the top of its head. The paint looked wet. She judged that she had just enough room to stand, but she crawled over to another painting, covered and leaning against one of the supports under the center ridge of the roof. Probably one she had seen yesterday.

It wasn't. She brought it nearer the light. It was a partial painting of a man and woman—the man's clothing was quite complete. The other was the clothing of a woman and the soft background of the two figures was largely finished. It was clearly a lady's dress with a large white collar that met at the midpoint of the neck. The tips of the large collars were rounded in a sweeping arc down over a dark blue bodice that showed two buttons other than the one that presumably gathered the dress at the throat. The lady's right sleeve ballooned, and the other was obscured under the armpit and chest of the man's suit coat. The lapels of his suit were broad, like some she had seen in pictures of her father about the time that she was born. The shirt was white with a sheen that suggested starch, and the tie was in a sharp, small knot. The tie was black with small splotches of red and yellow, and it passed between the sharp tips of the shirt collar and disappeared under a vest that showed its top button under the man's coat. The coat was black, although some blue had been used in the painting to denote the outline of the broad lapels. The lady wore a necklace that faintly showed on the painting. The fine line of the chain was almost undetectable; and the form of the small object at the bottom of the chain was unclear, partially painted.

The faces were little more than brush traces in a faded blue. Her hair was not shaped but appeared cut just at the shoulders. The outline for the cheeks was high, for the lips broad, and for the eyes large and widely set. The nose was unclear, not yet outlined. The outline for the man's nose was distinct, long and straight under heavy brows, and the hair suggested many waves. Only the chin on the man was otherwise distinctively lined in. Strong, extending well below the single line designating a mouth that gave no clue of smile or seriousness of set. The paint was quite dry; the canvas on the sides of the stretching boards yellowed, probably by time. Something begun years ago and never finished. Could it be his work? He had indicated that he had begun painting in Alaska. She guessed that it was his work, and it was easy to tell from the nose and chin that it could be William, or possibly a brother or his father.

She looked further around the attic. The painting of the drop zone was not present, and she found nothing she had not seen the day before other than the incomplete portrait. She decided they were two lovers. It was William and the girlfriend that he would not admit to, or had not yet met—or no longer had back in 1952. She put the paintings back as she had found them, and hurried down the stairs. She closed the stairway and looked at her watch. It was almost noon. She tried to determine where he would keep any special papers or letters.

Then she stopped and sat at the table. What if he came back and found her? She had no suitable excuse. She should not be here. It was out and out intrusion and would be terribly embarrassing, and would likely end their friendship. He was right. She ought to get on with her life. She knew that she had reached out to him for help, but she also wanted to help him. And she knew that he needed help. She was confident that something lay in his past, and possibly not so recent past. Something before Alaska, before he left the Army; maybe something that happened in a war. Maybe in the Vietnam War. She had to find a way to get him to talk about the Vietnam War.

She felt that the paintings had given her a little insight into William's past and she decided not to leave—not yet. There was little table or shelf space to lay anything down, much less drawers or cabinets. She went into the bedroom. It was a small room, and the floor space not occupied by the large double bed was under a huge, roll-top oak desk. She found a switch on the wall, but the ceiling light did not work. There was a light at the end of the desk on a swivel chair, but there was no room between the desk and the bed for the chair. She pushed the slide switch on the stem of the lamp, and the bulb and shade threw light in small circles above and below the lamp. She moved it to the top of the desk, but the lack of depth of the desktop did not provide room for the lamp. She held the lamp in one hand and rolled back the top of the desk.

There was a typewriter, a black metallic model that she had seen in antique shops and junk sales. There was standard paper beside the typewriter, and she could see a ribbon in the guide at the center of the machine. The small desk cubicles held pencils, a stack of military decorations, ribbons she thought they were called, two small books of poetry, one by Scott, the other by Abraham Lincoln. She did not know of Lincoln as a poet, but it was a thin book. She nearly snagged her finger on one of several large fishhooks with red and yellow feathers attached to them, and she tipped over a bottle of ink, relieved that the top was fastened tightly.

The middle drawer of the left pedestal was where she found it. A dark brown suede secretary's folder, a silky brown ribbon tied in a bow to keep it closed. She moved the light and the folder to the bed and pulled on the ribbon. It untied smoothly, and she turned the folder on its side and let the contents slip to the coarse blanket that served as a bedspread.

There were no letters, but there were poems. The paper was old, single sheets of heavy manila paper, browned with age around the edges, and containing three poems. Her hands shook as she placed the papers in order by the dates in the upper right hand corner. She started with the earliest: July 12, 1951.

> My friends who went east to study in Spokane
> > Asked why I chose to go west.
> Even while leaving I had no answer
> > I had no thought of a quest.
>
> I knew not myself why I was going there
> > I went as though I were drawn
> Toward something special or maybe someone
> > In sunset, not in the dawn
>
> I did not go there with the thought to find you
> > Such sense I did not possess
> I could not in any way know to desire
> > The magic of your caress
>
> And even that day, the first that I saw you
> > Walking as if in a scene
> Though I wanted to speak and to say hello
> > You seemed far, distant, serene
>
> And later they told me my sense had been right
> > Your family, name and place
> Found comfort in mansion, opera, and dance
> > And dipped to win the yacht race
>
> I made sure that you saw me, but stayed away
> > I thought my chances were small
> You said hello, and as I stuttered, you spoke
> > We met there in the long hall

I shall ever remember, will not forget
    The pocket watch and its fob
That you thrust upon me and told me to take
    And show I was not a snob

You did not tell your parents when we would meet
    We stayed just out of their sight
Until emboldened by love you took me home
    On that cold Seattle night

We should have seen and obeyed the signals clear
    Known then what our love had wrought
And protected you from your father and me
    And the hurt the night we fought

I shall never be able though still I try
    To amend failing you so
But the sting of his words was all I could take
    And so I landed the blow

I knew it was only his pride that I hurt
    I pulled back and walked away
But I think that I then forecast for us all
    Sorrow akin to that day

    Rachel heard the rattle, the engine of the old truck at the front of the house, then on the side. She placed the papers back into the folder. She knew they were out of order, but she tied the bow and returned the folder to the drawer. She rolled down the desktop, placed the light on the chair, pushed the light switch, and listened. It sounded like he was just beyond the wall. The truck engine had stopped. She tiptoed to the kitchen door, opened it quietly, and stepped onto the stoop. She could not see the truck. She heard him whistling just around the corner, on the side of the house. She stepped softly, but quickly, around the corner of the house, away from the side where she still heard the whistling. She felt foolish. Like a child again, but without even the excuse of fun for her actions. But she stayed at the corner, listening for the sound of him opening the door. When he did, she walked the few steps to her car parked at the curb. He would have driven right by her car. She would have to give him a reason for it being there. Maybe. But now she was going on back to Boston. Her full time job at the printing shop started in just four days. William had not helped her with her father, and maybe there was nothing he could say or that she could do anyway. She found that almost as hard as accepting that she could do nothing about her mother's illness. She was meddling. She knew it. She could help none of them. She would go back to work. He had said he wanted more privacy. Let him finish his bird painting. Maybe he would forget seeing the Honda. He probably had not looked at the poems in years. But had she turned off the light in the attic?

CHAPTER 8

Stephen stood beside the 14th Tee as his Uncle Robert lined up the golf shot, the shiny persimmon wood resting on the soft green grass just behind the ball. Robert took his short backswing, customary now for this family leader, nearly eighty years of age. He was the surviving male member of the clan, save for Stephen himself. The club came forward on its predictably accurate arc, struck the ball, and sent it some one hundred and eighty yards, straight down the fairway.

"Good shot, Uncle Robert," Stephen said as he waited for the elderly man to accomplish the most difficult part of his tee shot, finding the tee, often lofted by the club head to another spot, and then bending down to retrieve it. Stephen remembered when he had first played this game with Robert and his great grandfather. Fourteen years ago, when Stephen was twelve, and his great grandfather swung as Robert did today. But Robert's golf swing back then was smooth and fluid, his slender build allowing a full turn in the back swing.

"Yeah," Robert grunted as he headed toward the cart. Stephen knew that his uncle would ignore his shot—for several reasons. First, he could not see where the ball landed anyway. Stephen spotted the long shots for both of them. Second, he wanted the time to get to the cart without hurrying his less than limber legs, and third, the drive was the weakest part of Robert's game. Not in accuracy, but in length. The drive was the strongest part of Stephen's game. That is if he avoided the tendency to throw the club at the top and then to bring the club across as it met the ball. When that occurred the ball went straight initially, but then bent lazily to the right to land in the taller grass just off the fairway—if he was lucky. Otherwise…

He addressed the ball, twitched his right knee slightly, and then began the back swing. He was careful to keep the hands inside as he came back and then pull down with his left hand as he began the forward swing. He struck the ball solidly and it took off brisk and low, straight and angled toward the left side of the fairway. It might have been an acceptable shot if he had not hit it so far—well over two hundred and twenty-five yards. But it was a pull and the length took it well into the evergreens that bordered the left side of the fairway. He would be hunting again, and the tree limbs were still wet from last night's rain.

"Good shot," his uncle called back.

Robert always managed to see the direction of the ball if it was one of Stephen's bad shots, even if he could not tell you where it landed within ten trees in either direction. Stephen said nothing. This was about the time in his rounds of golf that the tee shot normally went awry. He knew it was the impulse to swing too hard and to think too much standing over the ball before he swung. He would correct that on the next tee.

By the time they were lifting their golf balls from the cup on the green, he had forgotten the vow on the tee. He had made an eight-foot putt to save bogey on the hole. Robert had bogeyed also on the par four, but only because it took him two woods and a nine-iron to get on the green. His putting had been masterful: a twenty-five footer that rolled to a stop four inches from the cup. Robert tapped it in despite Stephen's distinct call that it was good, requiring no further play on the ball. But Robert always tapped them in, a reminder to Stephen of the superiority of his short game over that of his young, grand-nephew.

Robert's tee shot on the fifteenth did not go so far, rolling to a quick stop at no more than one hundred and thirty yards out. It had been a weak swing. Stephen watched his uncle shuffle to the cart. He did not even stop to put his driver in the bag, but clutched it between his legs as he sat.

Stephen hurriedly teed the ball and briskly went through his routine. The ball shot low and long off the tee. He was already walking toward the cart with concern for his uncle when the ball rolled to rest. It lay in the middle of the fairway, two hundred and sixty yards from the white tee that still sat upright in the tee box.

He started the cart and glanced at his uncle's profile.

"Robert, I really have some work I need to finish at the office. If you don't mind maybe we could cut our round short today."

"Well, if you want, but you shouldn't be going back to the building today, Stephen. It will be six o'clock before you can even get there."

"It's okay. I have no plans for this evening."

"What about Julia?"

"Not tonight. She has a staff dinner with her magazine folks."

❦ ❦ ❦

Steven guided the cart to the center of the fairway and picked up his uncle's ball. He looked for his own ball along the right edge of the fairway and was about to forget it when he saw it at the longer distance and near the center of the fairway. He did not comment on the length of his drive, and neither did Uncle Robert.

"You still making all the shows and concerts with her?"

"Most of them. I guess we have some good theater here. But it isn't really my thing."

"No better theater except in New York," Robert said.

Stephen thought that might be true, but then he still knew little about the theater. For a while, he had pretended for Julia more interest than was honest. He had hoped to learn to like it more, but he had not. He still preferred the Mariners and the Seahawks games, even on television. He thought that she had come to realize that. She had not asked him to the last comedy opening. He especially did not enjoy the stage comedies. He found reruns of "Cheers" and "Taxi" on television much funnier. The lines in the stage shows had too much in common with the current TV situation comedies, which she even liked. In all fairness, he had seldom watched them. He favored any sport, even auto racing.

He dropped Robert off at his car and put his bag in his trunk for him and said goodbye. He drove the cart over to his Explorer, opened the rear door, and threw in his gear. He had tried to get Robert to let him drive him home, but his uncle insisted that it was a short run—just south of the Broadmoor area near the shore of Lake Washington. He was right; so Stephen had let it drop. It had been a pleasant June day, one of those Seattle days that was about to go the entire daylight period with no rain. Fortunately it was toward the end of June, and the rainy days had lessened. July and August were his favorite months. Great sailing. The family sailboat had not been out in weeks. He was the only one who sailed it now; he had taken Julia out on their third date. It had been like old movie scenes of Grace Kelly and Bing Crosby. He thought Crosby a little old for the part, but his Grandmother Grace viewed often the scene of the crooner and his rendition of "True Love." But Stephen found the blond Ms. Kelly and the majestic sailboat more attractive. Julia also was a blond.

❦ ❦ ❦

In his office on the twenty-second floor of the Grace Building he snapped open the lid of his ox-blood leather briefcase. He had never used it to hold a brief even though he was a lawyer, one year out of Stanford Law School. That was a miracle. With a good mind and plenty of family money behind him, he still had been in the lower third of his class. Started there and ended there—he was consistent.

He was not confident that his life as a lawyer was going to work out. At school his friends envied his guaranteed position with the family law firm and the automatic climb awaiting him up its rungs of success. But he had not enjoyed the studies. Not nearly as much as the hobby he developed in reading about and visiting the string of Spanish missions along the California and Mexican coastline. It was all a matter of discovery for him. He had never thought of the entire region belonging not to the Native American Indian but to the Spaniards when the infant United States expanded west. The Spaniards had already taken it from the Indians and then our government took it from the Spanish. He found the number of books and good histories of the region limited, but he read all that he could find. It was a story that still was not told in a balanced way in the English histories. He thought about how the period might be treated in Spanish and Mexican histories, but he never had tried to find one in English translation. It was a story that some citizen of the United States of America, some Anglo/Saxon, white, protestant son of a wealthy family should write.

He had written an article, published in a small university alumni newsletter. He had gotten a call from his grandmother within a week. Some of the alumni had disliked it. "California Retaken" was the title, and he had tried to link the history of the region and its passage from the Indians to Hispanic America and then to the present day with its flow of the tired and poor Hispanics yearning to be free, or at least employed. His effort at combining a serious story with what proved to be some poorly phrased humor had not worked well. Still, the editor of the newsletter loved it and wanted a sequel, but he never wrote one. Stephen had kept a copy of the article clipped from the newsletter. He liked reading what he had written. Not even his best law school brief approached giving him the satisfaction he got from those ten inches of double column print. Julia had laughed when she read the article, but he didn't know whether she was amused with the attempted humor or with the idea of him as a writer. At any rate, writing was not worth incurring again the wrath of his grandmother. Few things were.

The weather was still holding fair as he looked out the window toward Elliott Bay. The Belltown section held a number of tall buildings, most of them several stories taller than the Grace Building, one of the early multistoried office buildings in the area. He removed the folder with the list of the last two years' contributors to the Carolyn Grace Blandon Foundation. Three names had caught his attention—the largest single contributors of 1999. One was a firm big in the lumber business, an annual contributor. A second was the owner of a fine glassware company whose wife had died in the same year. The third was a man named Jennings, apparently an Alaskan. None of the Foundation staff knew of prior contributions by the man, and the family name had no prominence in the area. A quick phone call to the Alaska senior senator's office had provided no immediate help, but the courteous woman had promised to call him back.

There was a file on each major contributor to the foundation, but the file for Mr. Jennings had been started and little more. There was a paper, a legal paper dated earlier in the current year and indicating that the man's attorney was a Mr. Leland Caudry, not of Alaska, but of a place called Boothbay Harbor, Maine.

CHAPTER 9

William pulled the paper from his typewriter and placed it on the other typed sheet on his desk. The poetry had come easily as he had sat on the bench over the past few weeks. He had made some penciled notes on paper, mainly to preserve some phrases that he particularly liked and thought that he might not recall in just the same structure, much as he had done years before, carrying word pictures in his mind or on notes in his pockets for days before he decided that he was not likely to improve the expressions. Once the words were on paper he had found little reason for change. Of course, he had then as now written just for himself. He put the two sheets of poetry away and closed the desktop.

In the kitchen he was drinking the last of a glass of water when he saw the light of the attic through the cracks between the ceiling panels. Before winter he knew that he should put some insulation down between the rafters above the ceiling. He did not want another drafty winter. He pulled down the stairway and climbed up to turn off the light. He tried to recall how many days it had been since he had been up here. He was glad he lived alone. He had come to forget so many things, and they all seemed to be routine matters. Just as he reached to pull the light cord he remembered the drop zone painting. It was still in the side storage room, in the wooden box he had asked them to encase it in after it had been framed. He backed down the stairway and went out the door to retrieve it. He had meant to bring it in, away from the damp.

He carried the box around to the front door and recalled why he had left it in the storage room in the first place. The long drive back from Freeport had left his legs stiff, and the walking was painful. He had decided to come back out and get it the next day, but he had forgotten, just like he had forgotten to turn off the attic light. He set the box on the floor in the front room near the wicker love seat.

She had never come back. He had wanted to tell her how his truck engine had turned over the first time and had run fine on the trip to Freeport and back. He had not moved it since. It was not like him to leave the truck in the wrong place so long, and it was not like he had owned it for a long time, it was just that in his scheme of things, it was to be parked under the tree on the left side of the cottage, not on good grass on the other side of the building.

He looked at the box that contained the painting. What should he do with it now? He had planned to give it to her, but she probably would not be back again. And that maybe would be best. But then he knew that it wasn't best. It had been so clear as he typed the poem that it was the young woman who had stirred him. Increasingly he was dreaming of her—of Carol. He was picturing her face, the curves of her body, almost hearing her voice—something he had stopped being able to do thirty years ago. He had been able to dream such dreams for a while in the fifties and sixties, but they all, even the nightmares, ended with the combat in Vietnam. Despite his many efforts to keep all the positive thoughts that he could about that American experience, he resented most that it was there that he had lost the memory of her face and voice.

And he had no picture. He had failed even to get that from the firm. He might have been able to get it from her family, but he never tried. So he had no picture and her face wavered, grew faint, and then was lost. Despite his efforts, he had never been able to create it in his mind. Contrary to what he had told the girl, he had started a painting in the late sixties. But, he could not remember Carol's face. Later, even looking out on the green, flowing Kenai River from the deck of his Alaskan cabin, he could not bring himself to try the portrait again for fear that she would look ugly, something that he would never want. So the partial painting had been moved to Maine and now sat in the cottage attic. In the limited light, her image up there at times appeared ghost-like. And the man at her side, he looked like a ghost as well. And why not?

Still it might be good to do something with the drop zone painting. He had thought he might scrape away the heavier paint, turn the canvas to a landscape view, and paint his impression of Boothbay Harbor. He had already pictured in his mind a composite scene. He could pull the white steeple of the church nearer to what she called the old boathouse, and then draw in some other feature that he could not yet identify, maybe the footbridge, as the third point of a triangle, an old master's approach at composition. It was a scene at the center of his life now. A scene helping to bridge the years since his days in Seattle,

Japan and Korea—the same years that he had filled with service to his country and with the years in Alaska of which he now was not so proud. It was not the fault of Alaska whose awesome beauty and life on the environmental edge had drawn him. It was his fault that he had let that place freeze a heart already hardened in the previous thirty years. He tired of the arithmetic. It all added to the same thing, long years of guilt and fear at best, waste at its worst.

There were times that he had been given a chance, even as late as the Kenai. Paula, the woman with the craft shop near the fishing guide's office. She had talked with him of his painting, had gone with him to his chalet to see the work. And she had criticized it. So much that he scraped his freshest work away and tried again, producing the moose portrait, his best. She had offered more, for she clearly was lonely too, but he shoved her away with excuses of saving her from an old man set in his ways and selfish. He did not think then what he found nettling him now: that out of guilt had grown the inability to love. Or she may have unleashed another fear—that he could love again. He had run. More than his move to a milder climate for his arthritis was the reality of his flight from Paula and her offered warmth. There had been other Paulas, women that he could never love or, maybe, women that he did not want to learn that he could love. That was why he had written the last poem. It was a letter to Carol.

He prepared for bed. Tomorrow he would get back to his painting. He felt that he had so much that he wanted to finish. And he knew that his time was not unlimited.

CHAPTER 10

Peggy listened closely to Rachel and munched on the peanut butter-filled stalk of celery.

"I think you're inventing this air of mystery about your brigadier, Rachel. He does seem lonely, but what old person living alone wouldn't be? You probably could have stopped a derelict on the streets of Boston and told him of your problems and got as much advice. I think you should stay away from Boothbay Harbor. Spend the weekends and holidays here with me. I know this med student that you would really like. He's a riot. You wouldn't believe his operating room jokes."

Rachel knew that Peggy was still trying, and she had not found the two or three men she had dated unlikable. She just had no real desire to spend time with them. Not on a date. She preferred to spend time in groups of young men and women—no complications.

"Rachel, you know you're drifting. I admire you. I don't have half of your capacity for getting things done, or getting people to cooperate. But Rachel, you aren't doing anything with your great personality. No, I take that back. You're becoming so, so self-absorbed that I can't believe you're the same person. And while I'm at it, you running a paper-folding machine is like my favorite singer shoveling coal."

"That all you have to say, Peggy?"

"Well, I can get specific if you want. But I don't want to hurt you."

"No. Go on. You're on a roll."

"Well, let me take the easiest one first. You wouldn't spend an hour with your brigadier if you were able to accept the situations with your mother and your father..."

"Now that is really glib, Peggy. If I had no problems, I would have no problem. Thanks a lot."

"If you don't want to listen, fine. I'll stop talking."

"No. I'll listen. Go ahead."

"Well, I guess that's about it. You just are not handling the other problems very well. You're not the first girl whose mother has a mental illness. You're not the first girl whose father went outside his marriage for love."

"No. No. No more." Rachel rushed into the bathroom and slammed the door. She looked in the mirror. Peggy was right about her mother. She knew she was running, had vowed to stop, to spend more time with her mother. But she had not. Even Peggy saw that she was not going as often to see her mother as she should. She could do that. And she would. But her dad. Peggy was wrong there. This was different. Her mother was ill. And she was wrong about William. Maybe she was making more of William's story than she should. And she was curious. But she could help. She could not explain it. She was no psychiatrist, but the man needed someone to care about him, and she found no evidence that there was anyone for him, anywhere. But more than that, she was the one to help him; maybe she was the only one who could. She could not explain that to Peggy, or to anyone else. But she was as sure of that as of anything in her life.

Peggy was right about another thing. She was drifting, and she needed to get hold of the tiller. She opened the door and Peggy was not there. Then she heard her in the small kitchen.

"Like some hot chocolate?" Peggy called out.

They talked well into the morning but only skirting the matter of her father's girlfriend. They talked of more frequent and longer visits with her mother, notice to the printer that she was seeking a job dealing more with people, and just one more visit to William just so he would not be offended when she no longer visited him. And they would talk again about her father after she contacted him and learned specifically what he was doing with his life. Peggy had the last word.

"How original, the college girl is going to call her dad."

❦   ❦   ❦

In August she went back to the Harbor and arrived late in the afternoon and walked directly to the bench before going to her motel. There was no sign of the truck and she guessed it was in some repair shop or junkyard. She sat on the bench and watched the evergreens across the harbor sway in the breeze. She was no closer to knowing what she ought to do about her father, or how well she could live with whatever she did. She feared that they were not the same.

When she and Peggy had talked last about her father, her roommate had dispatched her dilemma as if it were trivial.

"Rachel, my father and mother divorced when I was thirteen. I saw no signs of it coming. I was not abused. My mother was not abused. My father was not abused. They just split. Both have been remarried over four years and say they were never as happy as they are now. I don't know what kind of therapy that revelation is supposed to be for me, but there you are. I love my father's new wife, and I despise my mother's new husband. It doesn't seem to make a damn to either of them what I think of their new mates, and I guess that it doesn't."

"But Peggy, that's not the same."

"Maybe not. Maybe it is. That's my best shot, Miss Morality, now let's go shopping."

Now she went to the door and knocked. There was no reply. She tried the door. It swung open; she stepped inside. She reached in her shoulder bag and took out the small silver flashlight, and she walked through the front room, almost tripping over a wooden box. It looked the size of a coffee table with the legs removed.

She pulled open the middle drawer of the left pedestal of the desk. The folder was there, and she opened it on the bed to find the poems still in the chronological order she had left them. She guessed he had not even touched the folder since she had tied it closed. She took out the second poem dated December 24, 1951.

> I tell myself that it could have worked
> My pride made it so hard
> I proved the things that he said were true
> My background your life marred
>
> And while we waited for one more year
> A war stepped in our way
> And I came back to learn you had gone
> To your mom, there to stay

> I thought your love had been just a play
> I failed us then and there
> I thought it your choice and did not write
> I said you did not care
>
> And back to the war and pain I went
> I hoped there to forget
> But that black fight just told me clear
> I could not leave you yet

She came to the third and last poem. The word jumped out of the text. It was not unexpected, but it left her drained and cold. She turned the page over and slipped the short stack of papers back in the folder.

When she was back on the path and headed toward the Inn she resolved to leave the next day. She had invaded his privacy again and it was hard to determine if it would help her in any way to help him. Just how successful had she been in getting him to think about his past? Maybe she had succeeded even less than she had thought. Her own needs and curiosity had driven her at first and maybe he recognized that. She hoped he was somewhere this evening with someone. Someone who asked nothing of him. Someone honest, who accepted him as he is, and who enjoyed his company with no secret prodding into his past. A painful past that might help no one for him to remember.

Rachel did not check in. She visited the desk and they agreed to forget her reservation. They had people waiting for a room to become available. By ten o'clock she was driving through the darkness of the Maine summer. She had not had dinner, and she was not hungry. She choked the steering wheel as the pavement of the Interstate flashed under the beam of her headlights. She felt the hot tears on her cheeks. She felt so confused. She knew of nothing she had ever felt like this before. She imagined these silent cries for help that she wanted so much to respond to. But she didn't know how. Not for her mother or for William.

CHAPTER 11

Stephen and his Grandmother Grace sat in the hospital waiting room with Blake Halsey Grace, the granddaughter of Robert Grace, the old man he called, "Uncle." Blake was a fellow lawyer with the Grace and Fallows Law Firm. She was three years older than Stephen, a fact he knew to avoid in conversation although she was sensitive that all recognize her three years seniority over him in the firm. He could like her, and they could be friends as they had been as teenagers. But she maintained this distant air with him, as she did with all the men in the firm except with her grandfather. The three of them sat now expecting no miracles, waiting to be told that the cancer had finally taken him from them. Blake had been the last to leave his side, an honor that he thought that Grandmother had maneuvered to gain. But Blake was a strong lady. Maybe stronger, if far less manipulative, than Grandmother Grace.

Blake had said nothing when she came out, foregoing the seat that Grandmother patted for her at her side. She sat instead in the chair next to Stephen, but gave him no word or signal. She, like Stephen, always spoke of her grandfather as, "Uncle." Like Stephen, she had no real uncles. Stephen's mother and his father had each been an only child. If—when—Uncle Robert died, Stephen and Blake would be the remaining members of the old Grace Brothers clan. Except, that is, for Grandmother Grace. She was still formidable. But only because of the weakness of Robert. A weakness that hid behind a professed need to maintain harmony in the family. All the lawyers at Grace and Fallows knew that the harmony meant continuing to give the old lady, now ninety-five, whatever she wanted.

The doctor removed the green mask from his nose and mouth as he closed the door to the long hallway where they all had last seen Robert—no longer looking at or talking with anyone, but in a sleep that heavy sedation gave him as an option to waking pain.

Stephen watched the professional turning of the head and the compassionate look in the doctor's tired eyes. He felt Blake's hand on his. They rose with Grandmother to accept the decision of the Almighty. That's how she would speak of it, Grandmother Grace. Stephen had developed no better concept of it all while being reared by this old woman, actually his great grandmother.

Blake turned and fell against him, her arms about his shoulders. He pulled his forearms free to embrace his cousin and to hold her, the only way to keep her from falling as she fainted. He turned and let her down on the couch. The doctor called out for help, and from somewhere two green-clad people appeared. A man and a woman. The man pulled something from his pocket and handed it to the doctor. Stephen guessed it was old-fashioned smelling salts, just like those the assistant high school football coach had seemed to relish using. Blake was back with them quickly, but she was ashen. She and Stephen were two of the few in the firm really fond of the old man, and the only people anywhere who truly loved him.

He drove her home and told her that he would have someone from the firm drive her car to the house later in the evening. She had regained control once in the car. He drove through the late afternoon Seattle rain. They were going to the old home that she and her mother had shared with her grandparents in the Capitol Hill area. She never spoke of her father who left the family when she was still a child. Her mother had died of Leukemia when Blake was seven. She was alone with Robert by the time she was sixteen and her true grandmother Grace—Robert's wife—died.

Blake had not yet married and was given to saying that she never would. Stephen often thought that she, not he, should be the heir apparent to the inside track in the firm. Both had only done what was expected of them in gaining law degrees. But she had graduated with honors from Yale, and no one in the firm doubted the sharpness of her mind or the common sense of her thinking. That had been Robert's strongest, and underestimated, strength: common sense. Somehow Stephen could see her name in a brass plate on the door of one of the top-floor senior partner offices well before his. But he was a man, and some of the members of the firm still spoke openly of the expectation that the front runner of the Grace offspring would perforce be a male.

"You'll be moving fast now, Stephen," she said as if reading his mind.

"I hope not too fast," he said. "I still don't know where the boy's room is."

"You're too modest. It's wherever you are from now on, and where you want it to be."

"You don't mean that do you?"

"I certainly do. You could get support to take the firm in any direction by the top echelons. All you have to do is join in a campaign to undermine the power of Grandmother Grace."

"Would you do that if you got the chance?" He asked.

"In a super-short minute," she spat out and lighted her second cigarette on the short drive.

Stephen unlocked the door and entered his houseboat on Lake Union. Grandmother did not like him living here. She liked less that he leased and had not bought. The prices for both had jumped after the Tom Hanks movie but were back to a less insane growth rate now. The rent was not a problem. His income from the trust was ample even without the salary that he now drew from the firm. He could have bought, but the house on the lake was not what he wanted as a home. He did not yet know what that was. Except he did not want the museum that Grandmother Grace called the family home. The only right the big stone mansion had to that name was that she had driven Stephen's grandmother away from it and had locked his adult father inside it, allowing him out only to marry, and then had trapped the bride and groom there as if in the web of a spider. He owed Blake for most of what he knew about his family. It was not a great deal, but she had passed on things that Uncle Robert had said, usually after his heavy drinking in the years after his wife had died. When she had told him of these things, she had respected his feelings—his hurt, his loneliness. He felt that he owed her for that friendship.

They would make jokes about the fortunes of the Grace family when they were teenagers. But it tended to cover a melancholy that they both felt. Stephen was confident of that, and he guessed that he felt it more. She would recite the lineage in the manner of the Bible: using the term begat to link one generation to the next until she broke up in laughter. He had been uncomfortable with her monologue, but still he laughed, aware that the tragedies were greater on his side of the family. Maybe she had come to realize that and had ceased the bizarre humor at some point. For a time he had put it totally out of his mind, in the last years of high school and most of college, but his position in the firm that provided the legal advice to the Carolyn Grace Blandon Foundation, caused him to confront it all again. He had laid it out on paper in as simple terms as he could, less the details of how some of his people had died. As he had typed the names and dates of births and deaths, he could see why Blake at sixteen, had ended one monologue with "The Graces kill off their young."

Blake's side of the family was not complicated. Her great grandfather was Ralph E. Grace, younger brother of Richard Todd Grace, Stephen's great grandfather. Ralph and Mary Pruett Grace had a son in 1929 they named Robert Everett Grace. That was the "Uncle" Stephen had just lost. "Uncle" had a younger sister who died just after birth. He married Norma Triscomb Halsey who gave him a daughter that they named Ellen—Blake's mother, who had married Ronald A. Dubois in 1970. Blake had been named Blake Halsey Dubois at the time of her birth in 1971. When Blake's father deserted the family, Ellen's father considered it good riddance and had Ellen agree to a legal change of Blake's last name to Grace. Stephen thought it curious that Ellen's name had remained Dubois until her death at age twenty-seven.

Old Richard Todd Grace was born in 1900, and the lanky lawyer, who reminded some according to Grandmother of Abraham Lincoln, won the hand of ravishingly beautiful Beverly Carswell in 1922. Stephen smiled, recalling that it was his Grandmother who gave that description of the match. They had but one child, Carolyn Susan, born in 1930. Carolyn married a young naval aviator, John Blandon, just before the outbreak of the Korean War. Their son was named John Todd Blandon, born in February of 1951, just months after his father's fighter aircraft crashed in the sea off the east coast of the Korean peninsula. Strangely, even for the Grace family, Carolyn also died in a Pacific plane crash just three months after the birth of her son. Neither of the parents' bodies was ever recovered.

John Todd married Dorothy Wentworth Darby in 1973. And in an eerie accident, the young couple perished in an avalanche while trekking in the Himalayan Alps of Nepal in 1981. Stephen put down the pencil. There was this feeling of near emptiness, but of lingering disbelief, that any family could be so unlucky. And there was the question he did not like to entertain—was it something that one could inherit. He felt no bitterness or anger. Not anymore. Or at least not toward them. He had been born their son, Stephen Todd Blandon, just six years before their deaths. But he could not really remember them. People had told him that he should be able to remember them, at least in some way. But he did not. He had tried, but he could not recall a voice or a face, except for the photographs. Only the photographs and the little that Grandmother Grace ever said to him about them—that was all he had. The Grace home that he had always known was a place of old people, of harsh words and a tense struggle between his guardians, Richard Todd and Beverly Carswell Grace. He was always in between, but the continuous discord was not over him, he was just caught in the maelstrom. The battle raged until his great grandfather, the only father he had ever known, died in 1988, an apparently strong man even at age 88. He simply did not wake up one morning. Stephen had played golf with him just the weekend before, with him and Uncle Robert.

Stephen had leaned on Uncle Robert and Blake after his great grandfather died, his great grandmother becoming even more distant toward him than she had been before her husband's death.

When Uncle Robert died, among the affairs of his estate, handled by Leonard Fallows, a senior partner of the firm, was the key to a safe deposit box. The contents were bequeathed to Stephen. Blake smiled at him during the reading of the will, but did not ask him about the box, then or later. But it probably puzzled her as it did him.

Mr. Fallows' secretary called to arrange for Stephen to meet with her boss to receive the contents. Fallows greeted him in a cordial manner and offered him coffee, which he declined. Stephen had been wondering for days just what Uncle Robert would have seen fit to leave him. It was all in one manila envelope that the senior lawyer handed to him as soon as he had turned down the coffee.

"You may open it here, or take it with you," Fallows said. Stephen took it as a polite preference that he take the packet with him and leave.

"Have you looked at what is in here?" Stephen asked.

"I saw the nature of it, but I have not examined the contents. I just slid the material from the box into the envelope."

"Thank you, Mr. Fallows," Stephen said, and returned to his office several floors below.

He dumped the contents of the envelope onto his desk. There was nothing of apparent value. Folded charts of Puget Sound, some quite old, and possibly of collector interest, but Stephen knew that they were intended for his use. He and Uncle Robert had been the surviving sailors of the family. There were other papers, clippings from newspapers of family events, mostly marriages, deaths, and tragedies. There were photographs. There was one envelope, yellowed by age. It bore something that he had never seen, a wax seal embossed with the stamp of the Grace family coat of arms. The seal had been cracked and the envelope flap opened. The envelope bore no address or name. He tipped it to remove the paper inside and a fine chain slipped out and fell to the top of the desk. It had a pendant attached. He picked it up and noted that it appeared to be silver-plated and nearly covered with the purplish-black oxidation common on silver. It did not appear to be an expensive piece of jewelry. There was a note of one page, hand written.

∞

Robert,

Please keep this safe.
Beverly thinks it long destroyed, but I couldn't do that. She must not know that it still exists.
My Carolyn only loved two men in her life—myself and this man.
Possibly some day it will be needed. By someone. Perhaps you can then give it to him.

I would bear you no grudge if you do not.
I was not able to. God help me.

Richard

 He looked inside the envelope again. There was no clipping, no picture. Nothing to depict "this man" in any way. Maybe there had been a slip of paper with a name on it, his grandfather's name. Maybe it was a clipping of the newspaper obituary of his grandfather. Was it simply a picture of his grandfather? But that would make no sense. There was no problem between his grandfather and great grandmother Grace. He was a hero. She had his picture on her grand piano. It had always been there. What could it possibly have been that would make his great grandfather so secretive? His great grandfather had always been Stephen's favorite, even ahead of Uncle Robert. While Stephen did not feel comfortable with anyone, and he did not feel that the Grace mansion was a real home, he came closest to feeling at ease with his great grandfather. He could see how his grandmother would have loved him—her father. Was it a picture of his grandfather? But if there had been a picture, why had Uncle Robert removed it? He sorted through the pictures in the box, but all were of his grandmother as a child and young girl, except for the obituary picture of his grandfather. Had that slipped out of the envelope? It must have. What good did it do to leave the note with nothing to explain its meaning?
 A locket. He looked at the necklace. Could it be a locket? It must be a locket. He put down the pictures and newspaper clippings and ran his fingertip

around the pendant, searching for some release or locking device. But there was none. His short fingernails allowed him no entry into the grooves of the oval pendant. He needed a knife.

Uncle Robert would have left a clue to the meaning of the note. His strength was common sense, and so far all of his other affairs they had found to be meticulously handled right up until his collapse.

He took a letter opener from the desk drawer and slid the edge into the crevice of the pendant. It opened. It was a locket and the hinges worked despite the clumsiness of his hurried efforts in prying it open.

There was a picture. It was surprisingly clear and retained sharp contrasts of dark and light values. It was a black and white photo, probably clipped to fit in the oval container. The woman was Carolyn, his grandmother. The man was not his grandfather.

"Oh, hell," he said aloud.

Even his great grandfather, the one person of all the Graces that Stephen faulted little, had not gotten it right. Why do this? He asked himself. The old fellow should have tossed the locket in the Sound. And if there was something that he, Stephen, now ought to do with this, why had the great Richard Todd Grace not done it himself? Fear of Beverly Carswell? Maybe. But if the old lady would have objected, it seemed that there would have been ample reason to do so. And what good did it do for him to learn of this now. That was all so long ago. And yet…

He put the locket, photos, and clippings back in the envelope and set them aside. He wanted to leave the office now, but he took two memos from his inbox and read them and attached a note to one instructing that some files be returned to him along with the memo. He tossed it into the outbox, and decided to leave for the day. Things were still a little off schedule following Robert's death. Maybe no one would notice his early departure. He grabbed his briefcase and the envelope and headed for the elevator.

When he got home he removed the locket again and stared at the man in the picture for a long time. Then he took his great grandfather's note and the locket and dropped it into the gray, fire and waterproof safe box that he kept in his closet. They were probably safe enough here, and even if his house were to sink they would likely be able to recover the box and its contents. And what if they could not? Maybe that would be for the best.

The cool of September was on the lake as he stepped out on the deck. He recalled Blake's comment on his ability to dictate where the boy's room would be. He had done nothing to test such power. He should take her to lunch. She had few friends around the firm, including a couple of guys who only wanted a one-night friendship. Maybe she had some of those. Well, anyway, he ought to share lunch with her. She had been especially considerate toward him since Uncle Robert had died.

He was not particularly hungry, and it was a little early for dinner, but he thought he would drive over to Angelo's Restaurant and get some spaghetti and a good beer. It was his and Julia's favorite place, but she was out of town again. He flipped on the four-wheel drive as he sped over the wet Seattle street. The windshield washers barely kept ahead of the steady rainfall. Who was the guy? The man in the locket?

CHAPTER 12

The early October wind whipped through the trees at the head of the cove and swung down over the water and through the town of Boothbay Harbor. William was going for the first time to the Tugboat Restaurant. He had driven the truck to Portland, found a Tall Shop and bought himself a blue blazer, a white oxford, button-down shirt, a pair of brown loafers and a black and gold, diagonally striped tie, broad stripes, like he had worn years ago. The tie was a little broader than he liked while not as wide as those rags they wore in the forties and seventies. He would have preferred one of the mid-width ties of the fifties, but this one would do. He stepped down from the truck in the restaurant parking lot, his refinery complete with the sharply creased khakis he had picked up at the laundry just this afternoon. He had felt relieved because he had no backup trousers to wear if the laundry had failed.

He had seen the tugboat shell of the restaurant many times, but he was surprised as he entered to find he was looking at the spiral passageway that would lead up to the boat's pilothouse. There was a waiting area and lounge near the doorway to the passageway, but Rachel was not there. He turned to the left and walked over to the bar. He was about to order a vodka when a waitress stepped up.

"Are you Mr. Jennings?"
"Yes, ma'am, I am."
"Right this way please."
She was seated in the far-right corner toward the harbor.
"Hello, William."
"Hello." He sat.

"I wanted to see you to apologize for my meddling in your life and to tell you that while I initially really did not like you and then approached you only because of your fencing off the bench…well, I did—and do—care for your well being and happiness," she said.

"Wow, you must have rehearsed that for a week."

"I have. And I thank you for agreeing to come here tonight."

"What is this? The real goodbye?"

"Well, no. I mean, I don't know. I just needed to talk to you and explain some things."

"Let's start over," he said. "How are you?"

"Great, just great. You are looking dapper."

"And you look…beautiful," he said.

His embarrassment he knew had to be obvious. He chuckled.

She laughed.

"Would you like some wine?" He asked.

"I'd love some."

He picked up the embossed folder enclosing the wine list. "You have a preference?"

"No, you pick for us."

"Is that in vogue with today's women?" He asked.

"You have some hang-up with today's women?" She shot back.

He felt his face color again.

"What do you think?"

She hesitated. She had left this. She had not come here to probe those areas again.

"Yes. I think you do." A voice told her to stop, but she shrugged it off.

"Well, now, I can see why you might think that, seeing as how you are given to reading a man's mind, or his private papers," he said.

He could see that she was shaken by his words. Her blush was bold and long.

"William, that's why I needed to talk to you. I'm sorry…"

"It's all right. I knew after you were there the first time, at least I guess that was the first time. And the reversed paper was obvious another time. I guess that was your last visit." He looked at her questioningly. "I haven't seen your Honda driving around my cottage, alone, for quite some time." He smiled. He did not want to make her uncomfortable. He didn't even want to engage in the light banter they had known. She nodded. She reminded him of a schoolgirl just corrected for some minor playground infraction. He smiled more broadly.

"What?" She asked.

He couldn't be that honest. He could never explain how he felt. She could misunderstand, feel insulted, and even think of him as coarse and fatuous. He could not stand that. He could not tell her anything approaching his feelings, but he could tell her about Carol. And that was what he was going to do. Tell her about the person that her very first visit, her face, her pounding on the door, her making fun of him, so many things, had brought back into clear memory and into his life, let him feel again, memories that he had been unable to capture for half a century.

"I was thinking of a story, a long story that you might appreciate hearing. But first, let's try some Beaujolais. I ordered Beaujolais one time for a woman just your age, in a little restaurant in Seattle, Washington. She told me what to order. She knew wine much better than I did."

It was the story that Rachel had hoped that he eventually would tell her. She listened intently. Above them as he spoke hung the inevitable climax. How would he get by it? How could he visit that again and in any way make this sharing with her worth the pain that he would feel?

He began.

Carol came to the University at the start of his senior year, the fall of 1948. She was among a group of freshmen girls that upper classmen considered it their privilege to stand near the freshmen girl's dormitory and watch as they came and went during the early days of the semester. He did not believe it likely that he would see a girl that would impress him, and he did not believe in love at first sight—not then. In his final year at the University, he figured he had seen all types, and all sizes. He was just curious about this year's "crop."

She was walking with two other girls, seemingly unaware of anything other than the three of them. But her animated gestures and her facial expressions were those one might see in a quality cinema. Not overacted, but played out in a manner that at once convinces one watching of the genuine and honest nature of the performer and the important message she is delivering. As a critic he suddenly lost his old and relied upon criteria. She was on the stage alone. He was deaf to the tired and vacuous quips of the men beside him. When she walked out of the scene, he left also to find out her name, her home, her schedule, and if she liked Puget Sound Olympia oysters.

Carol Grace was her name, and she was from a wealthy Seattle family. She had not identified a major, but the girl in the arts and sciences administrative offices was also from Seattle, knew Carol, and had at one time shown interest in William. She shared with him Carol's schedule. No likelihood of his being in one of those classes. He looked more closely. Art 101. The girl explained that it was a basic course, for freshmen really, but she thought that it might be open to seniors. He would have to check with someone else on that.

"Thanks, Lana," he said as he turned to hurry out of the office.

"Good luck," she said. "You'll need it."

As it turned out there was no problem in getting in the class. He enrolled late, but it was under-subscribed and, while his advisor guessed William's purpose for taking the course, he had no objection.

"Won't make a lot of difference, William. It's not a class you need, and you'll have enough credits for a June graduation without it. If that's what you want, have at it."

And he did. She only nodded when he said hello at the first meeting of the art class. He talked later to a fellow senior who was also a Seattle native.

"William," he had said, "She is out of your league. Her daddy owns banks and half the land around Lake Washington. You couldn't afford to take her to lunch."

William had been unperturbed—initially. But he found that other friends had the same view. Maybe they were right. He knew women, even in his senior class, who dated only men who drove their own cars, some new, post World War II production, and who wore coat and tie to classes, even to the college sports events. But most of all, they dated the men whose families had money.

He would see her outside the class, on the campus, in the hallway of one of the academic buildings and in the student affairs building. But he never tried to walk near her. And he did not try to talk to her in the art class. Yet he ceased to have interest in other girls. George told him he was stuck on her. He denied it in as light a fashion as he could muster, but as Thanksgiving approached, he knew that he had to talk to her. He needed to talk to her even if it was only about her interest in art, or her view of the University. He might ask her if she liked oysters. Then again, he probably could not afford the restaurant where she ate oysters.

Their shared class was at two o'clock each Tuesday and Thursday. On a Thursday he got there fifteen minutes before the class start time. He stood against the wall by the doorway. He saw her move around a group halted near the top of the stairs and walk toward the room.

He thought that she looked at him and slowed, and then picked up her pace again and walked toward him with her eyes on his. She continued forward. She was wearing a beige woolen cap, a small, round cap, fitted loosely to her hair and leaving ample dark brown, wavy hair showing all around. The hair was shoulder length, and tossed out from the neck by a light gray, knitted wool scarf, wrapped once around her neck, the two ends hanging well down on her black sweater. The skirt was also wool, and a gray, but darker than the scarf. The shoes were oxfords, black, and she wore off-white socks rolled at the top. She carried one textbook and a spiraled notebook. Her black leather bag hung from a long strap over her left shoulder. It bounced against the front of her left hip as she walked. Her manner was less animated than when she was walking with one of her girlfriends. Now she seemed to move smoothly, only the bag breaking an impression of a person in total control, like someone…someone important. He wished he had not taken up his post near the door.

She stopped two feet away. He said nothing.

"You going in?" She asked.

"Yes," he said, too softly and with too little certainty.

"Well, you're blocking the doorway."

"Sorry," he said, moving back two short steps.

"Haven't seen you here so early before."

"No, no I don't normally come this early." He was surprised at her directness.

"Why here today?"

"Because I wanted to…talk to you." He was more surprised at his own clumsiness. She would tell him to get lost.

"Oh, about what?"

"Well, you know. Like, do you date? I mean would you like a date with me?"

"Doing what?"

He should have figured this part out before. He knew that.

"Would you like to go to the game with me Saturday? It's the last one of the year."

"No, thank you. I really don't care for football."

William looked around to see if any of his friends might be close by. They were not. This was embarrassing. He had been told no on requests for dates before, but never like this. Not quite like this. He groped for what he might say next.

"Do you like rowing?" She asked.

"Rowing? You mean the canoes?"

"Well, I mean the boats, or shells. But yes, the canoes that you see out on Lake Washington with the University crews in them. Do you like them?"

"I have seen them out there, yes."

"Saturday they have a special fall meet with California. I'm free at ten o'clock. Would you like to see them race?"

"You mean, us, together?" He knew he was being clumsy, but he had not expected her to be so responsive, even aggressive.

She chuckled. He grew more embarrassed.

"I'm sorry," she said and stepped even closer to him to permit other students to enter the room. "But yes. I mean we could take in the races for a little while if you would like."

"Yes, I would."

"Could we meet at the main dock and boathouse at ten o'clock then?"

"Yes."

"Good. We better go on in. Now we are both blocking the door. See you Saturday."

Everything was that same way. Not the initiative that determined what they did, or who seemed to do more of the talking in any given situation. It was her direct, no nonsense, and enthusiastic way about all they did. On their third date, a movie downtown, she insisted on paying for her ticket. Only after William knew that his anger was showing did she back down, with the chuckle that had become familiar. She said she was not laughing at him, but he knew that she was laughing at whatever he was talking about. It just was not directed at him personally. It made him uneasy. He did not like it, but he had not yet decided how he could talk to her about it.

He never told George or his other buddies just how the first conversation took place, or how she had to explain the rowing teams at the races to him, but he let them assume that he was bold and certainly in charge. They pressed him when he announced that he was taking her to a fashionable, and expensive, seafood restaurant for an oyster dinner. Where would he get the money for such a plush outing? Were they insinuating that she would be paying? Only George's intervention moved the discussion to another subject.

As it turned out, she did pay, at least part of the check. She must have noticed his preoccupation near the end of what had been an excellent meal and conversation. He had spoken too soon when the waiter brought the cart of rich desserts to their table. He realized after they had ordered that he had no idea of the cost of the desserts or of the specialty coffees each had ordered.

"Please, William," she said and pushed a tightly folded bill across the table. "At least let me help tip our fine waiter. He helped make it a special evening."

William wanted to tell her thanks, but no. But he let the money lie there, noncommittal about it until he received the bill. Carol rather abruptly indicated she was going to visit the ladies' room, leaving him alone to read and count.

He did not have enough money. He picked up the bill, expecting it to be a one-dollar bill, or at most a five. It was a ten, more than enough to cover the meal. He placed the ten and a one on the tray. That gave the waiter better than a ten per cent gratuity. He knew that would be fine. He would give her the rest of his money after they left the restaurant.

They had taken a cab from the campus earlier and walked the last four blocks to the restaurant. She had insisted that it would be a comfortable distance for her, and it had been. The walk had been casual; both bundled up in warm coats with scarves and gloves. But now the darkness was accompanied by a drizzle that eliminated any strolling along the streets. He asked the restaurant staff to call a cab for them, and in less than a half-hour, he was spending another third of the money that he had left to pay the cab driver. He was nearly broke. He owed her more money than he had or was likely to earn for another week.

"I'll have to owe you the change to your ten for a week or so," he said.

"William, that's no big thing. It was a wonderful evening. I loved it all, including my contribution to the waiter's tip. Hold on to whatever was left for the next time we go out. By the way, when will that be?"

He did not like being short on money. He had never had a lot. The son of a central Washington apple grower does not enjoy deep pockets, but he had always had money for dates. Of course, he had to admit, tonight was not a normal date for him. He had never spent more than the cost of a movie, hamburger, and cola on a date before. Five dollars would have been a costly evening in the past.

"What about next Friday night? It's the last Friday before Christmas." It was also the day that he received pay from his job of clearing tables in the cafeteria in the men's dorm.

"Sure, what time?" She asked.

"Early. Is five thirty okay?" he asked.

"Yes, what's the plan?"

"It's a surprise," he said.

Later they were standing just under the eave of the doorway to her dorm. No show of familiarity was allowed here—no hugging, no kissing. He took her by the hand and walked around the corner of the building. He lifted his worsted wool coat high to cover her hair and invited her closer. She reached under his arms and hugged him. He bent his head to meet her lips. Their first kiss had been in this same spot the night of their first shared movie, but this was their first real kiss. They lingered. She seemed to melt against him, and he heard her moan, a deep, expressive message that simultaneously caused him to press her more tightly to him and to remember where he was. In the darkness he touched her cheek, her chin, ran his fingers down the pretty nose, and thought of the deep blue eyes. He did not want the evening to end.

"I don't want you to leave," she whispered.

"I know. I feel the same."

So they stood. The wool coat soaking up the rain, but shielding them from the wetness as their bodies generated a heat that warmed the enclosed space in mockery of the December cold.

He wanted to know how she truly felt. He was afraid that she could not love him; that they were too far apart, that—

"I love you," she said.

"I love you, too," he said.

He made his way slowly back to his dormitory, the cold rain soaking his hair and running down his face. His shoulders were wet under the coat, but he paid little attention to the cold. He lay in bed well past midnight. It had all happened so fast. He was unsure of himself when they were apart, but when together he succumbed totally to her smile and vitality that brightened up all the places they visited.

The following Friday night he took her to the Library. It was open until six o'clock, and they had fifteen minutes until it closed. He showed her where to sit, and then he went to a section of shelves and returned with several magazines and books that he placed before her. She glanced over them slowly and then picked up one, then another. Then she looked at him, seated across the table.

"This is what I plan to do next spring, Carol. I'm going to do something about the threat to our liberty and freedom."

She was looking at the magazines again, pages folded back to articles on post war difficulties in Eastern Europe, on Greece, on the United Nations, on Churchill's speech about an iron curtain. And a book about communism and Josef Stalin and the Soviet Union.

"What are you going to do?" She asked.

"I'm to be commissioned an officer in the United States Army. I plan a life of service to ensure that what we won in the war will not be lost.

"I'm glad you're telling me this, William."

"Carol, I'm not going to have much to offer a woman. The military is not a well paying profession."

"Army officers have wives, don't they?"

She still surprised him with her candor and aggressiveness.

"Well yes, but…"

"But what?"

"You know what you are accustomed to. I could never—"

"Yes, I do, and you seem to think that you want and cherish something in life that in some way I am not capable of appreciating or that I'm not worthy of sharing."

"Carol, I didn't mean that. I only meant—"

"Yes, you did. Regardless of what you thought you were doing you were about to tell me that I couldn't be the patriot that you can be. That I'm too soft or too spoiled, or just too damned rich to come up to your standards. I have seen people like you before. You think that everyone who has a wealthy father or mother lives in terror of losing their affluent way of life. Well to hell with your snobbish attitude. I won't let it mess up our happiness for one lousy minute."

They left the library quickly. He could not decide whether to try to explain himself one more time or to kiss her. Then he decided, and kissed her on the library steps under the spotlights that illuminated the white Georgian façade of this building of knowledge.

They turned to walk down the sidewalk and she tugged his arm. He stopped and turned to her.

"And by the way, I think that Mr. Churchill got it right in Missouri. They will try to keep the truth out to convince their people that the fluffy philosophy of Marx, Engels, and Lenin will really work. It hasn't worked in Russia, and it won't work in Poland or Czechoslovakia either," she said. "It will all fail."

"And I intend to help make sure that it does," he said.

"We intend to do that," she said. "together."

They walked arm in arm down the street toward their future and their dinner—a juicy hamburger with onion and mustard.

On Christmas Eve afternoon she picked him up as she had gotten him to agree, but in a taxi. He knew that she could have come in a chauffeured car, but he was more comfortable with the taxi. They were going to her home, and William was nervous. They had agreed to exchange gifts, and he had spent more than he should have on a silver plated locket. It contained a picture of a movie actor when he had bought it, but he had taken the picture out. She would have to decide on a picture to put in its place.

She was thrilled with it. He knew that she could afford genuine silver necklaces, although he had never seen her wear one. Or gold for that matter. She seemed to favor pearls; even the earrings she wore most often were small, single pearls.

Her gift to him was a pocket watch. He knew it was quite expensive and the fob was of more valuable metal than the locket he had given her, but he liked it, and he tried not to draw another speech on his snobbish ways. The initials, W. J. from C. G, were inscribed on the fob.

The meeting with Carol's mother and father did not go well. Actually, William did not meet her mother. They were escorted by a maid into what Carol called the library, and soon her father arrived. He was a portly man, balding, much shorter than William, and dressed in a finely tailored, double-breasted, blue suit. William preferred his own Harris Tweed sports jacket and gray wool trousers, but he knew his total attire cost less than his host's glinting, gold wristwatch.

He told Carol politely to go see her mother, and he took a seat behind the large wooden desk and motioned William to one of the two chairs in front of the desk. There followed a series of questions that told William more than his answers told Mr. Grace. The questions were about his parents, their work, their origins, his major, his income to cover college expenses, his plans after graduation, and his intentions toward Carol. Only his love for Carol permitted William to sit through the inquisition. It was insulting, and not far into the battery of questions, William decided that it was designed to irritate, deter, to run him off.

William sat mustering all of his patience and control. He gave answers that he knew were obviously independent, uninformative, and on the edge of impudent. When the rotund man came around the desk and took his questions and, increasingly, his own answers for them to a new level of personal attack, William stood and looked down at the man with no effort to hide his disdain and growing irritation. Then the man got too close.

"You will know yourself that when you deal with a rotten apple, all the good apples are apt to get tainted. The only answer is to demand that your apples come from the orchards of impeccable history and species, free of even the slightest hint of infirmity or inferior traits."

The man did not give any ground. He seemed to wait for William to speak. William remained silent.

"My Carol is a level-headed girl, and I can see the merit she sees in you, considering. However, I think it would be in her and your best interest for you to leave. I can explain your departure to Carol and her mother."

William shoved the man away with both hands, and Mr. Grace tried to find something on his desk to hold onto as he staggered backwards. All he succeeded in doing was raking the papers and green-shaded desk lamp onto the floor. He took one of the two leather-covered, wing back chairs over with him onto the Persian carpet.

William turned and walked out of the library and called out Carol's name. Almost immediately, coat in hand, she opened the door of the room opposite the library.

"Let's go," he said.

"You stay right there, young lady," came a woman's voice from the top of the spiraled staircase. It was a slender woman, striking in a long, flowing white shiny gown and tightly belted robe that matched her platinum hair. She looked like a movie star, and much too young to be Carol's mother.

"Mother, I'm going out. I'll be home before midnight, and I'm sorry we won't be sharing Christmas Eve, but Daddy seems to prefer it that way. Don't wait up. Good night."

Then they were outside and William's only thought was that they had no place to go and no way to get there. Carolyn guided him to the side of the house and toward a three-door garage, with apparent living space above. She knocked on the narrow door that led to a lighted stairway. Soon a middle-aged man opened the door putting on the coat of a chauffeur's black uniform. It was Roger, the family chauffeur, who had driven them before.

"Where to, Miss?" He asked.

"Anywhere, Roger, as long as it's not here."

They had driven aimlessly for over ten minutes when Carol said, "I know where to go. Roger, drop us off on the next corner."

"Are you certain, Miss?"

"Yes, you need to go home to your family. It's Christmas Eve."

Once the car was out of sight, "Around this way," she said.

They turned the corner and walked half a block and he knew before she turned in the door that this was the destination. It was not the finest hotel in Seattle, but it was nice. It was not likely that the doorman or the desk personnel would know her, but she might not care. He registered as Mr. and Mrs. Jennings, and they were soon inside room 904. They had no luggage. He could not afford the cost of the room, and they had not eaten.

"Are you sure about this?" He asked.

"I have only one reservation," she said.

"What's that?"

"Are you going to give me a hard time about who pays the bill tomorrow, or are you going to enjoy our room service dinner, a nice bottle of wine, and this lovely room, and my company?"

William enjoyed it all.

CHAPTER 13

Rachel ate slowly and said little but William's stream of words was interrupted only by the large bites of food that he chewed with some vigor before starting to talk again. She had suggested three different seafood specialties of the house, but he was set on steak, and ordered the twin tenderloins topped with gorgonzola. He had ordered another Beaujolais and she was not keeping up on her part of the implied bargain to enjoy the wine. Maybe the wine was part of the reason that his words flowed so easily. He seemed excited now to relive the days, and his love for Carol reached out from every part of the story. Rachel felt envy for the girl of fifty years ago—to be needed and to be confident of a man. She wanted to be able to give with the freedom and vitality of his Carol.

She reassured William that her seafood fettuccini was fine and that she just did not eat as rapidly as he, so he sipped the wine and waited and then successfully prodded her to share a dessert. He needed no prompting now to continue his story, but he waited until the desserts were served. She sipped hot coffee and nibbled away at her dessert after he quickly finished his and waded into 1949.

Carol's parents forbade her to see William again and, after finding out that she was disregarding their instructions, threatened to send her to college in Europe. Finally, to avoid the Europe trip, she promised not to see him other than in their shared art class. That was in March.

"What do you think they'll do when they learn that we still see each other almost every day?" William asked.

"There's not much they would do, actually. They could threaten me with the schooling in France again, but they suspect that they can't make me do anything now. Nothing they have means that much to me. They probably hope that I won't embarrass them in the gossip column. They would look over, but not forgive me for anything. It's a trait of the family."

"Not forgive you?"

"They don't forgive anyone, especially my mother, the Mrs. Beverly Carswell Grace. She is not one who forgives anything easily. She still bears genuine malice toward girls she knew in college that she hasn't seen in a quarter of a century. No, Mother does not forgive."

The second semester art class proved to be a good idea for William only because it gave him more time near Carol. As in the first class, he seemed to want to go too fast in creating a picture. When they did paint their first work in oils, he did not want her to see his painting.

"William, you have to be patient. It takes time."

"But look at yours, Carol. We've seen paintings for sale downtown that are not that good."

"Well, you're too generous, William. But you must know, I have been taking one form or another of art class since I was five years old."

"Well, that makes me feel a little better, but look at the shades of light you got into your painting. Mine looks like a kid's work with crayons."

"William, if you would permit me to suggest, you still don't put enough effort into mixing your colors. Mrs. Snowe is right. Half the quality of the color in your painting is determined before you apply the first brush stroke to canvas. My colors were made on the palate, before I began to fill the canvas."

"I just don't have a knack for this sort of thing," he said.

"That's not true. Have you forgotten what she said about your sketches? I wish I could do the sketches you do, William."

"That's drawing pictures, Carol. That's not painting."

"True. But you have talent, William. More than I do, I think. But you've got to give it a chance. Try to study the scene you will paint first. See the colors. See the dark and light values. See the painting in your mind. Then mix the colors you need. If you like we could practice mixing colors this weekend."

"Oh, no. Not our weekends. I'll try a little harder here in class, but our time together I'm not going to spend proving that I can't paint."

"William, you're impossible. You know you want to paint. That's why you're here."

He laughed.

"What's so funny?"

"I'm in this class for the same reason I enrolled in the first one—to see you; not because I want to paint."

"Then paint me," she said.
"Oh sure," he said. "And I'll redo the Sistine Chapel while I'm at it."
"You're impossible, William."
"We at least agree on that."

After that they spoke little about painting. Both were happy to share the time walking to and from the class together. From time to time he would admire her painting. She was doing a copy of a portrait by one of the masters. He watched her in one session spend nearly the entire hour mixing the paint that she used to color the woman's left cheek and chin. He thought it took her only ten or twelve minutes to apply all the paint she put on her work that day. Mrs. Snowe did not chide him for his idleness. William guessed she thought that he could learn more watching Carol mix than slapping on his bold blues and reds.

He had paid little attention before to the young men who drove their own car around campus, but now he did. He and Carol walked almost everywhere, but it was a long way downtown; so on those occasions they took a cab. Most of the time she paid the driver. They visited the Pike Place Market and she called out the imaginary shopping list she might be filling if she were cooking for him that evening. They would stroll through Pioneer Square and admire the imposing view of Smith Tower at the corner of Yesler. Sometimes they talked about the Canwell committee looking for communists in the city, especially at the university. Neither of them liked the young legislator and his snooping staff, but Carol said that her father fully supported the effort. She told William that her father had also defended the locking up of all the local people of Japanese ancestry during the war. Mostly they talked about light things—oysters and Dungeness crabs, hotdogs, the wine, the beauty of the bay and the mountains, the weather, school friends and little about their families. They talked and laughed, and looked at one another.

There were places they did not go, and lies that Carol told or implied to her parents, but the two of them were happy. They stole time alone whenever opportunity came and twice they revisited the hotel of Christmas Eve. They attended stage plays downtown and one evening, following the performance, they stepped into an arcade long enough to have a snapshot taken in a curtained booth. They waited as the strip of five small, black and white pictures flowed out of the machine. She would trim one down to go in her locket she told him.

As the time for June graduation approached, William raised more frequently his departure for service. He was to be commissioned in infantry, his preference among the branches, as they were called, in the Army. They did not speak of marriage, although William knew that was what Carol had in mind—an Army wife living on the meager salary of a second lieutenant. William had no intention of dragging her into that. Maybe after she graduated, and he was a senior first lieutenant, or even a captain, she could join him and they could be married. He dreaded the time when they would have to resolve this. She would not give in easily.

In late May, she asked.

"When are we going to be married, William?"

The argument lasted for one month. Then the Army came to his aid. He was to report to Fort Benning, Georgia, and wife and family were not welcome.

"I don't really care what they say. They can't tell me where to live. What city is close by? Atlanta? I'll go to Atlanta. I can see you on weekends."

When he left her at the train station for the long trip east, she was not convinced. Only his statement that he had been told that he would have no free time for almost three months had restrained her. After that time they would know where he was to join a unit and then, maybe, they could be together.

In September he learned that he would be assigned to an infantry division in Japan. His route would be through Oakland, California, and he did not have time for leave.

She flew down to San Francisco and they shared three days and two nights. On the last night, they sat in the bar in the Top of the Mark and sipped martinis until the bar closed.

They lay in bed and talked until the new day, and then he left to rejoin the Army and board the ship to the Orient. She later told him in a letter that she left the room shortly after he did, got an early plane back to Seattle, and told her parents of all their shared times together. She said that the argument ended when she told her mother that she was going to marry William Jennings, and that no one and nothing could stop her.

William found the training and garrison duty in Japan not to his liking. His unit was under strength in people—some regiments short an entire battalion—and the weapons were of World War II vintage. It was not the Army he had pictured that America would field to defend the free world against communism. He wrote little about such things to Carol, choosing to talk about the beauty of Honshu Island, the quaintness and courtesy of the Japanese people, and his growing attachment to the young men of his platoon, an organization of forty or so men including him as its leader. Often he was in charge of planning the training of the entire rifle company, some one hundred and eighty men.

He and Carol wrote almost daily and tried to be positive and upbeat. William thought that they generally succeeded. Carol was beginning to consider switching her education to nursing, but William suggested she stay with a four-year program—maybe commercial art or decorating, both of which seemed to be of natural interest to her. She reminded him that when he got his first promotion, she was coming to him in Japan. Then they would be married.

In May of 1950 he walked into the officer's club to find her newly arrived in Japan, now a member of the clerical staff of the American Embassy.

"I didn't trust you," she said. "I guessed you were already promoted to captain and just hadn't wanted to tell me."

"Captain! I'm still a second lieutenant. I won't make first lieutenant for another six months."

"Well, anyway, I'm here. I expect that my pay at the Embassy, plus yours, will be about what you would make as a captain. So we can be married."

He knew that they could be. He would have to get the permission of his company commander. He did not think Carol would like that, but he did not tell her. It was a formality anyway. It was a policy to keep young soldiers from jumping into marriage prematurely with the attractive Japanese women. He had counseled several young soldiers, but it seemed that once they decided they were in love, there was no delaying their marriage to their Japanese sweetheart. He did not tell Carol that either.

She lived in an apartment with two other single girls who also worked in the Embassy. He and Carol were more discrete, and had to be, than they had been in Seattle. There were few places they could meet that they were not likely to be spotted by the Embassy's or the Army's own security people. This all served to cause Carol to bring up the timing of their marriage more frequently.

Then in late June his unit was ordered into Korea. He took her for a walk beside the jade green waters around the Imperial Palace. It was a partially sunny day of broken white clouds and small patches of blue sky when they left her apartment. He thought she knew that he had bad news well before he told her, and he pushed it off until they had turned back toward her apartment and the heavy air of an afternoon rain hung overhead. When he did tell her, she said nothing. She looked up at him as if waiting for more. There was no more. There could be no more, not now. The first soft splash of a raindrop touched her forehead as her eyes welled over and tears slowly moved down her cheeks. She had an umbrella, but it stayed closed in her right hand, the tip toward the stone pavement. Her other arm hung straight down, her shoulders slumped. He reached for her. She stepped back, still looking up at him, the steady rain now pressing her wet hair against her forehead, streaking the mascara just below her eyes. He knew what she wanted him to say; what she wanted to hear, but he knew his way was better. The affair in Korea would be over quickly and he would come back and they could make proper plans for their marriage. By then he would rate the pay of a first lieutenant. He reached down and took the umbrella, popped it open, and held it above them. This time she did not resist as he wrapped one arm around her and guided her back toward her apartment. She did not mention marriage, not even when they said goodbye the last time.

There had been an attack against South Korea by the communist North Korean army, and American troops were needed quickly. They went in quickly. It was to William a debacle that should have suggested criminal charges in either the American Army, or government, or both. The units were utterly unprepared to give battle even to the forces of a lesser country like North Korea. Some American units were so unprepared that soldiers fled the attack of the northern tanks, dropping all sorts of equipment as they ran. Included were weapons that fired rockets designed to destroy tanks. The rockets bounced harmlessly off the communist armored vehicles.

By September they had been forced into the southeastern corner of the Korean peninsula, and things looked desperate. He had received but one letter from Carol—in August. She had written it in July, still lacking a specific address for him. He wrote frequently, aware in the first four months that he might not survive to write again the next day. By Christmas time they had driven the North Korean army back north to the border with China. Then the Chinese Communists entered the fight and forced them back near Seoul. He found little time to write. Most of his recent letters to her had been returned, an overprint stating that the address was not valid. He wrote to her father's law firm in Seattle, to the Embassy in Japan, and to the registrar at the university. The one reply he had received by February was from the office of the university registrar. It said that Miss Grace had not re-enrolled after an early withdrawal in May of 1950. In March, he received a brief note from the Embassy saying that Miss Grace had left the Embassy on good terms on August 28, 1950. They provided no further information about her. By late April he had located George's address in Seattle and wrote asking for his help in learning more about Carol's location.

In mid-May he was counting the days when he would be reassigned out of Korea—by July he had been told—when he received word that the division's signal officer wanted to talk to him and requested that he come to his tent at the division's headquarters location. He found the tent and the adjoining green vans with a small field of antennas later the same day, and was told that they could put through a radio/telephone call for him to the United States. The slip of paper gave the name and number they were to call. It was a return call marked urgent. It was to George.

The connection was poor. The volume of his friend's voice rose and fell, and the static obscured some of his words. It sounded like he had found Carol, but her location was not clear. Somewhere in the Pacific. Then George's voice came through, distinct and much too loud. "She is dead. Somewhere in the Pacific. I am sorry, William. It was an airplane crash."

Rachel leaned across the table and touched his hands. They were folded on the table in front of him beside the long empty coffee cup.

"You don't have to go on, William. I know it must be hard."

He sat looking at his hands, as if they in some way still held the telephone that had carried that stabbing message fifty years before.

Rachel looked around at the nearly empty restaurant. It was time to get him home. He looked tired, drained, his face white against the blue jacket that had helped start this evening in such a relaxed and upbeat mood. Now she did not feel like this man's friend. More like his tormenter, a persecutor in the disguise of an admirer—a Judas.

He left his truck on the wharf and she drove him to the cottage. He insisted that he could manage once he was inside. She left him. She would come back in the morning, maybe make him some breakfast. He looked so tired. It was the first time that he fully looked his age.

She got back to the cottage just before eight o'clock the next morning. He had already eaten, he told her, and she could smell the toast that he had prepared in the oven of the cooking stove. She accepted his offer of toast and coffee, and watched him as he put a little butter on two slices of bread before putting them under the oven broiler. He poured her a cup of hot water and gave her the container for the instant coffee. He had told her that he preferred it made this way, as he had prepared coffee from "rations" for years in the Army. She tasted the brown drink: hot, but little else to recommend it.

She ate the toast and waited for him to say something. Finally, he nodded toward the front room from his seat at the kitchen table. "I want to give you the painting of the drop zone. It's in the wooden container. I almost painted another scene over it—thought you were not coming back."

"Oh, thank you, William. I'll hang it on my wall. As soon as I get a permanent wall somewhere."

"You still bobbing about in your sea of despair?" He asked.

She did not like the words. She had not criticized him and his handling of his life. Then she reminded herself that she had sought his advice. She guessed that opened the door to criticism.

"I'm back in school, if that is what you mean. Peggy's still my roommate."

"What about a boyfriend?"

"None. Not interested."

"What about your father?"

"What about him?"

"Have you talked out things with him?"

"No. There's nothing to talk about. Besides, he doesn't live here anymore either. Lives with that woman outside Boston. He even has a new job. I guess he'll sell our house here."

"What about your mother?"

"About the same. I see her twice a month. It's so hard."

"And your father?"

"He visits her every week, on Wednesday. I only visit on Sundays. The staff knows that we visit at different times, and that we want it that way."

"That's good…that he visits her every week. That's good," said William.

"What's so good about it?" She asked, holding back tears since she had told him that her father was there every Wednesday. She was there only twice a month, and still had great difficulty in doing that. She felt emotionally drained after each visit. Her mother had nothing to say, just sat and moved a small toy horse around in her hands. She did not look at the horse; only turned it over and over in her hands as if it were in some other world. She smiled rarely. Rachel could not tell what made the smiles come and go.

"He's trying. It shows that he's trying," said William.

"Trying hell, how can you say that when he's giving all his time and love to that…that woman?"

"How do you know that?"

"What?"

"How do you know what he's giving—can give to the woman in Boston?"

"Well, it's obvious, William, he's a married man."

"Do you think it would be easier for him if your mother were dead?"

Rachel felt the cold air of the ill-heated cottage trickle down her spine. Then she felt anger.

"Are you trying to defend his behavior?"

"No. I'm just trying to help you. Rachel, do you think that you love someone less just because she is dead?"

"But my mother's not dead, dammit!"

"No, but she's different. There are things she can't do anymore. There is a life she once led that is no longer possible for her. Yet your father lives on in much the same life that he's always known. Except that she's different. He may be unchanged. Even the other woman may not represent any change. She may be just an addition."

"So what, William?"

"So, let's load this masterpiece painting into your car and go get you some coffee that doesn't cause you to make a face with each sip."

She knew that she could be horrible. It was so hard for her to hide it when she did not like something. When had she started to hide things anyway?

They went to a small restaurant on Commercial Street that she could not recall being in although she had walked by it many times. The waitress looked at them as if they were strangers, and Rachel did not recognize her. Many people came in to work at the inns and restaurants in the May to end-November period of the year. She often knew the waiters and waitresses who were there year-round. William led them to a booth in the corner, well away from the front door. He ordered two coffees. She watched him. He took charge naturally, without thinking. He had not asked her where she might like to sit, nor confirmed that she wanted coffee. After all, she might just as easily have preferred hot tea. She smiled as he liberally splashed sugar into the steaming coffee once the waitress had sat down the large mugs and departed.

"Glad to see the smile," he said. "You laughing at me?"

"Yes."

"My high sugar level in coffee?"

"No," she said as she stirred in her two small tubs of half-and-half. She hated sugar in coffee.

"No, I was thinking of just how difficult it must have been for you to give up control when your Carol asserted herself, like when you ate in a restaurant."

"Oh, it was bad. But I'm really worse now than I was then."

"No regard for women's rights?"

"Not entirely. Little practice. That and getting older."

"William, did you visit her home? Her parents?

"No. They'd never wanted to see me, and I ceased to want to see them after my only visit."

"What did you do?"

"I went back into the war until April of 1952. Then I took some metal shrapnel from a communist mortar and they flew me over to a hospital in Japan. Sagamihara. I remember the hospital too well. It was far from the center of Tokyo. After I was convalescent I would go into the heart of the city and visit every spot where we had sat, walked the same sidewalks, remembered her smile and her touch, and her laughter. Back then I could even remember her voice."

"Did you learn more about the airplane crash?"

"No, I didn't try to learn much until I did get back to Tokyo, but even the Embassy was not much help. The girls she had roomed with were no longer there. All three of them had been on a one-year hiring. Carol never mentioned that to me, I don't think. They formed a typing pool and later three other women replaced them. Carol worked her last several weeks in their mailroom. One man, a Japanese employee, told me that Carol went home to Seattle to be with her mother. The man said that the workers in the mail room were told that well after she'd gone."

Rachel hesitated. She just knew that he had done more to remember, or mourn, Carol.

"Did you ever visit her gravesite?"

"No."

She wanted to ask why he had not, but it was a matter on which people differed. Moreover, their reasons could be quite personal and private. She decided not to press him.

"You have visited Seattle since then, haven't you?"

"No, except to change planes at Seattle/Tacoma Airport."

"Would you think of her when you did that?"

"Yes, especially when I could view Mount Rainier flying in or out. She called it 'her mountain' and said that we would climb to the top some day. But we never did."

"What about your friend, George. Did you talk with him again?"

"No. I wanted nothing to do with anything there again. I have really visited my home only one time since I left there in 1949. I attended my mother's funeral in '65 between tours of duty in Vietnam. My father had died in '52 while I was in combat in Korea. I never went to his gravesite either." He held her look as he made the last statement. Was it a kind of defense declaration? She had not intended to offend him. She remained silent.

"I really have to go do a little work on my truck," he said.

She doubted that the truck was a problem. It was just time for her to go. That was all that he was saying. She guessed that he was right.

She did not leave the Harbor for two days. The first day she walked and ran again the roads and pathways of her childhood, but avoided Holmes Cottage and the bench. She looked in the windows of her family house. Now she wished she had brought her key. She wanted to go inside and walk around, touch the things that she had shared with her father and mother. She would visit her mother tomorrow. She had no good reason for not visiting her mother every day when she was in town, but she had not. When she got back to Boston she would call her father, and go see him. She would tell him what she always told her mother. Of her unqualified love. She was going to add that she would not judge him; that perhaps she did not understand all that she might at some time in the future. She hoped so.

On the second morning she ran for a change along Route 27 that hugged the cove west of their home—in the opposite direction from the street that ran up over the hill by Holmes cottage. She was about to cross the short bridge at the head of the cove when she saw a large bird in the marshes inland from the road. The rays of the low sun highlighted the rust-colored tint of the feathers on the wings and back of the bird. It was mostly light gray in color with a white neck and long black legs and black beak. It was Williams' bird, much larger than she would have guessed; the dark red patch atop the head brilliant in the sunlight. The head went down and bobbed as the bird pecked into the shallow water. When the head came up again it swung slowly to the side. The bird seemed to look at her. She could not make out the color of the eyes, but they were small. The bird rose from the ground, the sound of the wings' strong surge breaking loud against the bank of evergreens to the west. The bird stayed at a low altitude as it made a slow, majestic turn and flew away from her up the slight incline to the north. It dropped behind the low brush and smaller deciduous trees and disappeared. She had never seen such a bird, except in William's incomplete painting.

She continued her run along the road as it turned slightly toward the southwest, still hugging the bay. At the point that the road turned back inland, she swung around and ran back to the inn where she was staying. She wanted to change and go see her mother.

Her thoughts turned again to William. She would be back soon to check that he was all right and find out what it was that he still had not told her.

CHAPTER 14

The man and woman looked up at him from the small photo in its silver encasement. The locket shone now, meticulously polished and sitting prominent atop the eating counter in his kitchen. Stephen had removed the locket from his safe almost nightly now for over two weeks. He could no longer deny its presence or the lure of its very existence. He had gone over all the reasons why he should go out and drop the locket from the deck of his house into the deep, cold waters of the lake. However, he was left with two overpowering questions. Whoever this man was, could he still be living? And, why had Richard Todd Grace thought that there might be some value to Stephen in seeing the picture; of knowing there was a man loved by his grandmother who was not his grandfather?

He picked up the necklace and locket, dropped it into his running jacket pocket, and zipped it closed and walked out of his boathouse. He was hardly dry from the perspiration of his run when he turned the ignition key of the Explorer. He was going to see Grandmother Grace.

"Stephen, you aren't even dressed. What brings you here at this time of day?" His grandmother was finely dressed, as always. Even for bed her preparations took the better part of an hour; more if she lingered in her expansive, marble bath. He no longer could guess what she really looked like. Her hair was not real, still lustrous platinum. Her face was applied. His great grandfather had only one time looked like his great grandmother did now. That was when he lay a corpse, his face redone to look like a picture of him when he was twenty years younger. She no longer permitted anyone to come close to apply a mock kiss to her cheek. He guessed it was because her face would simply brush off. She had lost the resounding and commanding voice. Either that or she mouthed the words weakly to avoid cracks in her face around the mouth. He had been embarrassed, even felt guilty, when such thoughts about his grandmother—great grandmother—first came to him. That had been over ten years ago, and her image could have prompted such ideas years before that. He could only describe her face now as...colorful.

"Grandmother, I want to show you something and ask you some questions." He saw her bony hand clench more tightly the ornate mahogany arm of her chair as he removed the locket from his pocket. He wished he could see her face. Then as he opened the locket, her eyes snapped. He knew to be wary.

"Do you know the name of this man?" He asked and held the locket closer so that she could see the small photo clearly.

She grabbed at the locket, but caught only the necklace. She cried out as the necklace chain ground along the palm of her closed fist. The chain broke and he retained the locket firmly. She had not surprised him. She dabbed at the palm with a small handkerchief, the slightest evidence of blood transferring to the white cloth as she touched her palm.

"That means nothing, absolutely nothing," she said. She rose and walked to the table beside her bed, opened the drawer, and took a pill from a small container. She poured water in a glass from a crystal pitcher and took the pill. Then she returned to the chair.

"Do you know who he is, or was?" He asked.

"No. I have never seen the man in my life. I have never seen the cheap picture or the cheaper piece of junk jewelry that it is in."

The note. Surely she had known about the locket. Whether or not she had seen it, she had to know the significance of the photograph, of the man pictured beside her daughter.

"Grandmother, did my Grandmother Carolyn love my grandfather?"

"But of course. What kind of a silly question is that? We all loved him."

"You knew him really well?"

"Certainly. I knew him from the time that he was a baby. His mother was my best friend in college. She was my best friend until the day she died."

Stephen had heard this before. It was like lines in one of Julia's stage plays, spoken over and over again night after night. In the case of his great grandmother, they were spoken year after year. She would sit and talk in glowing terms about her Carolyn, model child, model student, and model young woman. She would tell of the romance that began when Carolyn and John were children, brought together by vacation visits in Carmel and here in Seattle. How they were thrown together again in time of war in Tokyo, realized their great love and were married. Then she would grow somber, dab at tears he never could see and tell of John's Navy fighter aircraft crashing into the sea. Then how his grandmother, leaving her son just months later with his paternal grandparents in Carmel, had flown to Hawaii as a volunteer to the USO. There she was helping host soldiers and sailors coming back for breaks from the war in Korea. In a voice that broke always at the same points she told of the crash of the plane and the refusal of the sea to give up her daughter, just as it had kept her hero son-in-law. If he asked now he knew she would run through the lines again, flawlessly.

"I'm sorry I came, Grandmother. I'll be leaving now."

"Good night, Stephen. The next time you come to visit me, dress properly."

"Yes, Grandmother," he said, portraying the obsequious manner upon which he knew that she thrived.

He did not know what she could tell him, but he knew that she was lying as he had seen her do so many times over the years, particularly with him, and most especially when he was a child and she thought him incapable of believing that his Grandmother Grace would ever lie.

He wished his paternal great grandparents were still living. His father had grown up in their home, but they were both long departed. Maybe they could have told him something about the stranger in the locket photograph.

When he got to his house, he found Julia's note on the kitchen counter. She was sorry she had missed him. She was sorry about a lot of things; saw no reason to go on with the facade. She was going on a working vacation with James to London. Be gone for two weeks. He did not know James, but she thought that she and James might be the real thing. "Ciao" was her farewell.

He dropped the note in the trash receptacle below the sink and felt the relief. Relief that their play was over and that he had not been there for the final act. He knew that she would feel relief also. They had fun together, but they were not even good friends, and they had known for months that they were not in love. He opened his briefcase and pulled out the papers that Blake had asked him to review. These were the only copies she said, and it would not do for the boys at the top to see them…not yet. He was impressed. They confirmed what he had already begun to surmise: there was a major reorientation needed in the firm, a need to catch onto the rocket of the twenty-first century. It would mean a significant reduction in resources piled annually against three old clients, and a revision of the billing practices for those clients in particular. Her figures made a clear case that they made no profit at all in meeting the legal needs of two of those clients. Yet the firm was doling out large salaries and still showing good profit. The firm simply needed fundamental changes. The kind that Blake had the insights to identify and apply. The question was how to get her into a position to accomplish such changes. That could take years, lots of years—unless she had the support of one or more of the powerful senior partners, or someone very influential on the board. Grandmother Grace was the one person who could most quickly make way for major changes, but Blake seemed quite ready to help undermine the old woman's position. He knew that Grandmother Grace had no protégé now, and he believed that his grandmother knew that as well as he. He was certainly a disappointment to her. Would she champion an offspring from the other branch of the Grace family? How would she regard a woman of the new era, a woman that she surely recognized was not the powder puff that Uncle Robert had been? Did he, did Blake, really want to be any more in the old woman's debt than both of them already were?

He pulled out a legal pad, wrote "SENSITIVE" across the top, and began making notes keyed to the paragraphs of Blake's tightly drawn argument. The men at the top held control, even in the recent days of his great grandmother's strong influence exercised through the now deceased Robert. If their weakness was only the failure of economies in managing the three major accounts, they would remain quite strong. Then he wrote an outline plan of action, one that would require some skillful manipulation within the firm. The kind of manipulation at which Grandmother Grace excelled. She just could never know that the recipient of her wiles, Blake, was the mind behind the old woman's "original ideas." In addition, he needed to insure that he, not Blake, was the person that Grandmother Grace believed she was ensnarling in her web. Because he had learned and accepted something that Blake had not, and, as a result, he was immune to the old woman's poisonous bite.

A twinge of disloyalty touched him as he closed his briefcase. The senior partners had never been unkind to him or anything but fair in their dealings with him. His great grandmother had provided the shelter for his upbringing. But it was like the rest of his life. There seemed to be nothing genuine about the total surroundings in the Grace private and official family. It had never been anything that he could identify clearly. It was more like something important was always missing, or left unsaid. Even with Blake, he left most discussions with this strong impression that she had been guarded, holding back. It made him wonder if there had ever been a member of the Grace family who just lived life, took it as it came and attacked each day with open, honest enthusiasm. As a child he had often felt this…this…lacking, and somehow related it to being smothered under a pillow. Now he had grown to manhood and he was coming to realize that the invisible pillow was all around him, like the lake fog that now engulfed his house on this chill fall night.

CHAPTER 15

Rachel's mother appeared to have changed little since her last visit. Several times she pointed to the large vase of white carnations. She did not smile as she pointed them out. Rachel was convinced that she did not know her. She did not know whether the flowers were being pointed out for her benefit. When she went over to smell them and caress the outer stems into a tighter display, her mother watched her closely, her eyes staying on her as she returned to the chair beside her own. She had brought nothing to read, something she vowed to correct the next trip. There were two magazines, both recent, on the middle shelf of the metal stand beside her bed, but she guessed there were no appropriate articles in them. Then she noted that she no longer knew what might be appropriate.

She looked at her mother and for the first time in years tried to look deeply, tried to see if there was something there that she was missing. But the eyes were not changed. They were the same eyes she remembered from the earliest days of her recollections. They were the eyes that steadied her as she stood to read the short portion of her first Thanksgiving school pageant; that were bathed in tears as she tried to convince her that her braces would not hurt and that she was still beautiful; that glinted when she explained how Rachel's two girlfriends did not hate her when they did not invite her to join them in play; that warmed her as she told her that her grandfather had gone to a better place where he would see Tilley again, and that looked up at her from the water and convinced her that she could make her first dive off the stern of the boat.

"Mother," she said, "do you remember my first role as an actress, my Thanksgiving reading? I was terrified. I don't think you knew how scared I was. I would have run off the stage if you had not been there."

She spoke to her mother of her grandfather and Tilley, asking her questions, but not pausing for answers. She laughed as she recalled in words the first time her father put her in charge of piloting the sailboat out of the crowded harbor. Her mother had not laughed then either, but her father had and it had angered Rachel.

"But I got it out, didn't I, and I needed very little help to get under sail once I was out in the bay." A uniformed woman came in. Rachel did not look directly at her. The woman left. She told her mother a story. She stopped to turn on the bedside lamp and moved it to where it softly bathed her mother's face. The windowpanes grew gray and then black, and it was 1991 again and she and her mother were taking the sun on a large rock ledge overlooking the sea in Arcadia Park. Her mother responded then to her question of how she and her father had met and how their courtship had developed and she listened to what was the most romantic story she had ever heard. She told her mother they should make a movie of that and her mother had chuckled and said that her father would never want to admit the wonderful things he had said to her on that very first meeting and when he asked her to marry him.

Rachel still thought it would make a good movie but could not escape the feeling that the sad ending might spoil the wonderful beginning. When she left she hugged her mother and kissed her on each cheek. Warm tears seeped between the closed lids and slid down her mother's cheeks to touch Rachel's lips.

Her visit with her father and Marianne, the attractive brunette, was in Marianne's house, now her father's home as well. It was a strained visit. Both he and Marianne tried, but the presence of Marianne's late husband—the picture in the shelves by the study fireplace—seemed a constant reminder to Rachel of her mother. She one last time told herself that she could not possibly understand how her father could do this. Then she forced a smile and tried to show interest in her father's new job—same work with a different design firm—a Boston-based company.

Marianne's dinner was superb, flawless. A delicate creation of sauce, petite chunks of lobster, and a variety of lettuces sprinkled with watercress and bean sprouts. It was the sauce, she and her father agreed, and he beamed when Marianne shared her recipe for the sauce. Rachel could not have remembered the first step by the time the meal was over, but it was not for lack of attention and courteous interest in the telling. She was somewhat soothed during the visit by recalling one of the few things that William had offered:

"Rachel, I can't speak for society and the expected norms of behavior, but I can tell you that what your father feels he controls little or not at all. If he can love—if he can feel for this woman—is it not right for him to do so? From what you say, she is not deceived; nor is he. If he cannot, no rule or expectation of society can change that. And no expectation of society can cause his memory of or love for your mother to go away. Society could even tell him that it is all right for him to forget her, but society's permission does not make it true. Your father is alone. You—or he—can wish it different. But he is alone."

Before she left Marianne's, and her father's, house, he told Rachel of his desire to give her the house in the Harbor, not because it did not have continuing importance to him, but the opposite.

"I know that you will retain it in a way that reflects our life together—all three of us."

He insisted that he would pay for its continued maintenance and any improvements that she might like. If she were to decide that she did not want it, he did want the option of discussing some things that he would want to keep if she did not want them. He asked her if she needed more money for her college expenses. She told him no. He was now aware that she was working, but he did not protest that or press to provide more funds.

The discussion about the house ended the evening in a most awkward manner. But they all managed warm good-byes, and Rachel embraced Marianne at length, said nothing, but responded with an impulsive strengthening of her hold on this new woman in her father's life just as their embrace was about to end.

"Thank you, Rachel," Marianne said softly.

Rachel left with no further comment. She had resolved not to cry and she had not, even on the drive to her apartment, but she could not subdue the thought of her mother and the feeling of guilt, a feeling she knew that she would never lose.

The apartment was too expensive, but Peggy had insisted that she could go the rent alone for a while if Rachel's finances got too close. What Peggy did not know was that they were always close because Rachel had told her father that her expenses were not going to be any greater than in her junior year, despite her move from the dormitory to an apartment. Peggy had wanted to go for an apartment the previous year, but Rachel had argued her preference for dormitory living. She guessed that Peggy had not believed her, but had respected her position.

Otherwise, the income from her work was permitting her to handle her finances pretty well, but it meant that she had limited time to drive up to the Harbor more than the two monthly visits to her mother. She had avoided going over the top and Holmes Cottage. Now she wanted more time at home for Thanksgiving. She wanted to open up the house, air it out before the holiday. Her class break would permit it, but not the schedule at the print shop. She decided to just tell the owner, and go regardless.

It did not go well. She was given the choice of working up until the day before Thanksgiving or give up the job. She decided to leave the job. She had not yet found another job dealing directly with people, but she had not really looked, and she wanted to go home.

Peggy was disappointed. Not in the loss of the job, but in Rachel's decision not to visit with Peggy and her father and stepmother for Thanksgiving.

"Rachel, you really worry me. I know you say it's to air out your house and all, but I don't think you should let yourself in for the depression you get when you go up there, and you are silly to be meddling in his personal things. I can't believe you did that. And regardless of what you say, I think that William should get his companionship from people nearer his own age." She had made a mistake in telling Peggy more about what she had learned from William—and how she had sneaked around, but Peggy did not even try to understand the loneliness of the man. She did not bother to remind Peggy that she had not visited William in recent trips home. She had planned to tell Peggy more, but had found her so unsympathetic that she had then tried to minimize the whole matter. But it had been too late. That, and her lack of desire to date anyone seriously. Both had strained their time together, but she knew that their friendship was still quite strong. She also knew how her actions looked to Peggy, and would to anyone, but she just did not feel that she was doing anything wrong; that it was not being curious alone, that she could help him. How, she did not know, but she could help him, and she believed that she had accomplished little for herself by avoiding William while in the Harbor.

She drove through the town of Bath with its history of shipbuilding, from three-mast sailing ships to, until the last few years, modern submarines. She always felt like she was getting close as she left the old town, but it was as she crossed the river at Wiscasset that she felt at home, and today the feeling was especially strong. She did not know whether it was the thrill of getting back into her home, or her plan to fix a proper dinner—ham—and invite William to have a real Thanksgiving dinner; not one delivered cold, hours after everyone else has eaten the holiday feast.

It was mid-day when she let herself into her house. She did not know just how much airing out she could do and still get the chill out of the rooms. She decided to open three of the windows on the southeast side and delay turning up the thermostat until she returned from her walk.

Her plan was to take a seat on the bench and see if he responded to seeing her there. After less than ten impatient minutes, she walked up and knocked on the door. There was the delay she had come to expect, whether she found him home or not. Then she saw his large form nearly block the light in the front room doorway. He opened the door.

"Oh my, William. You look a sight. Are you sick?"

"Rachel. Well, no, not really, but I am guilty of not getting up and starting this day off right. Come on in, if you can find a place."

Rachel took in his appearance and the room quickly. She had seen the front room full before, but never so cluttered. He had not just failed to shave this morning. It had been days since he had shaved. He was wearing the green forest fatigue shirt again. Now it had oil paint smudges on it, reds, whites, melon, and almost cream colors. She looked around but saw no easel.

"Been painting?" She asked.

"Not for a while. What are you doing back here on a Tuesday?" He motioned her into the front room and removed a stack of *Boothbay Register* newspapers from one of the chairs.

"Thursday is Thanksgiving, William."

"Oh, yeah. So it is. You planning to have the holiday with your father?"

"No." She sat in the offered chair and placed her purse on the table at its arm.

"Is he still not back home either?"

"He is at home. His home is not here anymore."

"You two made up yet?" He sat finally on the edge of the loveseat. She did not think that he wanted company.

"I guess. But that's not what I want to talk about. Are you ill?"

"I told you no."

"You said, 'not really.' That's not the same."

"Is to me. I'm not sick. There. That clear enough?"

"Don't get mad at me. I just asked, that's all"

"Maybe you ought to go to your Inn and come back tomorrow," he said.

"I'm not staying at an Inn. I'm back in my own house."

"Well, that's good. Then maybe you ought to go back to your own house and come back tomorrow."

"You're serious, aren't you." She said.

"Yes, I am."

"Okay. What time?"

"Why don't you come for lunch? Say about noon."

"Okay, see you tomorrow."

"At noon," he said as they stood and walked into the kitchen.

"Bye," she said. He closed the door firmly behind her.

She walked back along the street to her house. He had shown embarrassment, either for the way he or his house looked—or both. She closed the windows and turned the thermostat up to seventy-eight. A no-no. Even her mother would never set the thermostat so high. Her father could be quite pontifical when this error, among all errors, was made in his house. His specialty in structure design was heating and cooling. She smiled to herself as she sat at her mother's writing desk and prepared a list of food for a Thanksgiving meal for two. She knew that it was almost identical to the list made by her father when they had prepared the meal last year—the last for the three of them in this house. Peggy would disapprove of all this. She would probably contend that William was a father figure, even substituting for her mother as well. There could be some merit in the thought. But it was not quite correct. She knew what she could do for her mother—and for herself. Her mother's tears had not come again although Rachel had come back more often to talk to her. The doctors she knew doubted what she told them about her mother's tears, but it had happened. However, it had not happened again, and she treasured the memory. Who knew? William might be right about it all, but for her, she needed her mother to hear her. She did not have to be rewarded. She might not know if her mother heard, or understood. It was simply what she could do.

Someone else met her father's needs right now—she guessed. William had no one. She would try to help him. What she wanted from him she was not sure. Her excuses for returning to him were gone: Craig, her mother, her father. All that he could do for her and her problems with them, he had done. If those were her reasons, there would be no need to encourage more time with him. She knew that she wanted to hear the rest of his story but she wanted that most because she thought—hoped—that it would help him to tell it. Maybe what he had already told her had helped him. Telling of Carol's death had been hard, but he had done that well enough it seemed. Still it was a fine line; she knew that. He did look drained when they left the Tugboat. The telling could hurt him in ways that she might not know. If she now talked with her mother in a way that surely helped her more than it did her mother, did she extract his story more for herself or for him? She tried to muster all the objectivity and honesty that she could. She just did not know, but she knew that she wanted to help and she could never know if she had failed him if she did not try. In the most private of her thoughts, she was convinced. Carol would have tried to help him remember. She would have taken the risk.

She did her shopping and picked a ham. Unlike her father, her preference had gone to a small pre-cooked with a guide on the label for the proper oven temperature and time. It was less than two hours. She selected a bottle of red wine. There was little to pick from and the nine-dollar price for the bottle told her that she had not picked up a rare year or bouquet.

After she returned home and satisfied herself that she was ready for Thursday, she sat down before the television, and searched for a good program. Except for an account of the great storms off the New England coast over the last quarter century there was nothing of interest on the tube. Still she found herself searching up and down the channels—surfing—symptom of a disease not of television watchers, but of the producers choosing those presentations that could be made at least cost while still being acceptable to many. It bothered her that any serious criticism of much of the evening television fare was met with the assertion that what the people wanted was what was aired. She finally turned the TV off. In her mother's limited shelves of books, she found one of Colleen McCullough's novels. It had been there for years, the only book her mother had ever insisted that she read. She never had. The jacket promised the story of a man set to save the world, but whose life is threatened by the woman he loves. She opened to the first page, Chapter I.

When she awoke, she found that she had read just enough to get from Connecticut to Washington and to be introduced to a woman doctor, knee-deep in a bureaucracy of doctors. She would have to take the book back with her to school and read more. She had not picked up a book since she finished Grisham. It was two o'clock in the morning when she finished her bath and went to bed. She resisted the desire to open the book again. She was aware of how relaxed she was. Was it the bath, her familiar bed, or the thought of reading the book to her mother? Somehow her mother might remember the book that she had recommended.

The next day she arrived at his cottage at noon sharp. She did not have to knock. He opened the door as she stepped on the stoop. He looked like a different man.

He was wearing his blazer outfit again, but with no tie, and she could smell the food.

"I understand that you love sausages and sauerkraut," he said.

"Well, I do if they are prepared just right."

That did not seem to bother him.

"Not only that, but I have the finest beer ever imported from Germany."

Beer. A first here. But then anything other than chicken noodle soup was a new experience.

"I also have for dessert, coconut chocolate chip cookies, domestic."

He was in a good mood. He did not appear ill today. Part of it was he was clean-shaven, and he was so…so upbeat. The smell of the oils used in painting was distinct despite the strong aroma of the sausages and sauerkraut.

"Delicious, William," she said later, then fought off a second helping. He asked if she would mind, which she did not, and he had another sausage. She noted that his appetite was good.

"William, how did you learn that I like sausage and sauerkraut?"

"Lady at the meat counter in the grocery across the footbridge."

"Mrs. Maramount?"

"Don't know her name, said she had sold sausages to your family for years and your mother said that you ate most of them."

"That would be Mrs. Maramount."

She had enjoyed the sausage, but she was anxious to get to the dessert. It was not the cookies that drew her, but the promise of getting him to talk more about what he had done—and not done—after he learned of his Carol's death in 1951.

However, William seemed to be eager to talk again about his paintings—about the one he called the Drop Zone. It was not well done, although she did not admit as much to Peggy. The contrast of the snow covered mountains and the golden sky was good, but more in the nature of poster art, or commercial signs, and the perspective of the open area on the ground, his drop zone, was off, tilted a little too much toward the viewer. But she was struck by a single impression of the open sky and the broad, open expanse of the ground below—emptiness. She lay at times and looked at it before going to sleep. Was that all he had tried to express? Or was the impression intentional at all? Was it related to his loneliness? He was an amateur painter. The technique made that clear, even to her. However, anyone is capable of wanting to project something, whether he has the talent to do so or not. What did he want her—anyone—to see?

"Thank you for the painting. It was nice of you to get it so nicely framed. The frame looks expensive."

He chuckled as he moved both plates to the sink and placed the cookies before her.

"What?" She asked.

"You were not very impressed with the painting, I take it," he said.

"I didn't say that."

"No, but what you don't say speaks for itself." He walked into the front room and soon she heard the hum of his record player. The sound was classical. It was a familiar melody, but she could not name the piece. She liked it, but only in the way that she also liked popular music. She had not studied music, despite her mother's urging, and while she learned enough in basic school courses to score well on tests, she had soon forgotten most of it.

"Why do you not have a cassette or CD player? You can play those for hours without having to change anything."

"I like records. They require your full attention, and so you give it. It's a shame to waste fine music on people riding on elevators or sitting in dentists' offices. This way I select each record, and give it my full attention.

"Don't you have one of those long spindles so that you can stack several at a time? My mother used to have a portable record player. She could play five or six records at one time."

"No. Never had one of those. If I did and used it over the last thirty-five years or so, some of these records would be trashed by now."

"Thirty-five years? You have records that old?"

"Sure," he said and returned to the front room. He came back with a Margaret Whiting labeled record. "This one is over forty-five years old. Had the cover until some high water on the Kenai got in my storage shed. See, the record is like new." He returned the record to the front room and came back to the kitchen table.

"Okay, you can't avoid the subject any longer. What did you make of the drop zone painting?" He asked.

She was not comfortable on just how to approach this. He may not know just how…well…basic his painting was. She had to be honest.

"Well, the painting seems to lack something. It's so empty. Do you know what I mean?" She asked, and hoped that he did.

"Yes. What is it lacking?"

"Well, I don't know. Did you intend for it to look empty?"

"No."

"Did it just not come out the way you had hoped? Was that it?"

"Sort of."

She did not want to guess. She did not want to be overly critical of his painting. They were not talking about his ability to paint, but his idea or ideas.

"What would you expect to see above a drop zone? I mean if it were a busy training day for the Army, wouldn't you expect to see something above the drop zone?" He asked.

"You mean people using parachutes. Parachutists." She felt like a third grader.

"Paratroopers, or parachutists. Yes, that's right. Now why do you think there's none in the painting?"

"Because you left it out on purpose?"

"Right. Now why? Why did I leave the paratrooper out?"

Rachel restrained a smile. He was very serious. Maybe he had in mind something that was connected to his story—to Carol, to her death.

"So someone can step into the picture—be the parachutist?"

He smiled. That was it. It was not a sophisticated concept. He seemed to take some pride in the whole painting, beyond this revelation of meaning.

"I think I understand, but, William, at the risk of offending you, I don't see that as a big thing, artistically or otherwise. I mean, am I missing something?"

"Yes, but you will have to find it for yourself."

She was glad to leave the subject of the painting, but she could in no way get him to address the days following Carol's death.

It was growing late and she had things to do to prepare for tomorrow's dinner.

"William, would you join me for dinner at my home tomorrow?"

"I'd be happy to. What time? Can I bring anything? Wine?"

"Do you have a good wine?" She asked.

"No, but I could run down to the market and get some."

"You don't need to do that. I have wine, William, thank you. Is two o'clock okay with you?"

"Sure is, but I have to warn you."

"What?"

"I'll be forced to wear what I have on right now. It's the only thing I have clean in addition to being all the dress clothes that I have."

She felt a touch of embarrassment for him. Her father had some clothes still in the house, but while her father was not a small man, William would split his jackets down the back. She would have to find a way to get him another suit of clothes.

"Thank you for the delicious meal and the music," she said as she moved toward the door.

He smiled.

"And for the painting. I'm pleased that you gave it to me."

The smile broadened.

CHAPTER 16

She was nervous as she opened the door following his knock. He held a bottle of wine, the same brand as the one that she had bought, a Zinfandel.

"Happy Thanksgiving," he said.

"Welcome, and Happy Thanksgiving to you."

He wore no coat other than his blue blazer despite the cold, blustery day.

"I'm running a little behind," she said. "Why don't you just look around. That's the study in there. It has always served as my father's office at home. Not much of his work evident in there anymore though. And…thank you for the wine."

"Can I help with anything? I'm not totally dangerous in a kitchen."

"No, I don't think so, but—"

"Yes?"

"I failed the basic test on special meal preparation, I'm afraid. Did not set the table. If you want to help, you could do that. I thought we should eat in the dining room. But if you don't mind, sit the places close together; not on each end of the table."

"Any other instructions?" He asked with a chuckle.

"Yes, don't break anything."

"Table all set," he said later, coming into the kitchen.

"Just in time," she said, and picked up the ham.

"Here, let me do that," he said and took the platter from her.

She moved quickly to place two of her mother's woven potholder pads on the table and stepped back as he set the platter of ham down on them.

"Smells great," he said.

She did not mention to him that he had used the wrong china. She had forgotten to tell him to take the china from behind the lower doors of the breakfront. Instead he had taken the china visible behind the glass of the top of the display.

"Beautiful china," he said, admiring her mother's special white china, being used for the first time in six years. Probably the last time it had seen a dishwasher, she thought. He did not seem bothered that she took the time to wipe the plates and cups.

The wine was not bad, and her ham gravy was excellent. She hoped that he would recognize that it was not store-bought, but made from drippings, flour, and water, with a little seasoning. He ate it as if he thought it was good. She was a little disappointed that he did not compliment it. Her mother would have been impressed—and surprised.

Halfway through the meal he asked about her father and Marianne. She told him everything, including the visit with her mother and the tears. By the time she finished he had helped himself to seconds of ham and potatoes and extra gravy. He had complimented the tossed salad. She was glad of that. She remembered the Waldorf salad from the previous year and hoped that he had not.

She had baked a pumpkin pie. It was one of the reasons that she had forgotten to set the table earlier. She was glad she had asked him to do it. He was right. The white china was beautiful.

He cut into the pie with the side of his fork and she made another attempt to restart his telling of the events of 1951.

"Did you make no effort to contact your friend George, again? I mean…ever?"

"Yes, but it was many years after that. In 1998 I was in the waiting room of a doctor's office in Anchorage, Alaska. I picked up a brochure about an education project involving Eskimo children along the Bering Straits. It looked like a good project involving both private and public funding. There was a list of contributing organizations. One shocked me. I hadn't seen the name in writing in years: Carolyn Grace. He paused. She waited. He put down the fork and took a drink of hot coffee.

"That's good," he said. "That's good coffee."

"Thank you," she said.

He sighed. It was a big sigh. One that expanded and then deflated the large chest, and dropped both shoulders.

"The full wording was The Carolyn Grace Blandon Foundation.

"I thought that it could not be her; that it was some relative, maybe a distant cousin or something. As a matter of fact, by the time I left the doctor's office I was only bothered by the coincidence of names. I had another night and day before the doctor would have the test results back, and since he had asked me to come back in two days, I decided to stay in town.

"By noon the next day I was curious and called the local chamber of commerce office. They couldn't help me, but gave me a number down in Juneau that I called. They gave me the number for the foundation in Seattle. I felt my stomach sort of flutter when I knew it was a Seattle foundation. The girl there connected me with a fellow who told me that it was Carol, my Carol. She had died in an airplane crash in the Pacific in 1951. Never found her. Her husband—I nearly dropped the phone when he said it—her husband was a military pilot who died in a crash before she did. His name was Blandon. I hung up the phone."

She waited to let him rest. He had not moved the fork from beside the small dessert plate, but he still held it, and the whiteness of his knuckles told her that he might put a curve in its handle at any moment. What had the news of Carol's marriage come to mean to William? Had he been able to make sense of it at all? It made none to her. However, she only knew what he had told her.

"What else?"

"Nothing else." He drained the coffee from the cup.

"Let me get you some more," she said.

"Thank you," he said absently as she went into the kitchen.

She tarried in pouring the coffee, watching his shoulders drooped and rounded like his curved, ladder-back chair. Then he sat tall, braced his shoulders back, and took another bite of pie.

"Great pie," he said.

That was the only insincere compliment she had gotten today, but it was a good signal. He was back in control. She had been uncomfortable when she left the table with the feeling that he was close to breaking down. She had seen the misty eyes before, but this time she saw his chin quiver. It had in turn made her uneasy and she hurried from the table into the kitchen. She hated the idea of seeing him lose control.

"Would you like another piece?" She asked.

"No. I have to be running pretty soon."

"Why?"

"Well, I'm sure you have other plans for today. Young girl like you."

"Knock off the 'young girl' bit, William; I'm here for the duration. I want to know what happened. So tell me."

"You know. That's all. Except that I tried to contact George and learned that he had been in business in Denver since '69. Then I contacted the foundation again, and they linked me up with a guy named Robert Grace, Carol's uncle. He was just great. Insisted that I only talk to him, and he gave me all the information that I wanted about the foundation."

"What about Carol?"

"The foundation was Carol, or Carol was the foundation."

"What about Blandon?"

"I didn't want to know anything about Blandon; still don't."

"And you have learned nothing more?"

"Dammit, girl, what more does a man need to learn? Is that not enough?"

He rose. She could tell that he was sorry for his outburst. She wanted to stand, put her arms around him, and tell him everything was all right, or would be all right. But they were not all right, and she could not make them right. Now she was sinking again. Sinking into embarrassment, and shortly after that she knew the guilt would be waiting, the guilt that said why open his wounds when there is no medicine to keep him from hurting. She started to stand.

"Don't get up. I can see myself out. Thank you for a wonderful meal. I haven't tasted gravy like that since I sat at my mother's table." He bent and kissed the top of her head. She again started to rise and he pressed a strong hand on her shoulder. "It was nice of you to ask me here, and I feel badly about leaving, but it's better for me to go on. I'm sorry."

She listened to the soft steps toward the door on the carpeted floor, on the slate at the foyer; then heard the door open and close. She repeated the curse word repeatedly and she began to cry. She was not cursing him, or the events of fifty years ago, or the emotion of using her mother's china or the missing of her father. She was not mad at herself, not really. She was cursing the limitations to our abilities to undo things done, to our abilities to exact fairness from the events of our lives, and to our abilities to find words or actions that can really help people we care about. It made no difference which of them she thought about. The result was the same. She felt helpless, spent and defeated.

She drove by the cottage the next morning. She guessed that he was not there. The truck was gone. Late in the afternoon she drove by again and knocked. He was not in the cottage. Back home she watched the Patriot football game and thought a lot about her father. The Patriots had a new quarterback, and he was really good-looking. But what her dad would really be enjoying was that the guy was just so under control. Patient. He was patient. Seldom went for those long bombs like Terry Glenn used to catch. This quarterback seemed happy just to get the team down the field. She liked him. The team had already won as many games as in the previous season. They were fun to watch again. And she missed her dad. She left before the game was over and went again to the cottage. She sat on the bench until the cold air drove her back to her car where she sat, and waited. After ten o'clock she decided that he was probably gone for the night. She drove back to the house, her mind contesting whether he just did not want to be seen or had been in an accident in that old truck.

Early the next day she drove by again. The truck was sitting beside the cottage. She sighed. He was all right. She steered the car toward Townsend. It was a long way to Boston. She noted that the trip back always seemed to last so much longer than the drive up. She had cleaned out the refrigerator and turned the thermostat down to fifty-five. She did not think she would be using the house anytime soon.

CHAPTER 17

William sat on the bench in the afternoon sunlight. It was not warm but it was pleasant. He had nothing to do, so he sat and watched the few high clouds driven by a wind that would bring in colder weather later in the day, at least, the radio had said that. It did not much matter to him. He could not paint the outside of the cottage until spring regardless of the rain or no rain. The paint might not be any good. He had finally put the cans in the storage room in the side of the cottage, and the freezing weather would probably ruin it. But he didn't want to go to the effort to carry it all back inside.

She had been gone for over three weeks. He could hardly believe it was so near Christmas. Maybe she would be back up and would invite him to dinner again. No. Not likely. Something had happened that last visit, there at the dining table in her warm and comfortable home. It was reality. That was what had happened.

He had wanted for the first time, or maybe for the first time that he had let himself admit, to hold her and comfort her. But he no longer knew if he could keep them apart in his mind. It was her voice that he heard in his dreams—not Carol's—and it was her smell, the fragrance of her hair like when he had bent to kiss it, turning to leave before he could let himself believe that she was Carol. He had nearly made a fool of himself, an old fool, with a young girl who had given him back memories that he had thought forever lost, or forever separated from him by his own barricade. He did not know which.

He had come back that night and finished the poem, his letter to Carol. He wanted her to know that the young girl was not at fault; that he had intruded upon her reality with his memories and past that could only bring her sadness. He wished that he could give Rachel more. She had given him so much.

He had driven the truck hard the day after Thanksgiving. He had gone up to Bar Harbor, took the ferry, drove around the island, and watched and listened to the waves against the rocks well into the night.

Now the wind lessened as he pushed himself from the bench and walked out to the sidewalk and down the street. He needed a little exercise. The knees had gotten tighter in the past few days, as had his fingers after he had stopped his oil painting. He turned back after five minutes or so and walked back up the street and started up the hill toward the bench. The cold air was making him short of breath. The slight burn seemed to start low in his chest and rise to his throat. He should sit down right here on the grass beside the road until the feeling went away, but he looked up at the bench. It was not that far away. He walked a few steps and the burning increased. He stopped and looked down toward the wharf and harbor. It was beautiful at this time of year. The bay was free of sailboats and he saw no one on the wharf. He started up again. The burning came back, but not as great. He would sit down at the bench. It had gotten a lot colder. He would not sit long. He should get on into the house.

The pain in his jaw hit just as he reached the bench. He let himself down. The pain was more intense. He leaned back and closed his eyes and took shallow breaths to lessen the burning in his throat and chest. He told himself it was the cold again, but he knew it was not. He knew what it was. He was feeling a little warmer again. Comfortably warm, and he opened his eyes to look out at the sky above the trees and the water of the harbor. The sky brightened, the wind washing away the few clouds, and the blue turned to a soft, silvery gray.

The figure at first seemed to be moved by the wind; then it appeared to rise and fall like a bird in flight. It came closer—a large whorl of white gossamer, near transparent. The ends seemed to flow over one another and billow in the open space. Then he saw her. In the flowing fabrics, surrounded by them, but just in part. Her brown hair, flowing like the wispy whiteness about her. Her face. There, and then partially veiled by the layers of white. The curves of her body, seen and then hidden.

It was as if he were rising from the bench, into the air, toward her. He looked back. He was still there, his head leaning against the back of the bench, his eyes closed. He turned to the figure. Now she flowed toward him more rapidly. He reached toward her, saw her come near, so near, her hair billowing. It was Rachel. She moved fast; too fast. He reached for her, but she was too far away. Then she was gone. He looked back. He looked down. She was gone. There was nothing. Nothing below or above, behind or in front. He looked back for the bench. Nothing. He was floating, and he seemed unable to govern where he went, and he had no feeling of being anywhere.

He saw the small spot out there, a tint of green. He watched it. He tried to make himself move toward it, but it stayed far away. It grew slightly larger. Then larger, and closer. Another whorl of fine silk the color of the aqua lagoons of the ocean. She was coming back. It was her again. She was closer. She extended her hand and slowly drifted toward him. She beckoned. He could not move. Then he saw her face. It was Carol. She floated to him, her hand reaching, her eyes and lips smiling as her hand touched his. Her fingers were warm. He felt her guiding touch, a prompt, a hint of drawing him on. He felt himself filling with her even as she linked both hands with his. Then he was at her side, joined by their extended arms and an inseparable touch. They were moving now steadily in the same direction. He knew not their heading, only that they were soaring—and that they were one.

On the knoll, at the bench above Boothbay Harbor, the figure sat quietly. It was a man, apparently asleep, no hat, a bulky ivory sweater covering his great shoulders and chest. It was a fair day, high, wispy clouds being driven by a wind that no one could feel. The sky was a light blue and the air chilled. But the face of the man turned upward to the heavens bore a faint smile, and he was not bothered by the cold.

CHAPTER 18

Rachel unlocked the door of the apartment and put her book bag and purse on the small table that sat in the foyer. She picked up her mail. There had been none in their box downstairs. That meant that Peggy either had skipped her one o'clock or had come back between that class and her last at three. Peggy was not too preoccupied with classes now. She was in love, and Rachel liked Thomas, an investment counselor five years older than Peggy and twice as wise. A good match.

She went into the bedroom and changed into her jogging outfit. She preferred running in the morning, but she had increasingly left her class work to be done at that time because of her part time work at the department store. She could get more work than she wanted between now and early January. They were just a week away from Christmas, and they had wanted her to work tonight. She had been tempted, but she needed some quiet time to finish the letter to William. Actually, she had decided to write another one, a different letter. Make it seem less aloof, or less—uncaring. It was not easy. She had decided against going home for Christmas. Her dad and Marianne had made that less difficult by insisting that she spend Christmas with them. And Peggy certainly did not want to be bothered by her presence, here or at her home where Thomas was to spend the holidays. She knew that Peggy was expecting a proposal during that time. She hoped her friend's dream would come true.

She took her stationery from the night table and carried it with her mail into the kitchen. She would take a try at the letter before she ran. She made a cup of tea and set to the task. She sipped at the tea and looked at the blank paper. Maybe she should go on up to the Harbor for Christmas. She wrote, "Dear William," and sipped more tea. Maybe she should run first. She rose from the table and pulled her running jacket off the table. All the mail came with it.

The note was on the top, unfolded enough for her to pick up Peggy's clear handwriting. "Call Mr. Caudry in Boothbay Harbor. It's urgent, he says." The number was listed below the writing.

"William," she said aloud to herself as she dialed the number. He's ill.

"Oh my," she said aloud. Urgent. Who's Mr. Caudry?

There was no answer, but she waited and the recorded message said she had called a lawyer's office and to call him at home if it was urgent. The deep voice with clipped words gave the number. She called the new number. There was a pickup after the second ring.

"Hello."

"Mr. Caudry, this is Rachel Connor. I'm returning your call. My roommate left me a note that it was urgent."

The words were crushing. She heard little after he told her that it had been the heart. Her feelings were like those she felt so long for her mother. But the finality of the message lost her in grief and tears, and she put down the phone. She lay on the bed and sobbed, her body under no control until the crying subsided and finally stopped. She sat up on the side of the bed briefly, then went into the bathroom and washed her face.

The phone still lay on her bed, bleeping loudly. She picked it up, depressed the button, and then dialed the lawyer's office again to get his home phone number. She had failed to write it down. She needed to know what she could do for William. The lawyer told her, and that she did not need to be at the Harbor until two days following.

She stood on the wharf early in the morning some forty hours later. Mr. Caudry arrived, introduced himself, and pointed toward the boat they were to use. She was as surprised as Tom. She looked again at the writing above the pocket of his shirt. Boyd Cruises, it read.

"Hello." He said.

"Hello, Tom."

"You folks know each other, good," Mr. Caudry said.

She and Mr. Caudry walked to the stern of the double-decked boat. She had seen it in the harbor for years, but most of that time it bore the name of one of three boats that took tourists on tours of the bay and runs out to the islands. Now it was painted a new coat of white and bore a new name, "Stealing Home." She liked it. Tom had gone into the cabin and the boat was pulling away from the dock, a young boy in his teens stowing the ropes that had tied the boat to the dock. "I explained to Tom Boyd our mission. He bought this boat a little late to make much money this tourist season, so he was anxious to get the work," Mr. Caudry explained. Tom came out to the bench where she and Mr. Caudry were sitting shortly after the boat cleared the harbor, and he and Mr. Caudry examined a chart to confirm their destination.

It took them over an hour to get there. Tom stayed in the cabin. He had glanced at her several times, but had made no move to talk with her. His task as captain of the boat in part explained that. She knew that no further explanation might be needed than the same thing that kept her sitting in silence—the urn that Mr. Caudry cradled in one arm.

They cast his ashes on the sea, one small mound poured into her palm that she waved out toward the rolling waters. She turned her hand and saw the gray shadow of the ash still clinging to her palm. She instinctively started to wipe her hand on the leg of her jeans after the throwing gesture, but caught herself. She closed her fist on the traces of ash and kept it knotted the rest of the boat's run.

Mr. Caudry and Tom seemed satisfied with the mission. Rachel did not know what to feel. The lawyer had told her that this was in response to William's wishes, although Rachel's participation was all Mr. Caudry's idea after she had asked if she could help. She knew that and appreciated it. Burial at sea was not a new idea to her. She had grown up with stories of such practice and occasional reports of its use by the descendents of seafaring families. But the cremation was new to her. She had never known anyone before who chose this…disposition. She guessed that he could have been buried at the big cemetery, Arlington, in Washington. But then it was his business, and she had pried into his business far too much as it was. Tom took her hand to help her step from the boat. "I'm sorry, Rachel," he said.

"Thank you."

She and Mr. Caudry walked several steps away from the edge of the wharf and he told her that the cottage was locked, and would be until after the estate was settled. He was serving as Mr. Jennings' executor. She would be contacted at some time pertaining to the old man's will. She would be invited to come to the reading of the will here, in Boothbay Harbor. She did not have to be present, but he would call her once a time was set. She looked back at the boat. Tom was still standing where he had stood as he released her hand. She could not make out the look on his face. Nor could she identify what she felt, or whether she felt anything at all.

"He refused to take any payment, Rachel," Mr. Caudry said as he noted her and Tom's unbroken exchange of looks.

Her eyes smarted. Tom looked away.

She felt clumsy in avoiding the lawyer's offer to shake her hand, but he withdrew it quickly. They said goodbye and she walked over toward the car and stopped, turned and began the long walk up the hill.

When she arrived at the bench, she knelt. Someone looking on from afar would have been reminded of a person at prayer, kneeling at an altar of faith. But someone up close would have seen her slowly moving her right palm softly over the grass, as if brushing something off the grass, or off her hand onto the natural, green carpet below the white bench.

CHAPTER 19

Mr. Fallows leaned back from the table in the Grace and Fallows executive dining room. He still had not told Stephen why he had invited one of the newest lawyers, albeit the Grace heir apparent, into the exclusive, walnut-walled dining area. It was small, a part of its appeal. They had other rooms if they needed to hold a large luncheon, but this room was for the inner circle, and only the most select clients. The service had been prompt and he had taken Mr. Fallows' lead in eating the tuna salad quickly. Mr. Fallows cleared his throat, a signal in case he did not already have Stephen's attention. He did.

"We have some good and bad news, Stephen. One of our most recent contributors to the foundation has died, and we have been informed that the foundation is named in his will. You should recall the name, a retired Army general, a William Jennings. We don't really need to send anyone to the reading. We can retain a lawyer in that state to handle it for us...."

"Alaska or Maine?" Stephen asked.

"Maine. You already know the file then?"

"There's not much of a file to know. Did you know him?"

"No. It's one of several of Robert's matters that I sort of inherited. It was a special file to be handled exclusively by Robert, although I don't see anything unusual about the donation or the man.

"May I look again at the file—the one that you have?"

"Of course, but as I say, there's nothing special except that Robert marked it special."

"Would you consider letting me attend the reading of the will; that is handle whatever comes out of this?"

"Yes, as a matter of fact that's why I wanted to lunch with you, to ask you to do just that. Robert viewed the man with some special regard. I just thought a personal representative of the firm and the foundation would be appropriate. I was concerned that someone might be offended if we just as a matter of routine asked you to cover it."

"You mean my grandmother."

"I didn't say that."

"No, sir. You didn't."

"Well, I'll have my assistant call you when the file is ready for you to pick up. If you would respond to the letter from the man's executor, a lawyer named Caudry, you'll then be the one they will inform of their next step. Well, good. That's that. Enjoyed your company, Stephen. Drop by and see me. Let me know how you're doing." The senior partner rose and moved for the door like he was late. Maybe he was.

Stephen sat back down and poured the remainder of the wine into his glass. He was the great grandson of Richard Todd Grace. He was well supported by a trust. He was a lawyer with Grace and Fallows. But he did not know when he would be in this dining room again. He had been thinking that he did not need or want any of this. Now he sipped the wine and looked at the chandelier hanging from the high, polished wood ceiling. Maybe this wouldn't be too bad. Not too bad at all.

Two days later he met Blake for lunch. He told her of his first ever meal in the executive dining room. She had never eaten there.

"Uncle Robert never took you there?" He asked.

"No. He would have been the last; always afraid someone would think that he was giving me a special break. Which, of course, he should have, but never did. Why were you up there?"

"To be assigned a mission. Be present at the reading of the will of one of the foundation's recent donors."

"Hardly seems like a task for the executive in charge of the boy's room location, does it?"

"No, but I'd like to know why the man gave so much to the foundation. Based on what I can learn, he must have donated his entire wealth."

"Maybe he had cancer. Maybe he thought it a worthy cause. How much was it?"

"Come on Blake. Over one million."

"That's not so much."

"It was the largest in 1999. It's the largest single gift ever from someone not related to the Grace family."

"Is that so? I haven't followed the foundation that closely, being on the wrong branch of the family and all."

"You make too much of that, Blake."

"Really? You talked lately to Grandmother Grace about her love for little Blake?"

"You should try to be more considerate of her, Blake."

"Oh, like you do?"

"I mean you may need her someday. More than I will."

"What is that supposed to mean?"

"Just what I said. I don't want to talk about it now, but later, I will."

"You're not about to pick up your bat and go home, are you? You would leave a few million dollars on the playground if you did."

"It's not out of the possible," he said.

"No. I have always known that about you. Uncle Robert told me twice when you were in law school that he thought you'd get up and walk out; said you were too much like your grandmother."

"Like Grandmother Blandon?"

"Yes, like your Grandmother Blandon who died flying around the Pacific for some unknown reason."

"She was with the USO, entertaining servicemen."

"I don't think Uncle Robert thought that was what she was doing."

"What did he think, that she was a pilot on a spy mission for our government?"

"No. I don't know what he thought she was doing, but it might have been closer to that than entertaining servicemen. There were three people in the plane that went down. Her, a pilot, and a minister. I think Robert thought the minister was the clue."

"Clue to what?"

"I don't know. He never said much, and only then after he had too much to drink, like the weekend after Richard Todd died. Then he hurt my arm telling me never to say anything about this in front of anybody, especially Great Grandmother Grace. You know, he was afraid of her. He really was." Blake lit another cigarette.

Stephen sipped again at his martini. He was glad they were coming back—the martini. He had not known they had been gone until he came back from Stanford. They packed a good kick. Like Blake's lunchtime musings.

The call came two days after he advised the lawyer in Boothbay Harbor that he would represent the foundation at the reading. Mr. Caudry said he was a little surprised they were sending one of their lawyers up to Maine, but he offered to accommodate Stephen's availability. They agreed on two o'clock on Tuesday. Mr. Caudry said that the time would be good for the other party.

He went through the files on William Jennings again, but found no insight as to why the man chose this particular foundation. Maybe Blake was right. The foundation did good work, and had a solid reputation. He had read that the foundation had made grants to two programs that supported activities for Native Americans in Alaska. Maybe that was the connection. Maybe that was all there was to it. Anyway, Stephen had never been to Maine. He had been to Massachusetts one time, in the late eighties with his great grandfather, Uncle Robert, and Blake to see the Seahawks play the Patriots. They had visited Plymouth Rock as well, but he only remembered how cold the wind was that blew off the bay, and that the Seahawks had lost the game. The Patriots had gone all the way to the Super Bowl just before that, and lost. He had been glad. He was a die-hard Seahawks fan, but the Patriots were going to make the playoffs again this year, probably would not get through the first round.

Stephen was pleased that the lawyer had been able to arrange for the reading this week. They were between Christmas and New Year. He was surprised that the other party did not ask to wait until the New Year. Maybe none of them had to travel as far as he did. As it was, he had left Seattle on one of the busiest flying days of the year, but all had gone well, and he enjoyed the rental sedan as he sped up Interstate 95 north of Portland. He would not arrive in time to look around Boothbay Harbor in the daylight. The girl at the rental car desk told him how lucky he was to be going to the Harbor, even if it was the off-season. He had not thought of that. He had lodging for two nights, and a flight out on the thirtieth.

Once he was settled in the motel in Boothbay Harbor, he pulled out the file on Brigadier Jennings. He had penciled in the response he had gotten from the Alaska Senator's office. The lady gave him a fair amount of information and offered to mail it to him, but he thanked her and told her that the phone response had been enough. It was in fact quite thorough indicating that someone had gone to some lengths to put the information together, but other than William's work on the north slope, there was nothing to indicate a specific link with either of the foundation funded projects. He also had added information gained by phone calls to several offices in the town of Boothbay Harbor. He had asked for nothing that would violate anyone's privacy, and people had tried to be helpful, but the truth was, they told him, that no one knew much about the man, except Leland Caudry and a Miss Connor. He pictured the Connor woman as an old maid schoolteacher who lived next door to the Brigadier. That was the most important thing he had learned—the address and directions to the cottage.

CHAPTER 20

It was mid-morning when he slowed the car and turned into the short drive at the side of what had to be Holmes Cottage. He turned off the ignition and sat, looking out toward the ocean that lay beyond the knoll and the house-lined harbor below. The clouds were thin, permitting light, almost a glare, to penetrate and bathe the natural beauty before him. He got out of the car, and was hit by the cold breeze off the cove below and to his right. He turned the collar of his suit coat up, and turned to get his topcoat from the back seat when he saw the bench. It was white. Seemed almost featured by a ray of light from a thinner spot in the clouds. He walked over, touched the back of the bench, and looked up and across the narrower finger of the harbor, at the church. He sat.

Why William left Alaska, Stephen did not know, but he could see how a man would buy such a piece of land. He had only glimpsed the cottage as he pulled in, attracted by the scene of the bay and ocean. But for the wind there was little sound, and the view of the church across the harbor was serene, peaceful, almost unreal, more like what is often captured in a painting. He did not know what brought William to this place, but he could see what could have kept him here. Too bad he did not have more time to look around after the reading of the will, but he needed to get back, and he guessed there would be little here to explain the Brigadier's connection with the Foundation. The answer probably lay in Alaska, someone William had known who was involved in one of the Native Alaskan projects. He looked at his watch—still nearly four hours until the meeting with Caudry.

She slowed her pace as she started up the steep street to the top of the knoll. She at first had decided not to run today, but she had grown nervous about the will reading at two o'clock, and compounded that with two cups of coffee before she realized she had used her father's caffeine-loaded blend. She seldom had anything but one decaf for the morning and she felt like she could not sit around the next five hours. She hurried and changed to the light green running suit, her oldest and favorite. Now she was running slowly but directly to the spot she had put off visiting for well over a week.

As she neared the cottage she glanced toward the bay. She stopped. A man was sitting at the bench, She could see only the left side and back of his head and the shoulders above the top of the bench. He turned. She looked away, in the direction of her run and her home. She looked back. He was standing. She walked toward the bench. She came closer. "Hello," she said to the tall man, now moving around to the end of the bench, turning down the collar to the coat of a resplendent dark blue pin stripe suit hanging on a frame well over six feet tall. He was looking at her as if trying to place her from somewhere in their past. She did not know him, had never seen him—she did not think He stepped forward.

"Hello," he said. "Beautiful place here, isn't it."

"Yes. Yes, it is," She said, and stood there.

"Well, I have to be going. Have a nice day," he said, but did not move.

"Don't leave on my account. It's a place where lots of people visit. I was just running by." She turned to leave.

"I'm visiting here, just arrived last night," he said. She stopped and turned back toward him. He had a nice smile.

"My name is Stephen Blandon."

"Rachel Connor," she said. Blandon. Blandon.

She saw a look of surprise on his face again, just briefly, and then it was gone, replaced by the large smile.

"You live here? In Boothbay Harbor?"

"Yes, when I am not away at college. May I ask, are you here in some way connected with William...the late Brigadier General Jennings?"

"Yes, as a matter of fact I am. I'm an attorney, here to represent the Blandon Foundation."

His hair was dark brown, and wavy. The eyes were light blue.

"I know this seems a bit forward, but I recognize your name. I'm told that you were a friend of Mr. Jennings."

"Yes. Who told you? Mr. Caudry?"

"No, two or three other people in town told me you knew Mr. Jennings as well as anyone here."

"Why were you asking about that—those things?"

"Well, my law firm; actually the foundation, is interested in knowing more about the man."

The man. She somehow did not like that. His nose was long and straight.

"I'm interested in getting to know Mr. Jennings better. He's a very generous man, and the foundation likes to know our donors well."

"William, uh…Mr. Jennings. He contributed to your foundation? I mean, he gave you money?"

"Yes. I just would like to know him better. That's all."

"He was my friend, but I didn't know him until he came here."

"When was that?" He smiled again

"I guess about a year ago…a little more than a year ago."

"Hey, you must be getting cold," he said. "I am, and I'm not wet like you are. I'm sorry. Do you think we could talk somewhere? Today, I mean. I'd suggest a cup of coffee somewhere right now, but I guess you…well, clearly you've been jogging, and…"

"Running. I don't jog. And I do need to get home.' She turned to leave again, but stopped to say, "You will be at the reading of the will at two o'clock, won't you."

"Yes."

"I'll be there too. Maybe we could talk more then, after Mr. Caudry finishes."

She was not sure how much she should tell him. She did not know what was going to happen to William's belongings. She did not know what would happen to his poems and his paintings.

She looked at him still more closely. The strong chin, the broad forehead, the easy smile, the slight stoop as he talked to her as if trying to lessen the distance created by his being well over six feet tall.

"He wrote poetry." She said it impulsively, as if she wanted to say more, did not want to go, despite the chill she was feeling. He looked a bit surprised at her comment too.

"He was a poet?"

"Not a published poet. He didn't write a lot of poetry. He wrote about himself, and his past."

"And he read the poetry to you?" He asked.

"No. I read them on my own."

"Where are these poems?"

She hesitated. Could the poems have special value? Could they threaten someone? She could not think of how they could be of value to anyone. Living.

Except to her. She should not have mentioned them—but he would probably learn of them anyway.

"I'm not after his poems. I'd be interested in reading them, but I don't want to take them. I assure you," he said.

"Why? I mean what kind of a foundation is it that you need that kind of information?"

"I told you. I represent it. I'm one of the firm's lawyers. And Carolyn Grace Blandon was my grandmother."

Rachel grasped for the back of the bench, but she was too far away. He caught her.

"Are you all right? Hey, can I run you somewhere? I am really sorry to hold you up like this. Are you all right?"

She let him move her around, and she sat on the bench.

"I'm okay." She felt betrayal. Carol had not just married, she had a child—a boy—father to this young man? If that were true, how large would the rupture in William's heart have been if he had learned of this man and this man's father? His hurt had been so great to learn of her marriage that Rachel could not imagine his reaction had he learned there was a child from that marriage.

"What will you do with the information you may learn here about Mr. Jennings?" She asked.

"What do you mean? Like the press, or media?"

"Exactly."

"Nothing. I want the information for the foundation files, but I certainly don't intend to put anything overly personal in there. We like to know a little about our major donors; that's all."

"Well, I don't think there is much to learn. His home is pretty bare." She was becoming more wary about this man, this grandson of a woman that William had died still loving. Did he know that—this man—did he know about William? And what did he know?

"He did have some boxes, foot lockers he called them." Should she help him? What about William?

"Where are they?"

"I don't know. They used to be in the front room. They may be in the attic."

"Maybe we can look after the reading. If Mr. Caudry will allow us. He said there was another party to be present at the reading of the will. Are you going to be there in that capacity?

"I don't know, Mr. Caudry just told me that I could be there if I wanted."

"Is there someone who will inherit his belongings—this cottage?"

"I don't know. I thought that he had nobody, just as I thought that he had no money. I was sure wrong on that. He was also a painter," she said.

"What?"

"He painted oils. One is very good."

"Okay. Well, I'd be more interested in the boxes."

"The paintings are in the attic." She was trying to think quickly. William was giving everything to this foundation—to this man. Maybe, just perhaps, the paintings and poetry would have no value to them. She should be more cautious, but…

"Look, I'm not after this man's wealth or any of his personal property beyond what he has willed to the foundation that explains his donation—no property."

What about someone else? She would like to have the paintings, but who would have legal claim to them if not this man's foundation? Might William possibly have…? No. No, he wouldn't.

He looked at her at length. Then he sat down beside her on the bench.

"You were really fond of this man, weren't you," he said.

She wanted to tell him to mind his own business, but words that had been prisoner to the last long week, sought expression.

"Yes. Yes I was quite fond of him."

"Do you think we should go now?" He asked.

"Yes."

"Do you think, after this executor's meeting is over, that we could talk?"

"Yes."

He stood and extended his hand. She took it, and he pulled her to her feet. He did not let go.

"Can I drop you off somewhere?"

"No, thank you. I live just down the hill. I'll be fine. I'll see you at two o'clock."

He watched her trot out to the street at the front of the cottage and turn to run down the hill. She smiled at him

The reading was in Mr. Caudry's office. The lawyer was informal, something that Rachel appreciated, and guessed that Stephen Blandon did as well. The older lawyer sorted his papers, and she looked at the profile of the man to her right. She could not dismiss his good looks. Yet he carried them well. He did not seem so conscious of himself as so many beautiful people did—men and women. He turned to look at her. She did not look away. She felt the blush.

She thought that she ought to look away, but his eyes seemed as caring, warm, and familiar as—as a friend of many years, but, then, not of a friend…

"Miss Connor, Mr. Blandon. We are ready to begin." She turned to look at Mr. Caudry. He was smiling at her. She felt her face grow warmer. She looked directly at the lawyer. Guilty, counselor.

"Yes, Mr. Caudry," she said.

It was all quite uncomplicated, even the part about William's sister. The sister was not named in the will, and he had left her nothing. He had merely informed Mr. Caudry that he did in fact have a next of kin, but that she would not care when he died. She lived in central Washington. He had not seen her since his mother's funeral. Rachel remembered William's stories of severed relationships. It hurt her. Mr. Caudry said that the sister had acknowledged the news of her brother's death. That was all that the lawyer offered.

He addressed Stephen as he explained that it was not yet clear the value of the securities and stocks that were to be left to the foundation. Possibly in the area of a third of a million dollars. Stephen nodded as if accustomed to such sums of money. Rachel could hardly believe it. William had not lived like a man with a thousand dollars in the bank, much less three hundred thousand.

Then the lawyer spoke directly to her. William had left to her the Holmes cottage, all its contents, and the land.

"This shall include the truck, even if it should become permanently inactive and attached to the land as she so often fears, and this shall include the bench." The lawyer read this last slowly, and smiled at her.

How much did he know of the early contest over the fence and the bench?

"To Miss Connor is also bequeathed the sum of one hundred and fifty thousand dollars for such use in the furtherance of her education as may prove pleasing to herself and her loving parents."

At this she could not restrain the tears. Stephen offered the broad chest and long arm and she accepted. Mr. Caudry left his office. He probably knew that he could transact no more business right now, and that he was neither needed nor wanted.

She invited Stephen back to the Cottage. She could share with him the poetry, and they could look for the boxes. Once she mentioned hot tea, he insisted on making it, and so she went into the bedroom and took the folder of poetry from the left desk pedestal. She looked further for anything pertaining to William's past and specific reference to the Blandon Foundation. She found something new in the right pedestal, top drawer: two new sheets of poetry. She found no papers on his past.

"Any luck?" He asked.

"No, but there is more poetry." She handed the poems she had already read to Stephen, keeping the one that she had seen, but had never completely read, and the newest that he had written. They began to read. He sipped at the tea and she was taken with the regret in the initial lines.

> February 7, 1952
>
> I want not to live again
> The days of fierce battle there
> To sit and to ponder why
> Quick death found the other guy
>
> It was I who was deceived
> In luck survived the strife
> Only to learn it was you
> I valued more than life
>
> But mine was a soldier's code
> I accepted not to leave
> Hills, vales, and rivers we passed
> I fought, and tried to believe
>
> I thought of us now apart
> I thought of you there alone
> I dreamed of having you here
> Or of me there in your home
>
> All this could once have been ours
> It might have been for us then
> I thought that I owed you more
> Owed wealth like that of your kin

> I cannot tell you my guilt
> For what my own choice has cost
> When I learned that dreadful truth
> Of the fateful airplane loss
>
> I know that I made you go
> I count toward my last breath
> I feign the desire to live
> But know that my lot is death

It was that last word that had shown clear in the spot of her small flashlight weeks before. She had thought it confirmed Carol's fate; that she had died. Now she knew that to be true, but the word expressed more. In the days of 1952 when he had written the poem, he still suffered with her death, and had contemplated his own.

Rachel glanced up at Stephen. He was still reading the earlier poems. She looked at the most recent poem—she assumed William's last.

> November 2001
>
> I have found you again. I touch your face and look into your eyes
> I brush your hair back from your cheek
> I watch you walk away, and return,
> I long to hear you speak
>
> Then I hear you, and the voice is hers
> But it is your smile; it is your laugh
> The words are ours. It is our time
> Can she speak on your behalf?
>
> I speak to you and watch your face
> Do you hear? We do not embrace
> I have said so little. I wish to say more
> There remains some veil. There remains some door

The Bench

It is not yours
The wall I have built
It is not of your making
It is all my guilt

It rushes upon me
Near sweeps me away
Why did I leave you
Why did I not stay

Or why did I not give you
In those last days, so sad
My full love, my commitment
My name—all I had

Oh I am not proud
Of the love in my life
Almost none at all
No children; no wife

And worse is the burden
That in all of those years
I confessed to no person
For the guilt or the fears

But I kept them away
They never got close
I said, I don't need you
Or said nothing to most

But it is quite true
That I did not conceal
That I did not miss
What I could not feel

And then I came here
And the cracks began
In the base of a bench
Where rusted water ran

I would not have renewed it
I would have thrown it away
But she came here knocking
On that cold, damp day

And what she awoke
Had lain still in my heart
Though I thought it had gone
Had left me bare and apart

Some was her caring
Some was her fire
Some was her laughter
At me, and my mire

But it was not to sink me
Or to watch me drown
That brought her back again
Took me into her town

The truth is that now
With all that has gone by
So strange that she helped me
And I do not know why

There is so much
That I do not know
Why I lost you
Why you had to go

But what is now so very clear
Is that I failed you in every year
That what you had that I did not
Was zest for life that I never sought

But that zest found me
When I again found you
And let me love you
Again, and true

And there is more
I do not understand
That name linked with yours
Of some other man

I think it now
A final test
A challenge greater
Than all the rest

But if I have
Found some new peace
Perhaps it helps me
To feel this, at least

That in those months
After I went away
I pray you found love
If for only a day

But the hurt of that thought
I must reveal
I am quite the flawed man
Prone to error still

That I feel the love
Again so great
Brings back the guilt
That will not abate

Then I sit on the bench
That wrought iron chair
And I know that our love
We will again share

Forgive me I beg that I did not live bold
That I wasted years, missed love untold
And I hope that you do understand
My love for you, renewed and true
Returned to me—your face and hair
Because she came, and I loved her too

Stephen took the pages of poetry from her, and placed both his hands over hers. She had made no sound, but her tears had dropped on the page, tiny splashes flooding the last stanza.

She removed her hands and turned the pages toward him for his reading. He had finished the first three poems. They made no comment. She rose to make more tea.

When he finished he looked at her, seated again across the table.

"It's her. It must be my grandmother. Do you know? Did he say?"

"Of course, yes, it is Carol. He told me, and he still loved her, just like he wrote in the poems."

"And it's you. You're the one in the last poem. It's you." He said it as part question, part conclusion.

She nodded. Her heart ached anew. She wished Stephen would say something more, anything. Her emotions were choking her. She did not want to break down again.

"Rachel, I know it's hard for you, but I have a flight out of Portland tomorrow morning, and I need to know more about William. Will you tell me? Tell me all that he shared with you?"

She wanted to ask him why he needed to hear personal things. And she was wary. The name of Carolyn Grace, and her memory, were so special, indeed sacred, to William. She did not know what might be harmful to that trust, and she could think of little that she could tell him that would help in any way. Just the close proximity in time of Carol's shared love with William and her love of Stephen's grandfather could bring discomfort. She knew little about the Graces or the Blandons, but there were likely questions to be raised in the minds of some of the members of those families.

"The poems explain William's link to the foundation, but there must be more. Did William just give up? Didn't he ever try to contact my great grandparents? Why would he go so many years with no contact and then give so much money to the foundation?"

"How much did he give?"

"Well over one million dollars. I was a bit surprised at the additional amount that Caudry says will come from the sale of stock he still held."

"And the money to me for my education—so generous." She did not want to tell him that she marveled at how William had lived; how he dressed, when he had so much money. She was aware that there had been ample years for him to amass an estate, especially if he had always spent so little on himself. He must have been delighted watching her respond to the truck. She smiled.

"What are you smiling at?" He asked.

"His old, beat up truck," she said.

"Maybe he was a Clint Eastwood fan."

"I wonder. He never said. I don't know that he ever saw a movie."

"Did he read?"

"I guess. He has some adventure novels here. I think he did."

Stephen paused. He seemed hesitant, then…

"Do you know how he met my grandmother, and when and where they spent time together? Would you tell me what you know about that?"

She recounted for him what William had told her about the meeting at the University, their shared time in Seattle, the scuffle with Carol's father, the only time that he saw Carol's mother, then their separation and the brief weeks they shared in Tokyo before he went off to war, never to see her again.

He asked her about the specific days they shared in Tokyo, but she was little help other than it started sometime in May and ended in late June of 1950. He was pushing hard on that period of time.

"Did he still have the watch she gave him?" He asked.

"No. He said that he carried it throughout the Korean War, but he never saw it after he was wounded. His unit tried to locate it, but they never did. No, he lost the watch."

Neither spoke for a brief time.

Then she asked Stephen about his parents, and listened to the unbelievable tragedies that had left him never to see his grandparents or to know his parents. She asked him about the details of the plane crashes that had taken his grandmother and grandfather. He knew little. If it were not for William's grant to the foundation, the young man might have had little reason to dwell on events half a century removed. It had not occurred to her that neither Carol's nor her husband's body had been recovered, although it made sense.

"Your great grandparents I gather never mentioned William, a Mr. Jennings, to you?" She asked.

"No, and my great grandmother told me when I asked about him, as a contributor to the foundation, that she had never heard of him or seen him."

"But William said that she did see him, even though they never formally met."

"I know. I find all you have told me about William's visit to my great grandparents' home bothersome."

He seemed less intent now on asking questions and more inclined to mull over what she had told him.

"Do you feel like looking now for the boxes, the lockers?" He asked.

"Yes," she replied and pushed herself away from the table. She then leaned over, gathered the sheets of paper and put them all, to include his last poem, in the brown folder. She tied the ribbon, thinking what a gift the poems were, but not his greatest gift to her.

"How do you get into the attic?" He asked as Rachel returned the folder to the left pedestal of the desk.

"The pull down, toward the door," she called out from the bedroom. "There is a light with a pull-string switch in the attic."

He was half way up the ladder-like stairs when she stepped back into the kitchen. The light came on and he pulled himself into the attic space. She followed him up.

"Well, a Sandhill Crane," he said, "And well done. Did William paint this?"

"The bird? Yes, do you know them?"

"Yes, I've seen them in central California and in the eastern valleys of Oregon and on drives down to Salt Lake City. Always in the spring and fall. They migrate. Have you seen them?"

"Yes. One. Above the cove just this last fall."

"Here? In Maine?"

"Yes. Why?"

"I didn't know they came as far as the east coast. Thought they were limited to the Michigan area. Normally you see more than one at a time. During migration they can number hundreds in a single flight. I always saw at least two at a time. The pairs can be inseparable, stay together for forty years or more."

"What did you call them?" Rachel was still standing on the ladder, her elbows on the rough plywood section that had been laid on a small portion of the attic's rafters. She was wearing a skirt, not the jeans of her earlier climb. She was admiring the painting of the bird that Stephen slowly tilted one way and another under the harsh attic light. It was good.

"Sandhill Cranes. Sometimes they are called Red-Capped Cranes. Most of them migrate all the way from the Gulf shore of Texas and Louisiana and mainland Mexico to Canada and Alaska."

"How do you know so much about them?"

"I don't, but I did a research paper in college on the threat of extinction of the Whooping Crane. They almost died out in the late forties, still are endangered. The Sandhills are more plentiful, but the main danger to them is the reduction in places to land and feed during their migration. They like wetlands. But now they are forced to invade the farmers' fields and are developing new enemies." He handed the painting to her. The attic dust was going to ruin his suit.

"Let me take your jacket," she said. "The dust up here is sticky with the salt air it has eaten up."

He began to peel off the jacket in the cramped space, and she carefully backed down the ladder with the painting in one hand. She laid it on the table and turned and he tossed the jacket at her.

"Stephen, that's no way to treat a good coat." She regretted the comment. It was so domesticated, like something her mother would have said to her. Many men took care of their own dry cleaning requirements today. But he did not reply. She waited. There was no sound of him moving around.

As she moved the painting of the Sandhill Crane from the table and leaned it against one of the wicker chairs, she was struck by the bird's eye—now tinted in a yellowish-orange—subtle, but clear. She had not detected the color of the eye in the bird that she had seen; and she was sure it had not been colored in when she had seen the painting before. In the right half of the painted eye, in the direction of the light, there was a small, delicate crescent of reflected light. It seemed to bring the eye, the entire bird, to life. It was if he were standing in the room—William. She felt an embarrassment, uneasy that the thought reminded her of how death had scared her as a child, including the death of her grandfather. The nightmare she had never shared with anyone. It had been an embarrassment; somehow disrespectful of her grandfather, and now she felt the same about William. It was not the way she wanted to feel about him. She had looked around the room as she felt his presence. Now she looked back at the eye of the great crane, tried to look into it, and she smiled. She sighed. "It is very good, William," she said. Softly, but aloud.

"Stephen? Did you find the boxes?" No reply. Had he sensed her emotion, her silence? Or had he heard her comment? What would he think? She climbed back up the ladder.

He held the portrait in the spray of light from the naked light bulb. The two figures, the two young people, were wearing faces now. Both smiling. The man—a young William—with the strong features and dark, wavy hair, the light blue eyes. The girl, the woman, beamed. She had not thought William capable of such work—and a portrait at that. The skin tones were so real; the eyes like looking in a mirror, like…She looked more intently at the picture. The hair and eyes of the woman in the picture could have been her own.

"Is this him?" He asked.

"Is that William? Yes of course, can't you…?" Stephen had never seen William. "Have you not seen pictures of William?"

"No, at least not that I am sure of."

"Is that your grandmother?"

He did not respond for a brief time.

"Yes, it's Carolyn. It's my grandmother."

His voice sounded muffled, weak. As if he had not wanted to find what he had found.

He laid the picture down and began to crawl toward the stair opening.

"Could you please pass the painting to me? It's so dusty up here. And I would like to look at it in better light," she said.

He responded without comment and waited until she was off before he put his two hundred pounds on the old stairs.

His trousers were soiled at the knees, but she said nothing.

"Did you find the boxes?" She asked.

"What? Oh, the boxes. No, no not the boxes." His reply was given absently, as if the footlockers no longer held interest for him.

He had found something—William as a young man—but as a painting. Yet, there was something else. Something in the portrait. He had found something that he had not liked. Either in the face of the man or the face of the woman.

Rachel played at tidying up the cottage, waiting for him to speak again. She came back into the kitchen and found him sitting at the table with the painting in his left hand, his right forefinger nearly, but not quite, touching something low in the portrait. She looked over his shoulder at the oval shape suspended from a fine chain around Carol's neck—a pendant.

She suggested they go by the market, pick up some groceries, and eat at her house. He thanked her and said no with such detachment that she found herself a bit embarrassed. Disappointed. She would not risk suggesting a restaurant.

Neither did he.

They had driven to the cottage in separate cars, and she watched him get into the rental. He thanked her. He did not even extend a hand. Neither did she. He said goodbye and backed out of the short driveway.

She had not asked where he was staying. There were not that many places open. She could probably find out. Or she could follow him right now. She could still see the taillights of his car dropping down the hill in the dusk. She stood there.

The bench. It would crush her to sit now on the bench. She opened the door of her car and sat behind the wheel. She needed to get back to Boston, back to school, back to her life, but first she would stop by and talk to her mother. She had never before told her mother about William.

CHAPTER 21

Stephen looked out over the tops of the white clouds and the expanse of blue sky above that seemed to go on forever. It could have been a peaceful, restful flight for him, but it was not. There was an ugly tear in the tapestry of his life in Seattle, a life that he lacked the will to repair, but he had a right to the truth and he could find that truth only in Seattle. And he was tugged by the life he had glimpsed in Boothbay Harbor.

His regret had begun even before his car reached the Maine Turnpike. He should have accepted, with the same excitement that she showed, her invitation to go with her to her home. He could listen to her talk about her family, watch her move about the kitchen, enjoy her voice, and watch the excitement in her face, an animation that he had helped remove in the last half-hour of his visit. He smiled to himself recalling her standing in the street, hands on hips in the green running suit, her hair wet where it framed the face, aglow with the vitality of exercise. He had felt awkward with the situation, her beauty a distraction even as he sought to say hello, and further as they stood in the cold, all things suggesting they should let go, but holding on to a conversation that seemed to go nowhere. But it had and now he looked back with regret that he had learned so much from her and had failed to tell her about the locket—the locket that was in the inside pocket of the suit coat he had tossed down from the attic. He wished now the locket had fallen out; that he could have said that he had intended to share it with her. He smiled at the image of the old maid schoolteacher that he had assigned to the name, Miss Connor. He had underestimated her—and William.

The man intrigued him. She had said his paintings were amateurish. He could not agree. Both the crane and the portrait were impressive. He could not speak for the technique, he knew little about the application of the oils, but he could see the result, and the beauty of his grandmother was beyond what the old photograph had captured.

Did Rachel realize that the hair was hers, Rachel's own, whether or not it truly represented his grandmother? The eyes also were Rachel's. Could they also have been Carolyn's? Once he saw the painting, he knew it was created from the image in the locket. Her white, curved collar, her shoulder tucked under his arm and shoulder, the pattern of his tie and suit, the collar. He also would guess that the painting was from an image deep in William's recall. Were Rachel's hair and eyes that much like Carolyn's or were they substitutes, an inference of Rachel's presence on his faulty recollection of Carolyn? Even using the black and white photo alone, Stephen thought the hair in the portrait was not that of his grandmother. He had taken the locket out as soon as he had gotten back to his room and compared the picture with his mental image of the portrait.

The locket in the painting was an addition. Not present in the photograph, but of sufficient meaning to the artist to cause him to transfer it from his memories to the canvas.

Had Rachel guessed the reason for his preoccupation and even lack of courtesy in the last hour they spent together? Had she seen what he had seen—the striking resemblance between one Stephen Todd Blandon in the flesh and the man in the portrait, the man Rachel believed was a young William Jennings? What about the black and white picture of the hero naval aviator on his great grandmother's piano—his grandfather? Family resemblance was not an infallible indicator of blood kin, but the resemblance he had seen in the portrait in the cottage caused him to look anew at the man in the locket. While the camera on that day over fifty years ago may not have been of the quality of William's brushstrokes, why had he not seen his own likeness in the locket from the beginning? Maybe it was the kind countenance of the face in the other black and white photo that had looked down upon him from Grandmother Grace's piano all his life. Maybe he still owed that man something, just as he had thought that possibly there was something owed to the man in the locket, and he had found that there was.

The top of Mount Rainier joined the other volcanic peaks in welcoming him back to western Washington. They thrust upward through and above the white clouds that blanketed the entire western interior and coastline of the state. Beneath it, he found the familiar, gray drizzle of winter. Later he looked at the Space Needle where he and Julia had shared a New Year's Eve just a year earlier, like a pair of tourists. It seemed a long time ago. What was he going to do tomorrow—New Year's Eve? He wished he had stayed in Boothbay Harbor. Not because of any differences in the natural beauty and appeal of the two areas. They were both places where one should love to work and to play. It was who was there. He had left her with no sign of the feelings that had kept her in his mind since the wide concrete ribbon of the Maine Turnpike whined to him that he was leaving her.

He needed to see his Grandmother, but first he had to call Leland Caudry. He needed all the phone numbers that Rachel Connor had ever listed. He had to talk to her.

"I have the number for her family home, but she isn't there. Left for Boston this morning just after she came to see me. Said it might be weeks before she is back in the house, asked me to arrange some special security for the house and cottage, seemed particularly concerned that no one disturb the cottage in any way." Mr. Caudry spoke with the clipped speech of the New England native. He seemed eager to help, although Stephen had disturbed him at home. Stephen knew that Mrs. Caudry had not appreciated the call—said as much before handing the phone to her husband.

"I have a number for her in Boston, but I would have to trust you. I don't like to give out clients' addresses and phone numbers without their permission. Do you think she will want to receive your call?"

Stephen did not know. Before his insensitive dismissal of her invitation to dinner, one that she had not seemed to extend lightly, the answer might have been yes. Now he did not know what damage he had done.

"Yes. Yes, certainly," he said. He heard the lawyer chuckle and then the man gave him the number.

"Happy New Year to you both," Caudry said.

"Happy New Year to you, and to your wife," Stephen said. Mr. Caudry chuckled again, but with a bit less enthusiasm. Stephen hung up, eager to put a call through to Rachel.

"Hello, Peggy here," was the response.

"Hello, my name is Stephen Blandon, and—"

"Rachel, Rachel, it's him, Stephen. It's Stephen. No, I'm serious." Stephen heard it clearly, as if she had not even lowered the phone.

"You are the Stephen from Boothbay Harbor? The one from Seattle…?" It was still the one who called herself Peggy. She didn't wait for his answers.

"Oh this is wonderful," She said. "You see I'm getting married, and we're giving a party New Year's Eve, and Rachel, well Rachel won't go to anything, and…"

"Peggy! Shut up. Give me the damn phone." He heard Rachel's voice. There was a pause.

"Hello," came her soft, calm voice, as if nothing had just transpired, as if Peggy were some stranger, someone that the phone company had thrust briefly into their realm by the work of a virus in computerized connections. Stephen let it go. Peggy had already answered his questions, at least his immediate ones. The first time he ever saw her he would give her a big kiss. He liked this Peggy.

"Hello, Rachel. It's good to hear your voice."

❦   ❦   ❦

Grandmother Grace seemed to approve of his smart suit if not the late hour as he went into the drawing room after seven, late for Grandmother Grace if she had no social event for the evening, and the maid had told him that she did not. Never the less she was already prepared for sleep in as resplendent dress as she would have donned to attend a party at the governor's mansion.

"Why do you bother me so late, Stephen, and with no advance arrangement?"

"I want to show you something." Her eyes seemed to change focus; the pupils grew a bit larger. He had learned to read her as one does an attendee at a masquerade party, denied the language of facial muscle and hue of skin. He handed her a copy of Richard Todd Grace's note. He did not want the original torn or possibly destroyed by the old lady.

She read the note, stood, read it again, and then walked to the window. He could tell nothing watching her back, but she had never done this in response to him, or at any time when he was present with other people. Grandmother Grace was not one to show anything but her best side, and she viewed that as straight on. She was deciding what to say. She was going to tell him something. He hoped that it would not be a lie, something that would cost him days or months to unravel before he found it false. She turned abruptly, walked directly to him, and handed the paper back to him.

"I have no idea what this means. It's some fabrication by Robert for reasons that would escape me. It is nothing."

He took the locket from his pocket, opened it with a fingernail, and showed her the picture once more.

"The locket was in an envelope with the note, sealed with great grandfather's seal."

"Nonsense, Richard stopped using that seal—"

"Why would he seal it?" Stephen asked.

"I have no idea, and certainly Richard had nothing to do with this fraud. This is some invention of Robert's and whatever reason for it no doubt went with him to his grave, bless his poor soul."

"Grandmother, did you ever meet or see William Jennings?"

"I have already answered that. I will waste no more time on the subject."

"William says that he saw you, that he was in this house."

"I understood that this William is dead," she said.

"Yes, but he told someone of his visit here."

"Well he lied, or someone lies in saying that he told such a story."

"What I don't understand," Stephen said, tucking the note back into his breast pocket, "is what is so dangerous or so bad, that you would go to such lengths of lying to hide it. I would guess it's to avoid loss of fortune or scandal." He turned and walked to the piano. He picked up the photo of his grandfather.

"What was my grandfather like? I mean, how tall was he? How much did he weigh? Why are there no pictures of him around except for this one with his dress naval hat on? What color was his hair? Was it dark, like mine, like my father's was? Was it wavy like my father's?"

"Stephen, you are excused. Please leave. You have given me a headache, and all over a meaningless piece of paper. If you won't leave, then I will." She walked briskly from the room.

He was certain that it was a first in her life. She had been driven from her own drawing room. Not by him—by the truth. He had to find out how to discover that truth; how to confirm what he was increasingly inclined to believe that truth to be.

It was too late to do more today. He had already retained the services of an investigative service, had told them where to look, and he had pulled the documents from Mr. Fallow's files, a major breach of etiquette in the firm. Their search would take them to Monterey County and the cities of Monterey and Carmel, possibly to the records of the United Sates Defense and State Departments, and definitely to Hawaii. He had dispatched copies of the documents by registered mail. The originals he had returned to Mr. Fallows' safe. Interesting that the certificate of his grandmother and grandfather's marriage had been among the documents held by Uncle Robert and transferred to Mr. Fallows upon his uncle's death. The same was true of the certificate of birth of his father.

He called Rachel again late that evening. She did not seem bothered by the lateness of the call. They talked for over an hour. She was a football fan—a New England Patriots fan at that. "They are on a roll," she said. It was the only time a real lightness entered the conversation. Still, he could hardly believe the ease of their conversation and the number of interests that they shared. But he knew the value of going slowly, not cautiously, but slowly.

He had a feeling he had not experienced before, certainly not with Julia, that this could be a lasting relationship. She still had six months of college, and she apparently had not decided what she wanted to do with her life. It was important that she make those judgments. He only hoped that he would have a fair chance to fit within her plans. He was firm on one thing. He did not want one of those—no obligations; let's just see—relationships. Too often nothing of value ever came from those. Some couples he thought even destroyed the potential for a great and lasting bond simply in the untrusting contract at the beginning. No, he wanted to take a different kind of risk with Rachel, the risk that time and the continental breadth between them would cause the trust already there to grow.

Despite the late hour, when he got off the phone, he retrieved the seldom-used box of stationery from his desk, and sat to write her a letter. The sepia artists' sketch of one of the many Washington coast lighthouses at the top of the paper reminded him of her home.

He began his confession: not sharing the existence of the locket, and rudely failing to respond to her kind invitation to dinner. He regretted especially not sharing the story of the locket. He ended by writing that he had considered catching a plane and joining them for the New Year celebrations, but that he hoped there might be others in the future. After writing the last sentence, he thought it went too far and considered rewriting the entire last page. But just as quickly he threw off what he had come to view as a Grace principle of withholding information and honest feelings. He left the letter unchanged.

CHAPTER 22

New Year's Day Rachel lounged around the apartment, lunching on leftovers from Peggy's party, and watching most of three college football games. Surprisingly two were fairly well played, but most teams lost the precision of their play between their last games in November and the New Year's bowl games.

Her father and Marianne had invited her to spend the day with them. But she made them as uneasy as she was, so she told them she was going to Vermont on a ski holiday. She had considered that, but dropped out at the last minute. Now she admitted to herself the truth of what Peggy had said as Rachel took her early departure from the party last night. It was barely past midnight, and she was carrying a shopping bag loaded with food not likely to be eaten now that the bottles of champagne were popping their tops.

"She's hoping that Stephen will come flying in and save her from having to watch football games all day tomorrow." They had all laughed, not knowing that Peggy spoke with solid knowledge of her ex-roommate. Rachel had hoped that he might call and tell her that he was flying out to share the eve of the New Year with her, and he had called, but made no hint of coming and in no way indicated when he would call her again. She had not told Peggy of the call. And she had said nothing to him to encourage a future contact, even a phone call. What might William's Carol have said or done in the same situation?

At the start of the fourth football game, she gave up, took her latest Grisham novel to bed, and fell asleep. Her last reading was of Nate trying to get some sleep and to overcome the ailments of too much festivities and drink. At least she had not made that mistake.

The next week she attended to her studies with new commitment. She had maintained good grades up until the last school year. Now she vowed to attain a level of excellence she had not experienced since high school. Partly it was William. She may have violated his intent in asking to apply some of the money that he left her to the rent on her apartment. Mr. Caudry had no problem with the desire when she had last talked to him in the Harbor. The money would be hers to use as she preferred. And there could be no further education until she completed her current program, now her main focus. When Stephen had not called by the following Friday, she decided that her education was her only focus.

At mid-month, she drove home to visit with her mother over the weekend. She carried the drop zone painting that Peggy so disliked with her along with an easel she had found in an antique shop. The antique had been the painting sitting on the easel, so she had not paid dearly for the stand. She placed it in the study, near the fireplace where she could see the painting sitting on it in the flickering light of the fire. The affect of the natural firelight enhanced the golds and the whites of the sky and landscape. It could invite one to imagine viewing the scene from high on a mountain or high in the sky. But she had not easily guessed the perspective of a parachutist, and he had wanted to emphasize with her the notion of substituting oneself for a missing parachutist in the picture. Had William known the similarities of her hair and eyes with those he depicted for Carol in the portrait beside the man who had to be William. Could he not remember Carol's full appearance. Was it an intentional substitution or did she and Carol look that much alike. Or had he come to believe that was how Carol's hair had looked simply by being around her in the Harbor. She felt a slight shudder despite the warmth from the fire and was embarrassed with herself. Whatever had been his intent it was something for her to treasure and feel good about.

Had she been Carol to him? Or had she simply helped him, as his poems suggested, to remember and feel the love for Carol again. She so wanted to believe that she had entered the scene and made his life better. She hoped that his meaning had been that he knew she was doing that, he knew it and accepted it. Was he happier, even for the briefest time? She watched the soft glow of the painting and felt again the light touch of his kiss atop her head.

She had to believe that she had helped.

🍁   🍁   🍁

When she arrived the next day, she found her mother confined to her bed. The attendant encouraged her to get her mother up. She apparently had been balking on her daily walk down the long hallway from the patients' rooms toward the lounge and reception desk. Rachel was thrilled when her mother responded so easily to her efforts to get her to sit on the side of the bed and to accept her robe. Sun poured in through the large windows, and as Rachel walked with her, she twice turned and seemed to want to walk to the bright light, to walk through the glass window. When they returned to her room, she resisted getting back in the bed. Rachel tried to get her to sit in the chair. She would not do that either. When Rachel guided her back toward the bright hallway, her mother grasped the facings of the door. She did not want to go out. Rachel tried to laugh with her mother; she asked what she wanted, what she wanted to do. One of the male attendants came over and, with a smile toward Rachel, guided her mother back to the bed where she let him remove the robe and swing her legs up under the covers. He tucked her in, and she stared at the ceiling, the acoustic tiles running in all directions in designs that had meaning to lovers of geometry, or maybe to people like her mother.

She walked out and the man swung in beside her and put an arm around her shoulders. She held back the tears and appreciated his gesture. He was a large man, with a soft smile and a tender touch. He said nothing. She knew there were no comforting words. It would hurt to tell her that her mother's lack of cooperation was someway directed at her personally. It would be even more hurtful to remind her of the truth. That her mother knew her not at all. What had happened to her mother's little toy? Probably taken away from her for her own protection. His large, black face smiled at her as she waved goodbye. She doubted if he knew how much it meant to her to know that her mother had his powerful tenderness there each day—just to touch her.

A week later Stephen called. He seemed unexcited by the conversation, and rambled about bad weather and his boring work. What was wrong? She resented that he had even called. Had she imagined it all? Had the feelings been one way? She had featured him as a positive person, not one who would waste valuable time fretting about the weather. And it seemed to her that he should practically own the law firm, or at least that grandmother of his did. She could not see why if things were so bad that he wouldn't just change them, or get grandmother to do so. She was glad that she had not called him. She had come so close. Not now. Not ever.

CHAPTER 23

After the phone conversation with Rachel, Stephen decided to call her each Friday. The conversation had not gone well. The entire time since he had come back had not gone well. He had far too much Champagne on New Year's Eve. It was as if he didn't care about anything. He was not a lover of Champagne and he spent the first and second days of the New Year remembering why. He could not recall feeling so sick. He guessed that regardless of the affects of the alcohol he was experiencing some type of depression, both before and after the New Year celebration. He didn't think he had felt such empty sadness since childhood, when he thought that the great arguments between Grandfather and Grandmother Grace had been caused by his mere presence in the big house. He learned better later, but the way he felt in those early school years was that all unhappiness in that mansion was his fault. If he was unhappy then, he knew why. Now he did not. It could not be her. He had just met her. Hardly knew her.

Things were not going too badly at work, except that it had taken far too long to think out a way to get Blake's ideas on the table in a manner that would avoid instant rejection. He had not yet decided to show her the plan of action that he had finally written. It was too dependent upon the cooperation of Grandmother Grace, and Blake would not want to depend on the old woman.

The next two phone calls to Rachel went better, but he thought that her attitude had changed. Maybe he had assumed too much. He guessed he should not talk so much about the firm. There was little good to say about it. Even football was a questionable subject now, what with the Patriots' big victory in the snow and just yesterday their defeat of the Steelers in their own back yard. Her Patriots were going to the Super Bowl, but it would probably be another big disappointment for her and her fellow fans. She might want to talk about the Super Bowl, but he surely did not. There just was not a lot to talk about.

The first weekend in February her Patriots proved him and millions of others wrong. They beat the Rams soundly. He failed to call her. Actually, he sat by the phone knowing that he should call and congratulate her, but he decided not to call. He finally fell into a fitful sleep and dreamed of airplane crashes and shipwrecks. The next day he drove to the yacht harbor. The family forty-one footer was up on supports, in dry dock. He climbed the ladder and removed the canvas over the afterdeck and unlocked the hatch. Below, the air still smelled of the refinish work that he had directed on the teak interior. He was thinking he might sail the boat around to the east coast in the spring. He would need a mate for the cruise, and it would take weeks, especially if he went all the way up to Maine. He did not know whom he would want on board with him for that long. Not anyone here in Seattle. He would like to know if Rachel sailed. But he had not asked her. He needed to make a note of that. Something for him to talk about with her.

He should have called her. But he didn't know if she wanted him to call. She had never called him. That bothered him a lot. She had seemed so active, even aggressive, and he had liked that. He would call her later today. The work on the boat had been done well. He was pleased. A new radio system was supposed to have been put in by now, but the equipment was to be shipped late from the manufacturer. Should be in by the end of March.

He refastened the canvas and looked at the job they had done on the hull. It also looked good. He had learned from Uncle Robert, if you cannot maintain a boat yourself, be prepared to pay big money to have it done correctly. There were too many men romantically tied to sailing ships who did not have the talent to do first class maintenance. They advertised that they had such capabilities, trying to do no more than pay their way to stay around the love of their lives. Maybe they were not so bad; he smiled to himself. But just work on someone else's boat.

He did not call. Not until the following Friday, and it was the shortest and poorest of their conversations. He even forgot to ask her if she sailed. But he did congratulate her on the Patriot championship and she merely said she hoped the Celtics and Red Sox could now get it together. The big win was something that he could have shared fully with her, and should have, and he felt worse when they hung up.

In mid March he received a call from the investigation agency. They had an interim report and wanted to know when and where he would like to receive it.

It would be oral only. Nothing written until he agreed on what part of their findings he wanted written, if anything. He chose a motel just off Interstate 5 a few miles above the state line with Oregon. The man asked why so far out. Time was valuable to him. Stephen told him that he would pay his normal rate for the travel. The man seemed more than satisfied.

The report was brief. First they found the proper records on file to substantiate the certificates of the marriage and the birth. But that did not mean that they were not fraudulent. It could mean simply that the fraud was well executed. They could find nothing irregular there. Other than the document of marriage, they could find no evidence of the presence of Miss Grace or Lieutenant Blandon in California in the time of the marriage, and they found every indication that she in fact was in Japan that entire period, and he was aboard an aircraft carrier at sea. His ship did not put in to Yokohama until late October of 1950, five weeks after his plane crashed off Korea. Still those records were not foolproof. Even the service records might not have shown a leave for him, particularly if it had been worked into some duty of escort or shuttling of aircraft. On the other hand, it had not been hard to lay out the days that Miss Grace was in Tokyo and the days that Lieutenant Jennings was assigned to his unit in Japan as well as when he was in Korea. The investigation so far was not conclusive, but it kept the questions alive.

"We had a little better luck in Hawaii," the man said.

He had found that the flight had crashed en route from Maui to Oahu. It was a private charter plane, and had nothing to do with the military or the USO. The occupants included the pilot who flew out of Oahu regularly and whose body was the only one recovered, a minister from a mission on the tip of the island of Maui at Hanna, and the woman, Miss Grace, as the initial crash report in the Hawaii newspaper called her. She not only flew from Maui, but also had been staying at the mission at Hanna.

"The reason that I call this an interim report," the man said, "is that our next step would be to approach the mission in Maui. It still exists. Of course, there have been other ministers there since then, but the daughter of the minister who died in the airplane crash still lives there. She may be able to give some helpful information. That is your call—whether you want us to approach the mission. If we do, we would prefer to tell them that we represent you."

Stephen had hoped for more, but the report only made him more determined to learn the truth. He did not know what to ask them to do now.

"Please send me your bill, and make no written report. If I decide to do more and need your help, I'll call your listing as I did before."

They left the room together, the man going to the office to pay for the use of the room. That would be on the bill he was to give to Stephen later.

He pulled back out on the Interstate and headed north and went over the dates in his mind. His father had been born in February of '51. It was so likely that a child had been conceived in the May period of '50 when his grandmother was definitely in Tokyo. During a time that William was definitely there also, and during a time that Lieutenant Blandon most likely was not. It was possible that the conception was later, even after William was in Korea. But he did not think that. He knew now that he did not want to think that. The man was right. The answer could be in Maui. Stephen was going to Hawaii.

Four days later he drove along the narrow road that wound around the Maui coast, at the foothills of the great volcano. He knew that it was a fabled road, made so by journeys years ago when the route was without aid or assistance in event of problems with coach or auto along the way. The brochure still advised of narrow stretches, miles where one could not safely pass, and still long stretches without any human activity nearby. He found it a tame route now. A telephone on the seat beside him, tour helicopters flying regularly on a typically nice day like today, and cars before and behind him. It could actually be a sports car holiday were there not so much traffic. He had opted for a compact, and it was more power than he needed with the caravan he had joined. Still, he could imagine the concerns raised by such a trip many years ago—even in 1951.

The directions to the mission proved easy to follow. He would have needed to be asleep to drive by. He parked just beyond what he assumed was the administration building. It appeared much older than the stone church itself, but both had seen many years.

A woman in her mid forties was sitting at a dining room-type table. She was doing what he thought was embroidery, although the oval hoop was much larger than others he recalled seeing. She put it down and stood and removed her glasses and placed them on the fabric held taut by the hoop.

"Yes?" She said with a slight smile.

"I'm trying to collect some information. Some family information about my grandmother. As a child I heard that she once stayed here. I never met her, and I'm trying to get to know her better."

"You say she stayed here. At the mission?"

"Yes."

"What is your name? And her name?"

"My name is Stephen Blandon. My grandmother's name was Carolyn Grace...." He hesitated. "Her married name was Blandon."

"She hasn't stayed here. Not in the last twenty years or so."

"It would have been before that. In 1951, and possibly in late 1950."

The woman looked at him with apparent renewed interest.

"That's before my time, young man. Let me ask my mother. She may recall someone, but that was a long time ago. She would have been just a girl."

She went through a doorway shrouded by vertical strings of multi-colored beads. It was a functional doorway screen that let the air flow while providing some privacy. It did not block sound well. He could hear two women's voices, in whispers. They continued for some time until the woman returned.

"My mother will talk with you, but her memory is poor. She says that she doubts she can be of help."

She pointed through the doorway she had just used, and Stephen entered a room brightened by the doorway and the natural light of two large windows. He knew that the ocean was in that direction, but any view of the blue waters was blocked by a line of lush greenery just beyond a small mowed area of green grass. The grass opening was ringed with Hibiscus, the large, red blossoms that would live just one day and die.

Her back was to him and he walked around and to her side so that he might see her face. She sat in an overstuffed, burgundy chair that threatened to absorb her small frame. Her legs were covered with a lightweight throw, and her hands were folded on her lap.

"Good Morning, Mr. Blandon. My daughter tells me that I may be able to help you. But if it puts a demand on my memory, I would warn you that I don't recall things very well."

"I appreciate your taking the time, ma'am. It will help me a great deal if you can remember a few things."

"I don't know that my daughter told you, Mr. Blandon, but our family name is Clarewell. My name is Florence. Why don't you pull in one of the chairs from the table out there and put it where I can see you."

Stephen carried a straight back wooden chair in from the other room and set it to her right such that some of the light from the window struck the right side of his face. She turned her head slightly toward him. Her skin was olive, natural, not so much from sun, and cut with wrinkles. The brown eyes were alert.

"Now, this woman you want to know about, was her name like yours or something else?"

"It was Carolyn. Carolyn Grace…Blandon."
Mrs. Clarewell was silent for a short time.
"And she was what to you?"
"My grandmother."
"And she would have been here, just when?"
"Maybe in late 1950, definitely in early 1951, through the spring."
"You are talking about the woman who died in the airplane crash with my father. What is it specifically that you are looking for?"
"Did she live here for a while, and did she have her son with her? Was my father born here?"
"My, you seem to have a complete story already. Don't you know where your father was born?"
"They say he was born in California."
"Who is 'they'?" Her chin rose slightly, as if she was prepared to hear something she did not favor.
"My Great Grandmother Grace, and Uncle Robert, and Great Grandfather Grace before he died."
"Are your Great Grandmother and uncle still living?"
"Only my Great Grandmother is still living."
"My, she must be quite old."
"She's in her nineties."
"Well, well. My mother would be eighty-five this year if she had lived. Can you believe I won't draw social security for another year? This body though. Ah, now, that is another story."
She paused again. Was she about to share something.
"Why do you want to know these answers?"
"It's my father. I want to know for sure where he was born."
"Is he still living?"
"No, my father and mother died when I was only six."
"I see," she said, dropping again into silence. Then she asked,
"Is there some kind of court battle going on over money? I mean do you want the answers to win in court?"
"No."
"My mother said the girl's family was quite rich. Are you rich?"
"I'm well off. My grandmother is rich, yes."
"I don't believe you," she said, and for the first time moved one hand to the arm of the old chair, with some effort.
"What don't you believe?"

"I don't believe you have told me the real reason why you are here. I can tell such things."

He paused. He might as well tell her.

"I don't think that my grandfather was who they told me that he was. I don't think that my grandmother loved the man they call my grandfather. I think my grandfather was another man. A man that I never met either, but who died just a few months ago." Stephen paused. "I don't think he ever knew that there was a child, that my father was ever born."

"How sad," she said and looked out into the sunlight that still shone beyond the window despite the abrupt shower spattering the tin roof.

Stephen waited. Hoping.

"I will tell you what I remember that my mother told me, and what little I remember myself. But I will never tell this to a lawyer, or in a court. I don't want to harm the mission or its reputation. My mother paid for what she did twice over before she died. She only told me most of what I will tell you in her very last days. She feared for her soul, even after she had told the minister as well. But that was many years ago."

It was not cool, but the old lady began an effort to pull the throw up around her shoulders. Stephen rose and went to her assistance.

"Thank you," she said. "You are a nice young man. And honest when prompted."

She did not smile or soften her critique of his earlier effort to keep some of his information to himself. He waited.

"Your grandmother, Carolyn Grace, was here, and her son was born here. She stayed on for three months after the birth. My mother did not believe that she was married, but that the man who fathered the child was in the war in Korea. The flight to Oahu was to give her the opportunity to try to call the father in Korea or Japan. They crashed on the way there, so my mother never knew. Afterwards they came here to ask her some questions, the police and the newspaper. She said that she answered the police, but never talked to the reporter. The questions were about my father, she said, about why the flight was taken to begin with. She said she lied—told them she did not know, and they told her she would be contacted by Honolulu officials about the baby.

"My mother said that a man from the young woman's family, a Mr. Grace, came here just after that. He gave her money, and they tore the page out of the book that recorded the birth, and then filled in new pages. He gave her a lot of money. And she gave him the locket. I remember the locket the best, because I always wanted to look inside it. The girl looked at it all the time. After the plane crash, my mother took it from a drawer. We both looked at the picture, of her and a young man. Surely it was the man she loved back then. My mother told me two days before she died that the girl said the father of William, the baby, was the man in the picture. My mother said that Mr. Grace gave her more money and told her never to mention the name of the baby again to anyone. And she didn't until she told the minister and me"

"She said the baby's name was William?"

"Yes."

"And this Mr. Grace, he took the baby with him?"

"Yes."

"What was his first name, Mr. Grace?"

"I don't recall; I don't know if I ever heard his first name."

"Was he the woman's, Carolyn's, father?"

"I don't know? But I think my mother would have told me that if he was, but I don't know. He might have been."

"What happened to the minister that your mother talked to? Is he still alive?"

"Yes, he's right here. He's my daughter's husband."

"Do they know more about all this?"

"No. They know only what my mother and I have told them. But they won't talk about that with any lawyer, either."

He should tell her that he was a lawyer, but he was not here as a lawyer, and she knew that.

"Why did my grandmother not have the locket with her when she died if she valued it so much?"

"I don't know, and my mother told me that she had thought about that too. But she had no explanation."

"Would you recognize the picture in the locket if you were to see it again?"

"I don't know, but why would I need to?" She looked wary again as she had in the first few minutes of their discussion.

"You wouldn't. It's just that I have the locket now, and it's important, along with your story, to prove who my grandfather really was."

"Who do you have to prove it to?"

It was a good question. Himself actually, only himself. But he wanted enough information to shake one person who already knew it was true; who had known the truth—and the lie—for fifty years. He wanted to break the cold silence of Grandmother Grace.

CHAPTER 24

He called Rachel from Honolulu.

"Honolulu? What are you doing there, Stephen?" She asked, the edge of laughter hanging in her voice. She clearly was pleased that he had called. It was Sunday, and he had missed another Friday call.

"I'll tell you when I get there. I have to stop in Seattle, but could we meet in Boothbay Harbor? I have something that I want to talk to you about."

"Well, yes, I guess so. I was just up there last Sunday. When are you talking about? I have classes, you know. We're not all free to flit around to places like Hawaii."

"I'm not sure. But just as soon as I can meet with my grandmother, and you can get free."

"The least complicated for me would be Saturday, but if it's really urgent, I could miss some classes. I'm doing exceptionally well, I want you to know."

"I wish I could fly directly there right now, but I can't. Rachel, I really want to see you."

"And I want to see you," she said.

They talked longer than they had the last several calls, and he finally asked her if she could possibly meet him at Boothbay Harbor the next day. She agreed. Rather than indicate why they needed to meet so soon, he kept the conversation light, asking her if she had seen any of the spring baseball games in Florida. She had not, and yes, she would like to. Yes, she believed the Red Sox had a chance this year, but she thought that every year. He asked if she thought that the Red Sox could win with their new lineup, and she replied that she thought so. They did not mention the Yankees.

❦   ❦   ❦

Grandmother Grace was not pleased to see him. He wore a flowery red and white Aloha shirt under a lightweight tan sport coat despite the cool Seattle weather. And he wore white slacks and moccasins with no socks. She had hated it when he was in high school and insisted on wearing no socks. He had worn the outfit in Hawaii, but not on the flight back. It came to him as he was about to leave the boathouse that he should dress "appropriately" for his visit with her. So he had changed. All for her. She received him in his grandfather's study. She was sitting behind the desk as he entered the room.

"I heard that you had gone to Hawaii, and I can see you went native. That does not surprise me. Your conduct of late makes me wonder if you are the responsible person needed in the future of the firm. I wonder if you can really ever be expected to manage anything beyond your current meager trust."

Straight to the attack and with what she would view the gravest of weapons, the threat of near disinheritance, and the reminder of the comparatively small amount of the monthly payments he received.

"Grandmother, I would like for you to be quiet for a while. I want to tell you about what has been happening since Uncle Robert's death, and I would prefer not to be interrupted. You should know that I can prove what I'm about to tell you."

He knew that was not true and that she would probably know too well that he could not prove what he would claim. But he wanted her in a frame of mind to accept what he was prepared to do about the big lie of his life. He was betting that for the first time he would see her without a clever scheme or a set of intimidating deterrents to anything she did not want to happen.

He began with the locket. He would not bother to tell her of the constant thought now of his childhood in a house rife with suggestions that their life rested on a rotten base. He knew that she could not be moved by the past. He had to attack with the raw power that she understood—a threat to her wealth or social reputation.

He tracked for her all that he had learned from the files of the firm and the foundation, from his trip to Boothbay Harbor, from the investigative service and from his trip to Maui. He was guilty of suggesting hard evidence on points that were only supposition or circumstantial implications, but he saw her impatient switching of positions in the chair, alternate folding of her hands on the desk and seizing the arms of her chair and saw her come to the edge of outburst, and finally wilt.

He finished, and she confessed. But she regained strength in the process of telling her story, promoting her perspective. She told him what had been done, what she had directed when his great grandfather had lacked the fortitude to act in the interest of the family and its reputation. He watched her no doubt reenact her scenes with Richard and Robert. Richard who would not act; Robert who would dutifully do all the chores that she asked.

She had been the strong one, quick to assess the threat to all of them, and prompt to devise a plan. The plan was to create a life, a husband, a wedding that did not exist to cover the story of a daughter who had been killed after giving birth to a child whose father was a man that they had forbidden her to see.

Everyone can be brought around with money she said, and she explained how Robert had taken a stack of money to Hawaii and Monterey to remove one record of birth and to create another. He had blundered in the wedding certificate, for it would have been more favorable to reflect the marriage in Tokyo, not Monterey, and she had recognized his error immediately, but she decided to leave well enough alone.

The Blandons had been easy. Harriett Blandon had been her roommate at school and had married poorly, so poorly that her husband barely managed to support them and their son. And that son had been killed just short months before the birth of Carolyn's baby.

Blandon had died a hero in a naval combat aircraft, and was an acceptable father for her grandson. It had been expensive. Robert had given the Blandons far more money and stock than was needed for their cooperation. The stock came to make them far more affluent than she had ever intended or wanted. But the trust for the boy was her idea, as was the foundation in Carolyn's name. Harriett had even had the impertinence to suggest the foundation bear John's name as well. She had crushed that immediately.

Her schoolmate failed to recognize that the conditions of the trust required John to come to Seattle and join the firm once out of college. Grandmother Grace had picked a proper wife for him even before he was seventeen. It had been a splendid wedding. Few larger ever in Seattle. It was a shame that the two darlings had died in those horrid mountains. They were a perfect couple and she had exposed them to the most precious ideas for their social activities. What a waste, she lamented.

"Grandmother," he interrupted. "I don't intend to live this lie any longer. Some things have got to change."

"Stephen, you forget, your wealth and your future all rest on the fine reputation of the Grace family. You cannot undo all this and keep your life as you know it. I'm getting on in years. Most of what you see around you will be yours. It will be worth even more tomorrow than it is today. But if you besmirch the reputation of our family, the firm, your own grandmother, and the foundation, your wealth will shrink to that of any of a dozen families around here. Do you want that?"

"The question is, Grandmother, is that what you want?"

"Of course not, stop being ridiculous."

"All right. Here is the non-ridiculous part of what is going to happen. Blake has some good ideas, more than that, a feel for what is needed to make the law firm a more profitable and more responsible activity in our community. I think that Leonard Fallows would accept the merit of her concepts, should he be given a chance. Unfortunately, it's the other men that Robert and you have placed at the top of the organization with him who will resist any change. Especially since the changes will most directly affect them and their cozy relations with the clients they personally manage and coddle."

"You are still being ridiculous. We cannot turn our backs on our best clients, people who have been our friends for years...."

"Let me finish. Your special talents will be needed if Blake is to get the ear of the leadership, and apply what she has already identified as the vital first steps. All she needs is you to accept that she should and will be given this opportunity. You must create the opening for her, and give her just a little protection for a short time. She will prove her own merit. She does not need to be propped up like Uncle Robert."

"What about you? Don't you see what you would be doing? Giving an advantage to your natural competitor. You should do this. Not Blake."

"I don't want to do it. Besides, they are her ideas. All I saw was part of the problem. I think that she sees it all, and has already identified a new approach and solutions. I don't even want to be a lawyer, Grandmother. That was your idea. Blake loves the work. And she loves the firm, something that I will never feel, neither for the place nor for some of the people."

"Stephen, you don't mean that. You don't know what you're doing."

"Yes, I do, and I know it very well. I have other plans now, Grandmother."

"You are risking your fortune."

"No, no I'm not. I have my trust, though I would not die if I lost it. I don't need any more than that. But my fortune is secure. It's in your and Blake's hands. Grandmother, listen to me. If you don't do precisely for Blake what I have said, I will go to the newspapers and television and tell all about the big lie of the Grace family. I will do it. You must know that. Your lie has hurt too many people. I would not hesitate to reveal the truth."

"You can't prove it. I will deny all that I have told you."

"Yes, I can prove it," he lied. "But even if I could not, think of the people who will want to believe it. Think of the powerful people in this city, in this state, who wish you ill. Regardless it would destroy the ability of the foundation to get money. That's your ticket to all the galas and exclusive parties that you live for. Not to speak of what would happen to the part of the firm's business on which you really profit. Those accounts would dry up overnight. It makes no difference if I could prove it or not. I wouldn't have to, and you know it."

She rose from the big, leather-backed chair and walked around to sit in the chair beside him and turned it to face him.

"Stephen, you won't do this. I didn't want to tell you, but I am not well. I don't know how much time I have left, but the pain of all that would kill me. Is that what you want? Do you want my death on your hands?" She dabbed at the invisible tear with her handkerchief.

Stephen stood.

"Grandmother, I'm taking a leave of absence from the firm tomorrow. I spoke with Mr. Fallows late this afternoon, and he's arranged transportation for me in the morning. I'll call Blake in two days. By then you'll have met with her and you'll have informed Leonard Fallows of what you want to see happen in the firm. If you fail to do either, I'll be back here on the first available plane to tell the true story to the media. I suggest you call Blake right now. At any rate, you and I will have no need to discuss this matter again. Goodbye, Grandmother."

Stephen turned and walked from the room, summarily ending the conversation the way she had done hundreds of times, even to a small boy who had only asked to know more about the kind looking man in the sailor's uniform smiling down at him from the piano.

CHAPTER 25

Stephen laid the magazine on the armrest of the large recliner and stretched his legs. He sipped the orange juice, and smiled back at the flight attendant who quickly retrieved the magazine.

"Would you like something else to read?" She asked.

"No, thanks. I'll just finish my juice and take a little nap. It's a long flight."

"Yes, but let me know if we can do anything to make it enjoyable for you."

"Oh, it already is, thank you. It already is."

She smiled and returned to the small galley at the rear of the aircraft. It was a small jet that the firm shared with two other businesses in Seattle. It saved time for executives, and was far more flexible than the scheduled airlines. He was the only passenger today although it was company policy for junior people like him to share flights where feasible. He had told Leonard Fallows that this was an urgent family need. That was true, he just did not say for what part of the family it was urgent. He smiled at Blake's response the previous evening to what he had told her. He had laid out the whole story after arriving at her home just minutes after she completed a phone conversation with Grandmother Grace.

Blake had been wary of a relationship that left her indebted to his great grandmother. But she and Stephen had talked well into the morning. At a point she seemed to agree that she could handle Grandmother Grace with the threat that he had hanging over the old lady. Despite her excitement with the opportunity to get her concepts applied in the firm, she showed greater interest in Rachel and the story of William and Carolyn. Toward the end of the discussion she returned to Rachel.

"I won't ask you what your feelings are toward her. They're obvious. Does she share the same emotions?"

"I don't know," he said. "I intend to find out tomorrow."

"Good, but you know that I need you back here to help me."

"No you don't. I would be in your way. Actually, Blake, I don't want to be here. I don't know where I will wind up, but it's somewhere else, I know that."

"I envy you," she said.

"Oh, come on, Blake. You're getting exactly what you want. I've heard you say it a half dozen times."

"Don't believe everything a girl tells you, Stephen. I envy you and your Rachel."

"Well, why don't you try to develop a relationship with someone, Blake?"

"Oh, and what should I do to do that?"

"Take a vacation. Go someplace where people go just to have fun. To get to know other people. Take a vacation, Blake."

When he left she hugged him long and wished him good luck. He kissed her on the cheek and said goodbye.

"Take a vacation, Blake," he said as she closed the door. But would she.

He drained the juice glass, trying to picture Blake reaching out to someone. He could not. He turned his head, resting it against the back of the seat, and looked out the window. Under the perfectly blue sky, few clouds lay below, and beyond them were the eastern foothills of the Cascade Range and the pattern of fruit and nut orchards. William had grown up there. He would like to visit the area someday—maybe find the place where William had lived. He had driven through the country, but he would have to learn a lot more before he could expect to know when he was retracing the ground where his grandfather had walked. Maybe Rachel would know.

She would be waiting for him at the general aviation desk at the Portland Airport. The pilot had filed a flight plan that would have them landing at twenty minutes after two in the afternoon, more than two hours later than he had told her last night that the plane would arrive. He had left the message correcting the time on her answering machine right before they took off this morning. He hoped she would get it. He had called her from Blake's last night and told her he would be there sometime just after noon. He hoped she would get his later message. He wanted her to be there when he arrived. He wanted that very much.

The co-pilot woke him sometime later to tell him that they were attempting to get clearance to fly above some weather over the Great Lakes area. If that didn't work they would probably be forced a little farther south. That could delay their arrival at Portland. He thanked the man—the brass nameplate said it was Richard.

"I'm not going to worry about a little bit of weather, Richard, thanks." He was soon back asleep, compensating for the late night at Blake's.

Rachel was running the vacuum cleaner in her house at the Harbor. She had left her Boston apartment after Stephen's call well past midnight, throwing enough clothing in the car to stay for three or four days because she did not know what they might be doing. Or that they would do any thing beyond discussing whatever he wanted her to hear. But she thought, and she hoped there would be more—much more. She had arrived at the Harbor a little before five in the morning, and since then she had been busy giving the house a quick cleaning. She did not know if she would have time to go to the market for groceries. Maybe she would suggest that the two of them shop. She could fare no worse than she did the other time she had made such a proposal.

She put away the vacuum and took a shower in place of the bath she had promised herself. She spent more time deciding what to wear than she had taken to shower and dry her hair, but by eleven she was on her way. She smiled and accompanied the singing on the car radio as the miles ticked off.

She checked the note in her purse as she drove into the airport. It gave the information on his aircraft and a reminder of where to park to be close to the general aviation desk. It was after twelve and she hurried to find a space. She wanted to be there when his plane landed.

At the desk she learned that the flight had an arrival time of two-twenty. She was disappointed. She had almost run to the lounge area with the vision of arriving too late and not being there when he came down the corridor from the gate. She had more than two hours to wait. She took a chair, but it felt so like the seat in her car that she decided to take a walk. She started down the connecting corridor toward the main terminal. Two hours was a long time.

When she returned to the desk area where he would be arriving she noted that only thirty-five minutes had elapsed. She decided to repeat the walk.

Maybe she would stop at one of the sandwich bars and have a bite to eat. She had purposely omitted lunch, thinking that he might not have eaten and she could suggest a place on the drive back north. She had eaten nothing in over seventeen hours, and her stomach was quivery. She did not know how much of that was hunger, and how much was anticipation of his arrival.

She ordered a grilled cheese and some chips. A beer was appealing, but she was afraid that it would serve as a mild sleeping pill. She chose a coffee instead. The sandwich tasted good, and her stomach almost immediately settled down. But soon the wait began to weigh on her again. She wished she had brought the Grisham novel with her.

She rose again and went looking for a newsstand. Maybe a magazine or a paperback. She found a stand not far from the sandwich bar. She had read all of Grisham's works she thought, but maybe she had missed one. She found two of his novels, and confirmed that she was reading one and had read the other as well as those listed in the front of each. She looked at a novel by another prominent adventure writer, but knew that she found his work just a bit too technical, although clearly millions did not share her view. She finally settled on two magazines and returned to the general aviation area. She found two articles of interest in one, read them, and then began another article in the second magazine. She could not have told anyone what she had read in the first two paragraphs when she nodded off. She was not aware when she slipped into sleep.

❦   ❦   ❦

The pain in her neck woke her. It ached, and she did not wonder at the fact when she sat erect. She had slept with her head sharply turned down and to her right. She rubbed the side of her neck with her left hand and glanced at the clock above the desk. It showed ten minutes before three. She looked at the long list of flights on the board. Stephen's flight was no longer listed.

She hurried to the unmanned desk. She looked around. Surely he could not have arrived and failed to see her there. Had the plane not arrived at all. A young woman about her age came through the open doorway beside the schedule board.

"Has the Executives Express that was due at two-fifteen already arrived?" Rachel asked.

"Were you expecting someone on that aircraft?" The girl asked.

"Yes. Has it arrived?"

"One moment, please," she said as she turned and went back through the door. Almost at once she returned following a man wearing a blue blazer and red tie.

"Are you Miss Connor?" He asked.

"Yes. Is something wrong?"

"We called your name earlier. We were told that you were here waiting, but there was no response."

"What's wrong?" She asked. She felt panic. The airplane—Stephen's airplane.

"No ma'am. No please, nothing's wrong. They were delayed by weather. We now expect the plane to land at three-fourteen. They should be at the gate within a half-hour. I didn't mean to alarm you, and it looks like we have. Have you been waiting here long?"

"Yes, for almost three hours. Why is there nothing on your board?"

"We don't always post flights like the one you're waiting for. The earlier shift put it up. Probably the pilot requested it. When the plane was delayed and I saw the nature of the flight we just didn't update it. As you can see, the board is nearly full. I can assure you that we have not deviated from any established policies. But if you were distressed in any way, I certainly wish we had kept it up there."

She did not respond to the man. She was relieved there was no real problem. She was disappointed with herself that she had been so quick to fear....

She went to the ladies lounge and freshened up. Her eyes looked tired. And her skirt to her shirtwaist dress was a bit wrinkled, but she could overcome that easier than she could the look of fatigue around her eyes. She wished he would get here.

She returned to her seat and laid the two magazines in the seat to her right. She couldn't read, and she didn't worry now about falling asleep. She needed the reassurance. She wanted to see him walk into the airport lobby—safe.

When he came through the doorway he was wearing black slacks, a platted black leather belt, loafers, and a dark red, long sleeve shirt, the top two buttons unsecured. He carried a briefcase and lightweight, black leather jacket in one hand and a rather large black canvas bag in the other. His hair was a little messed up, like maybe he too had fought a bout with sleep, but the hair could not be greatly mussed for its tight wave and rather short cut. She stood. The unsettled feeling returned to her stomach and her emotions tossed between calling his name with happiness and crying in relief that he was safely on the ground. She walked toward him. She had the urge to run to hug him, but...

He dropped the jacket with the briefcase and the black bag and walked toward her. She did not run. But it might have been called a jog, and he caught her, his arms extended before they encased her and pulled her close to him. She cried.

"Damned," she said.

"And hello to you too." he said. He chuckled. Not enough to appear to make fun, or to take the occasion lightly, but to check his own emotions. She knew it. And that was all right.

CHAPTER 26

He offered to rent a car and she told him that she had planned to drive him and assumed that he wanted to go right up to the Harbor. He said Boothbay Harbor was exactly where he wanted to go because he had so much to tell her and that was the place for them to be when he did. He was well into the details of his trip to Maui and his visit with his great grandmother before they turned onto Route 1 from the Maine Turnpike. She wanted to hear it all but she wished she could watch his face instead of the road under the late afternoon light.

He interrupted his explanation of Blake's great opportunity with the firm and asked Rachel if she minded an early dinner. He was hungry and was already thinking of a good Maine lobster. She told him an early dinner was fine and suggested the Tugboat. He had seen the restaurant and motel on his earlier visit and said he would like that. He continued to talk about Blake and the law firm, and Rachel thought it was with a new enthusiasm. She thought that his might be a very short visit. He clearly expected Blake to make some quick improvements in the law firm.

She drove directly to the wharf and parked at the level below the entrance to the Tugboat. It had only opened for the season on the 4th of April, and she had not been by since the reopening. The table in the far corner was occupied when they entered the restaurant and despite the availability of a number of other tables, she told the waitress and Stephen of her favorite spot and he asked the waitress if they might wait for it. The waitress looked around at the empty tables and then softly said she thought that could be done. The waitress' name was Linda, and Rachel had spoken with her before as she attended the table—one time when she dined alone, the other with William.

She wasn't sure how long they waited but she drank her wine and Stephen finished a martini before the waitress escorted them to the corner of the restaurant. He had begun to tell her what he had learned in Hawaii, and now he continued his account in just above a whisper despite the empty seats at the nearest table. She could feel his warmth as he described the tiny lady in Maui who had corrected him as a mother does a child. He had liked the woman.

Abruptly, he reached across the table and covered her hand with his. It was large and the fingers were long. He drew it back and she thought, don't, keep it there. It was as if he wanted to say something else, on a different subject, but he smiled and continued his story.

"I have so much to tell you."

She had been touched by the comment by the little lady in Hanna when told that William had died without knowing about his son: "How sad." Rachel wished that her thoughts about William and Stephen were not so much like those of the lady in Maui. Both men had somehow been cheated. At first she thought William had been cheated more; and then she thought it was Stephen, but she felt disloyal to William. Still, there were questions that he had failed to ask years before that could have led to his son and grandson. But William had borne enough guilt. She could not fault him for not finding this young man before it was too late. If he were here, he would tell her not to fret now about the past. She knew he had learned that—late—but he had learned that, and would want her to remember it too. "Don't forget, but don't fret," he had said just the last fall sitting with her on the bench. She tried to free her mind of anything but Stephen here and now and returned his smile.

The waitress came, left, and came again. He talked. Gradually his words spoke of the present—of them, and he asked her questions. She gave answers that were short and effortless as she introduced him to her mother, her father, and Peggy, whom he said he already knew and liked. She smiled and pointed out where her father's boat had sometimes lay at anchor in the narrow harbor. But she hurried through her explanation of her father and the house that he didn't live in, and then smiled again as she recounted her recent visits with her mother and the reliving of many of their special times together. It all flowed briskly, easily, simply.

Most of the time he talked and she preferred to listen. It was a stream of happy words and memories and realizations, and one time he leaned back, paused, sipped his wine, and reminded her of William in his blue blazer. Stephen was dressed more casually, but he seemed to command the space in much the same way. It was partly their long arms and broad shoulders. It was also a zest that William had showed when he spoke of Carol and that Stephen showed as he looked at her regardless of his subject.

Even when she asked him about his time at Stanford, he seemed to launch from the chair, leaning closer, and sailing into a string of beautifully sounding names of missions and towns along the California coastline and in the big valley. His short history of the Spanish presence in California was salted with the names of explorers, priests, soldiers, sailors and political leaders. He had written an article about it all and she would not have been surprised if he had pulled it as a pressed, folded document from his wallet for her to share.

Her twinge of sadness briefly returned with the thought of how much William would have enjoyed sitting here and getting to know his and Carol's grandson—and the thought that Stephen could never be expected to feel what he had missed in not knowing William.

Two things had turned in her mind as she had driven to the airport to meet him. Seeing him again and telling him that she had decided to return to the study of law as she had planned when she first went to college. But after the dinner, standing on the wharf just outside the restaurant and looking out over the reflecting waters he told her that he had made a big decision. He was leaving the law. It was the first thing that had not gone right for her the whole evening. She had looked forward to his response when he heard that she too would be a lawyer. But now she had to remind herself that her choice of law was for her, not for her father and not for Stephen. It was her choice and her life. He told her that his secretary had reserved a room for him in one of the houses at the top of the hill overlooking the bay, and she dropped him off with a smile and the invitation to him to come to her home the next morning for breakfast. He thanked her for the offer to share her running the next morning, but said that he would limit himself to the short walk down the hill to her house.

She let herself in to the empty house and knew it would be a long night. A warm bath and a chapter of Grisham did not help. Around three in the morning, she feared she would never fall asleep. They had not kissed; yet this was the only man she had ever thought of being with forever, and he might be gone too soon. So much needed to be said. But how? What would Carol say? The hallway clock ticked away in a steady cadence: just tell him; just tell him. Yes, but how?

When he knocked on the door just after eight she responded with a cup of coffee in each hand.

"You open the door. I don't want to spill the coffee," she said. He swung the door in and stepped into the comfortable room that smelled of lilac and coffee.

"Caff or Decaff?" She said.

"Oh, high test for sure."

She held out the mug in her left hand. "Your poison from my father's own stock."

He almost missed the mug. The dampness around her hairline at the forehead and at her ears accented the dark hue of her hair, and her cheeks were a light pink. She looked like she had the first time he had seen her. She clearly had been exercising. Her hair was tossed, but soft beyond the wetness with a mixture of highlights and shadowed brown. She wore a green running suit, the same one he guessed that she had worn at the cottage that first time. It appeared comfortable but clung just enough. She had on running shoes. He knew the brand well although it was not his choice. A white towel hung loosely around her neck and she took the corner and passed it above her lips to remove moisture that he had seen as appealing. She had made room for him to step inside and close the door, but had said no more and made no move toward the kitchen or deeper part of the house. He had not tried the coffee. He stepped closer to her and tilted her head upward with the light touch of the forefinger of his left hand on her chin. Her eyes gave the answer to the question he had taken to bed with him the night before. The answer was yes. He should have, and now he did.

He dropped his free arm under her hand holding her cup of coffee, reached around her back and with slight pressure guided her closer. The kiss was long and he felt the coffee cup shaking. *Don't spill it.* But he did and she was soon down on her knees pressing a towel against the two near perfect round spots on her carpet. He knelt not to help but to share her laughter and to be close again. She had spilled her coffee too.

Midway through the breakfast she announced her plan for taking out a neighbor's day sailer. He was pleased. He had told her the night before of his love of sailing, and she had seemed enthused in saying that she also liked to sail. She had lost no time in arranging an outing.

"Just stopped off on my run this morning and made the arrangements. The boat belongs to my friend's sister and her husband. They're not out with it much any more. She was glad to have someone take the boat out."

"You really run? I thought you probably jogged."

"I invited you to a run. Do you forget so soon?" She asked, smiling.

"Well, we may be able to share that. I do some running, but I just didn't have any gear to join you this morning."

"Well, we'll just have to check you out, Speedy."

"Anytime," he said. There was a challenge in her eyes. In addition to having no gear with him, he had not run much since leaving Palo Alto. Rachel looked fit. Very fit.

Later at the wharf she was in charge from the start in getting underway and in heading the boat out of the tight space of the harbor. It was not a big boat, twenty-four feet, but he was glad to have her show her knowledge of the bay. It was busier than he thought it would be, but there was plenty of room once they cleared a small island off to port. Once out they had to tack little to enjoy the breeze and the cool but pleasant day. She liked being in charge, and she was easy enough, while a bit more assertive than the evening before. He thought about what he might have said that had made her seem less talkative and a bit reserved about halfway through the evening meal. He had not figured it out, but he knew the evening had not ended quite as he had pictured it. Not even a kiss. He had made no attempt to press things. Now he was glad that he had not. She may have been feeling what he was...maybe neither wanted things to be too casual.

They sailed to the northeast, toward an island that she pointed out after they were out of the small bay. When they gained the southeast coast of the island, she pointed out the high rock ledges, over one hundred and fifty feet tall, the tallest coastal cliffs in Maine. She named each, most heads: Burnt, White, Black. They sailed around the island—Monhegan she called it—leaving the seaward coast that she said claimed most every soul that ever went overboard from a ship or was swept by waves from the rocky shore. The quieter waters west and northwest of the island also provided a view of the picturesque small village that once sheltered a colony of artists. She said that some still visited there and painted, but the island was not the inexpensive haven it had once been. She asked him to drop the anchor at a point just beyond a flat rock ledge of an island that barely thrust above the water level.

He watched two small harbor seals play in the water as she decorated two paper plates with vegetables, fresh fruit, and a piece of cold salmon topped with a sliver of cheese. The wine bottle had been trailing along in the water of the bay and the white wine was a pleasant temperature.

While they ate, she told him her story of the girl lawyer in the movie that she and her father had watched several years before and then she told Stephen of her decision to go on with the study of law.

"Congratulations," he said, thinking that the money from his grandfather may have made that an easier choice for her.

"You will make a great lawyer. You care about people." He knew it sounded trite, but then her smile told him she had liked it. They talked for a while about law school and its trials and rewards as he had known them. He hastened to add that he was not the best source. He had never really wanted to study law. He simply gave no thought about not going until he was already into the first year.

"What did you want to do?"

"Please Grandfather and Grandmother Grace, I guess."

"I know how that can be," she said. "I guess you don't really have to do anything right away, but do you have any plans yet? About your work, I mean."

"Yes. I want to write. I want to be a writer."

"What kind of writing?" she asked. She did not seem surprised. Not like he was when he finally realized it late one night on his houseboat in Seattle.

"Well, history appeals to me, but I'm not sure yet."

"No poetry?"

"I don't think so. I haven't read much poetry, but what I hear and read that is currently popular is a little too vague for me. I guess I did learn one thing in studying law: how imprecise our language can be, even when you try to be efficient and clear with the words. I like that challenge. No, I would guess there is no poet in me."

"You never can tell," she said, putting the paper plates and napkins in a plastic bag to be stowed below.

"Would you like another bit of this wine?" He asked.

"No, thanks. I'm driving."

He followed her down the ladder, the near empty wine bottle in one hand, and the plastic, stemmed wineglass in the other. Once below he emptied the bottle into the glass and she held the bag open for him to drop the bottle into it. She twisted the tie at the top of the bag and dropped it in a nylon mesh bag hanging from the portside overhead.

"There. Now when you finish your wine we can get underway if you could just haul up the anchor and hope it is not stuck under one of these ice age boulders below."

"First priority, first," Stephen said and put the glass down and turned her to him. "Rachel, I want to tell you what you mean to me. I know we've hardly talked, and I admit I feel a little like a thirteen year old, but…well, I mean, actually, I've never felt this way about any girl, or woman. I know it's really moving fast, but, I know I love you, Rachel."

She almost laughed, but at the same time felt the tears forming.

"Oh, Stephen. I'm sorry. I mean. Oh, I really wanted to tell you first. I mean I swore the first thing when I got up that I was going to tell you how I feel. Regardless of what you would say I was going to just up and tell you."

"Tell me what?"

"Tell you that I love you."

The sun was low in the evening sky when they slipped the boat back up against the wharf just below the Tugboat Inn. While they stowed the sail and tied down the covers and adjusted the slack in the mooring lines, they spoke of the fine performance of the boat during the afternoon. Then they walked toward her house.

"What would you like to do this evening, Stephen? I can fix us some dinner at the house. Nothing fancy, but it will stick to your ribs."

"I think that would be great."

"Would you mind if we ate a little late?" She said. "I'd like to visit the cottage before it gets too late."

"No. I mean that'll be great."

"We have time to change and still enjoy the late sunlight," she said.

"Good, then I'll swing on up to my room and meet you at the cottage say, in fifteen minutes. That okay?"

"Yes, that's fine."

CHAPTER 27

They were sitting on the bench atop the hill that shaded the head of the cove and the near shore of Boothbay Harbor as the late sun flattered the far shore and the towering white church steeple with soft light. The small harbor was filled with boats, mostly like the one they had sailed, but including cruisers that would soon be off for some near or far port to satisfy the dream of a long winter or a lifetime. More boats would come to replace the wanderers and to enjoy this special spot tucked into the irregular outline of the Maine coast.

Rachel felt she could reach out and touch the church, and run her hand down the sails of the boats snuggling into the harbor. Never had this scene of her childhood seemed painted so vividly by the warm sunlight. Never had she felt as alive as she sat on the bench, close, but not quite touching him. She remembered their afternoon on the boat and even now in the cooling evening air she felt that warmth. He had told her as they stood in the cabin of the boat that he had experienced a feeling on the flight from Seattle that he had not known before. He could not know for sure he said, but he thought it was the feeling of coming home. It was new, but he could only guess that this was how it was—coming to a special place, shared by people you cared about and who cared about you. A place where you had a past and a future. That must be home.

Now in the coolness of the evening he had slipped on his leather jacket, and she wore a beige cardigan sweater over a rose blouse. A gray skirt completed a much more casual affect than the navy blue dress with gathered skirt that she had been wearing when they met at the airport the day before. The blue dress was of a shiny material, gathered at her waist and the neckline displaying a narrow, flat silver necklace that matched her small earrings and a set of three matching bracelets on her left wrist. He had noticed the dark blue shoes with the medium height heels when she hurried toward him, her dark brown hair, with the soft highlights, the hair that William had captured so well on canvas, bouncing as she ran, framing the smile that flickered between laughter and constraint. He had never seen such beauty. Closer, the depth of the blue eyes seemed to make the band of silver that lay around her neck all the brighter.

Now he turned on the bench to face her.

"Rachel, I'm not going back to Seattle. Not for a while, maybe not for a long time. I'm going to stay here to write."

"I'm glad," she said. "Have you thought of what you will write?"

"William's story. If you'll agree to help me."

"Sure, but from what you've told me, you can't write the whole story, not unless you want to anger your great grandmother."

"Oh, I don't plan to finish right away. By the time I finish the book Blake probably won't need anyone's help. I think that my grandmother will ensure Blake's role in the firm. She may even like doing it."

"You don't think your great grandmother will try to punish you in some way?" She asked.

"No. Blake and I are all she has. She wants us both. She probably can't act otherwise. The publicity may not hurt the foundation too much and the changes Blake can get will offset the damage to the firm. Even if they drop the Blandon name it won't mean all that much—except to Grandmother Grace. And it will most definitely embarrass her. That's what she will dislike most anyway—the embarrassment. I think that Blake will have shored up the weaknesses in the law firm by then; probably have cut off or reshaped some of the accounts that mean so much to Grandmother, socially that is."

"I hope all goes well, for your sake and for Blake," she said.

"Rachel, I want to ask a favor," he said.

"What's that?"

"I'd like to lease your cottage."

"You mean William's Cottage?"

"Is that what you're calling it now?"

"Yes. And yes, you can live here. I can think of no one that I would want more to live here, other than William, I mean."

"I can," he said.

"And that is?"

"Don't you know?"

"You mean me?"

"Yes, you. Wouldn't you like to live here, too?"

"Oh, I can't live here, Stephen."

"Why not? I mean, if I were not going to, would you...."

"Stephen, I can't live here and go to the kind of law school I want to attend. But I won't be far away. I won't be on the west coast, with all respect to Stanford."

"Well, they do have a couple of pretty good law schools down in Massachusetts, don't they? Or is it Connecticut?"

"I'm not sure I can make those universities."

"Oh come on, that's no way to start. Pick the best and go for it."

Rachel smiled. That's what Carol would have told her.

They kissed.

"Is it supposed to be like this? All so fast?" She asked.

"Isn't that what William told you about him and Carolyn?"

"Carol," she corrected.

"Our first argument," he said, and they kissed again, this time longer.

"You plan to write anything else?" She asked when they settled back from one another.

"Yes, and I may need you to visit the west coast with me to get all the facts I'll need."

"The history?"

"Yes. I'd like to write from the perspective of the mixed culture of what we now call Mexico, California, Arizona, New Mexico, and Texas. What it was like for the affluent and the millions of peasants as their culture and governments clashed with that of the new United States of America. I don't know where it will lead me, and I don't set out to be critical of our government in the nineteenth century, but just think of the strength of that mixed culture that so much of it has survived over the years. Oh, in Mexico it's not so surprising, but in California, in the entire southwest, we don't seem to know what to try to keep and what to try to "Anglicize" out of everyone. I know it won't be that simple, but I want to study it all. Maybe I won't find a history to write, but I think I will and I hope it will be one to help bring greater understanding. They talk about breaking down walls, but too many walls have been destroyed already. The walls are not the problem. We still just have not come to know each other, really."

"Sounds like a very ambitious effort, Stephen."

"You mean too big, too idealistic?"

"Oh, no. I envy you for that. I know you'll do it well and produce a work of great benefit."

"Why do you say that? Other than the obvious niceness of the thought?"

"It's nothing concrete. I mean no big set of facts. It's a feeling, really. Do you believe in fate?"

"I'm not sure. I would have said no, I think, a few months ago. Maybe."

"I feel it's like…fate. I feel that you are meant to do something great like that."

"William?"

"That's part of it. William. But it's also you. I don't know, Stephen. It's just a feeling that I've had almost since we first met. The same feeling I had that you would not stay here long. That you had to go back to some really great project." She sat quietly and so did he.

"You're not laughing at me," she said.

"No. I wouldn't want to have to explain my feelings and thoughts in a courtroom, and it may sound terribly immodest, but I think I can write something very special too. But part of that is you, Rachel."

"Me?"

"William found the same thing."

"William found his past, Stephen. That's all. And he had the courage to really look at it."

"You really believe that's all there was to it? Nothing about you—and this place?"

"This place? Of course I know this place is magic. I've known that since I was a little girl."

"Now you're making fun," he said. "I'm quite serious, Rachel."

"I know you are. But I don't know. I find all that a little…I don't know…unsettling."

"Because you don't understand it?"

"Yes."

"But you believe that I'm going to write something great?"

"Yes. Yes I do."

They looked out toward the bay. He waited to let her speak again.

"Do you think you'll write anything else?" She asked.

It was the very subject that had been pushing forward in his thoughts, even as he held his silence.

"Yes. Our story."

"You think we have one?"

"Oh yes," he said and looked out above the wooded peninsula that on the maps pointed into Boothbay like a large mitten. The sky was taking on a hue of light purple from the sun setting over their shoulder.

They both saw it. A crane, a Sandhill Crane that rose from behind the wooded peninsula, flew to the left of the tall church steeple, crossed the harbor, and spread its long wings to alight softly on the open ground beside the house below them. The red cap atop the crane's head turned slowly and the bird faced back to the direction from which she had flown.

They looked back across the harbor beyond the church, beyond the green trees along the top of the peninsula and watched the other crane rise high in the air, circle near the church steeple, and fly toward them to land some twenty feet to the right of the first crane. The two graceful birds faced one another, the rust colored splashes on the feathers of their backs and wings subdued in the shadows below the slope.

The two birds leaped high from the ground, the beating of their wings and their voices mingling and they floated toward one another, their legs and feet outstretched. Then they receded and returned to land at their original positions. The crane on the right bowed; then the other dipped her head and long neck. Low bows, courtly bows of respect and affection. They repeated the rising in the air, approaching, returning, as if in some form of minuet, landing again, bowing. Both birds turned to look at them sitting on the bench and retained their pose for some time. Then they lifted off together, moving wing to wing toward them, gaining altitude rapidly. The eyes, the four, faintly orange eyes, seemed to be ocean deep despite the sunlight toward which they were flying. Above the bench the pair turned, swooped down over the harbor, crossed it, and flew left of the church steeple and up and over the tree line. They did not dip on the far side. They continued to rise, their wing tips almost touching.

Stephen took her hand in his. She moved closer to him. They watched the pair of birds fly farther and farther to the east, higher and higher. Their wings seemed to touch, to overlap. The two became smaller and smaller; then they appeared as one.

"Do you think we'll see them again?" She asked.

"Not on this shore."

She pushed even closer to him. The speck of the pair of birds disappeared into the purple light.

"I wish I had met him. I wish he had known me," Stephen said.

"He knows you now, Stephen. William knows you now."

0-595-27348-3